HOPE'S LAST REFUGE

HOPE'S LAST REFUGE

PATRICK MORGAN

Phase Publishing, LLC
Seattle

This is a work of fiction. Names, places, events, and incidents are either the products of the author's imagination or are used in a fictitious manner. Any resemblance to actual persons, living or dead, or actual events is purely coincidental.

Phase Publishing, LLC first paperback edition
October 2021

ISBN 978-1-952103-33-9
Library of Congress Control Number 2021919362
Cataloging-in-Publication Data on file.

More from Phase Publishing

Also by
Patrick Morgan

Apparent Horizon
Realms
Viaticum

by
Colleen Kelly-Eiding

Favoured by Fortune
Face of Fortune

by
Christopher Bailey

Without Chance
Whisper

by
Dr. Robert Melillo & Domenic Melillo

Einstein's Desk

DEDICATION

For everyone out there who has to fight for the
freedoms, equalities, rights, dignities,
and opportunities they never should have
had to fight for in the first place.

And for my sister, Megan, who is and who always has
been a constant force for good in this world. Your
empathy, intelligence, and social justice advocacy
inspire me to be a better human being.

But truly the travesty, you've been robbed of your empathy
Replaced it with apathy, I wish I could magically
Fast forward the future so then you can face it
And see how fucked up it'll be
I promise I'm honest, they coming for you
The day after they comin' for me.

-Run the Jewels

ONE

Today is the first day in fourteen years that I wake up alone.

Before I'm really even awake, I just feel it and know it somehow. There's no need to stretch out a roving hand or an exploratory foot beneath the heavy, war-torn comforters. The truth is, I don't even need to open my eyes. I can just *sense* it; that emptiness there, the lack of a presence. The lack of life.

I do it anyway. Despite every logical, rational, practical part of my brain screaming out in protest, warning me that this is both a waste of precious time and a dangerous game I'm playing with a rusty emotional lockbox that may as well be a dormant volcano at this point, I do it anyway.

Eyes still closed, sleep still threatening just at the edge of my awareness to sweep me back in, I turn my body over and reach with one hand and one foot out along the cool, thin fabric. My fingers and toes search blindly, dumbly, for a warm mass that I can fully comprehend isn't going to be there.

Because nothing is there, because she's not there, and I know it. I knew it all along, and I still went through all the motions anyway because I'm human, and because humans are goddamn stupid creatures of habit.

And maybe I'll tell myself later that I was still dreaming or half-asleep, and that's the only real reason why I stretched myself out like that. But deep down inside, I'll know that it's all a lie. Because deep down inside, I've already accepted that my life will never be the same again.

Quite suddenly, and with absolutely no forewarning, that stark, simple truth shatters me into a thousand tiny pieces. And for the first time in five years, I find myself crying, and then sobbing, and finally wailing like a child.

If Ruthie were here right now, she wouldn't let me carry on like this.

That thought only makes it worse, though, and now I'm screaming into my pillow.

A short time later, this morning's unfortunate episode is just that: an unfortunate episode that I've already crumpled up, mentally discarded, and largely forgotten about. The forgetting part is still mostly manufactured right now, but I have no doubt that by the time I'm done with what I must do today, it will begin to feel less like effort and more like unconscious acceptance.

'Unconscious acceptance.' There's something to that, I think, when it comes to the way I live my life these days. I briefly contemplate making it into a sort of mantra for myself, but then I realize to do so would be impossible, since it would defeat the true meaning of what it means to be unconscious. Something about that revelation strikes a soft pang of bitter anger in my chest, and I vow to dismiss the idea of mantras altogether as payback.

Emotions are a dangerous commodity. I don't want to dwell on this morning's episode, but it's important that I realize I can't have something like that happen to me again. It's one thing to acknowledge a feeling peeking out and up from deep inside of you; it's another to let your guard down and watch that little fucker grab hold of the wheel and run the whole ship right into the rocks.

Teetering somewhere on the brink between psychological self-flagellation and a hardening resolution not to get duped again, I take it out on some berries, nuts, and greens with the flat end of a spoon.

Death is a natural part of life. Get over yourself, blueberries.

This isn't your first loss, and lord knows it won't be your last loss, so woman up, walnuts.

You knew this day would come, spinach.

Don't be a little bitch, blackberries. No one likes a crybaby.

Fuck you, kale. I hate you, I hate you, I hate you, I hate you, I hate you…

As it becomes every morning, the mixture before me in the dirty ceramic bowl starts to look like something a raccoon might shit out in the woods. It's a dark, thick paste that never fails to remind me how much I truly miss the halcyon days of blending up fresh smoothies and juices in seconds using a multi-speed electric blender. But the chunky sludge is nutritious and, more importantly, better than nothing, so I scoop it up in gobs and gulp them down whole.

When it's all gone and I've scrubbed the bowl dry

with yellowed paper towels, I take a light swig from my canteen, swish the water around between my teeth to rinse out all those pesky seeds, and swallow. There's that familiar sensation of not being quite as clean and clear orally as I'd like to be, but it soon fades into the background just like everything else. Who am I trying to impress anyway, right?

Now that I've had breakfast, it's time to see to the chickens. I open the door of a musty old linen closet and slide a stack of neatly folded towels and rags over to the side of the highest shelf, revealing a small safe.

1-2-2-5-9-1.

As I do every day, I try not to think of the meaning behind the combination—which, to someone stupid, might just be a string of random digits; and, to someone smart, might just be the date of Christmas Day in 1991. It's neither one of those things to me, but I've gotten good at not thinking about any of this.

Unconscious acceptance. Move along. Do what you came here to do and keep going. Anything else is too risky.

I check to make sure the Glock is fully loaded, even though I know it is. Some habits are healthier than others, and I fully believe that this is one of them. When I'm done, I holster the pistol behind me in the waistband of my pants, lock the safe, position the towels back in front of it, and close the closet.

In this house that I call mine, there are three exterior doors, eleven first-floor windows, and five second-floor windows.

The sixteen windows have all been thoroughly boarded up on both sides, and those on the ground-level have tubular steel security bars installed over the wood.

There was a stint when I learned to tell time from the quality of the sunlight streaming in through these windows, rather than from a long-dead watch around my wrist or from a cell phone and numerous other digital appliance clocks that all no longer function. That phase is over, though, and now time is mostly irrelevant anyway.

While it's theoretically still possible to open two of the doors, it would take a truly herculean effort from multiple human beings to do so without the aid of power tools and machinery. These doors—the front door and the back door of the house—are not only boarded up on both sides, they're also secured from the inside by heavy sheets of metal that have been drilled into the walls. That was done back when electricity was still a thing, of course.

Unless I've gravely miscalculated my situation during these past five years of relative solitude and safety, there's only one way in or out of my adopted forest home-turned-fortress, and that's the cellar door.

From the inside, it is twice-chained and twice-locked, and I wear the two keys in a janitorial ring that hangs from a silver necklace between my breasts. While the steel door obviously cannot be locked from the outside, I do keep it covered as best I can by rotting wooden pallets and logs of firewood. It's impossible to arrange the camouflage perfectly and then get inside and close the door behind me, but I do my best.

I'm confident that if anyone were to ever stumble across this place accidentally, they'd first assume it to be decrepit, uninhabitable, and long since abandoned. Even if they inspected it further, there's a good chance they'd overlook the area where the cellar door is located. And assuming in a worst-case scenario they still, for some reason, decided to try and break their way in somehow, I would hear them coming long before they ever made much progress.

The chickens are another story. Two words immediately come to mind: necessary evil. As much as I'd love to subsist on a completely plant-based diet from the modest secret garden I maintain in the woods not far from the property, scrambled eggs are a guilty pleasure of mine. With six hens, I get about two dozen eggs each week, which is more than enough to supplement my meals and my body with the protein I need to stay strong at my age.

Unlike the house, however, there's only so much fortification I can do with a chicken coop. I keep the structure locked at night (yet another key that hangs from my janitor ring necklace), but the fowl need to get outside during the day and peck around their fenced-in run. They're also not exactly the stealthiest or quietest of creatures. Even with no houses in any direction for twenty miles, these noisy but extremely valuable birds in their lightly secured coop are a constant source of anxiety for me.

It's a long, slow walk down into the basement. Recently, I've been experiencing flashes of what I can only describe as a kind of dizziness or vertigo while descending these creaky wooden steps. It's not something I can recall happening the first four-and-a-half years of my tenure here, but over the past five or six months, the feeling has materialized both more frequently and more acutely.

Am I just getting old? It's possible. I'm turning forty-four in a couple of months, but unless the old scale in the bathroom is broken (that's also possible), I'm weighing in just a bit over one-thirty-five.

Given everything I know about my family history, that's fan-fucking-tastic. Yeah, I'm not running six miles a day like I used to back in my pre-med or residency days, but I'm also not surviving on coffee, sugar, and hospital cafeteria food, either. I eat cleaner today than I ever have before, albeit out of necessity.

When my feet touch the cellar floor, I instinctively reach for the light switch and flip it on. Nothing happens, of course, and I'm left wondering why I just did that. It's been years since I had functioning utilities like power, heat, gas, and running water.

Why did I do that? Where is my head today?

I instantly regret asking that question, because the answer flies in like a barbed arrow and pierces me straight to the heart. There's a wheelbarrow over in the corner of the darkened room next to the extra gardening supplies, and I remember all too well what lies in the basket, still and swaddled in a blanket.

No, I will not go there. Not yet.

Actually, not again. I won't let myself do that again.

With newfound resiliency, I stride across the concrete cellar floor and find the workwoman's bench by memory. Right where I know I left it is my bag of homemade chicken feed. Next to that is another empty bag and a small shovel that I'll use to clean up and repurpose the manure as fertilizer. Next to those two items is my trusty old friend Jim Carrey, the nickname I've given to the mask.

There really is no acceptable explanation for why I reached for that light switch. I know my way around down here by heart. There's a flashlight I keep on this same bench, but I don't need it. Better to conserve the battery life. Better to stay in the dark.

My feet find their way over to the short series of steps that lead up to the exterior cellar door. Calm, composed, and centered, I slip Jim Carrey on over my head and fish the key ring necklace out from beneath my shirt collar.

There are six keys on my ring. The two I'm looking for right now go to the locks and chains at this door. There are two keys that I no longer use—one for the front door and one for the back door—since both doors to the house are now blockaded from both sides. One key starts and locks my jeep, tucked away and hidden in the forest about half a mile from here. And the last key unlocks the chicken coop.

These small, jagged bits of metal jingle in my fingers. I don't need any illumination to find the two keys for the cellar door locks, because they're the same two I use every day right around this time. This is just a day like any other. Nothing needs to be different. There is safety in routine.

No, there is *survival* in routine.

It takes longer than I'd like and longer than it should, but I find the keys I'm looking for and get all the locks and chains removed from the cellar door. As is my habit, I'm slow and quiet in opening the great steel beast into the outside world. The only sound is the steady groan of the hinge as it fights against the added resistance of the pallets and logs stacked against it on the other side.

When there's enough space for me to slip outside the crack with all my supplies, that's exactly what I do. Gently, I let the door come back to rest behind me.

Even with the nearest house more than twenty miles away—and presumably still uninhabited—there's no reason to be careless.

The chickens seem happy to see me this morning, which helps take my mind off the rest of today's chores. I clean the coop. I gather the eggs. I liberate the hens. The sun is shining outside, and it's a relatively cool morning, considering the season. I should be savoring this; or, if not that, I should at least be happy.

But it's harder than I thought to keep Ruthie at bay. I can't look at these chickens clucking and fluttering around in the pen without imagining her right here beside me. I can see the reflections of the birds in her soft brown eyes, excited and alive with their activity. We're a team, her and I. This is something we always do together. Or something we always *did* together.

No. I will *not* let this happen. Not again.

On to the garden. That's what's next on today's list. Get busy living or get busy dying. That's from a movie, I think. A good one, too. I wonder what it was…

This walk through the forest always affords me an opportunity to check on my traps and snares. They're sort of a point of pride for me, to be honest, given I was never what you might consider 'artsy-craftsy' or 'outdoorsy' before NDV.

I still don't know if I qualify for either of those designations, but what I *do* know is that if any living creature comes within ten yards of where the tree line clears and my property begins, they're in for a world of hurt and surprise.

Speaking of surprise, there's a mutilated rat's body half-hidden beneath a head of kale in my secret garden. This is exactly the kind of thing that Ruthie would have been able to spot and warn me about well before my own powers of discovery kicked in, but because I'm all alone, the sudden revelation of the rodent's torn, bloodied carcass absolutely throws me for a jolt. I don't quite scream, but I do fall back on my heels and land hard on my ass in the dirt with a grunt.

Something looks like it has *played* with this wretched creature. The missing parts, as well as those still intact, just don't add up to a natural death, at least not according to my own admittedly amateur estimation. My brain wants to hit play on "Circle of Life" from *The Lion King* soundtrack, but it's hard not to hear shades of "Psycho Killer" by Talking Heads instead.

A brief, callous thought arises that I should probably just let nature run its course on this poor soul. After all, the decomposition probably won't hurt my vegetables any. Gross as it is, the process might actually help them.

But the idea of a dead rat making its way through osmosis into my breakfast routine is just too much to bear. That gelatinous mush is barely edible enough as is some mornings without having to stomach a hint of Rodentia, too.

Before I can have any second thoughts, I slide one end of the little gardening shovel I keep out here under the ant-infested corpse and catapult it off into the dense forest underbrush, out of sight and hopefully very soon out of mind. Maybe whatever fearsome predator started on it will finish it now. But not here in my garden. This is a place of peace. We're all herbivores here.

Once I'm done tending to my plants, I make my way back along the wooded path, again taking time here and there to check on the traps and snares.

Obviously, I'm not actually expecting something to have changed in the short interim between when I came up here and now, but it's less about expectation and more about due diligence and repetition. Mistakes happen when you let yourself get careless. One day you're cutting corners, the next day you might be pushing daisies. There's no such thing as being too careful. Not in this fucked-up world, anyway.

By now, it's maybe mid-day. I wear this watch that doesn't tell time on my wrist out of some bizarre nostalgic ritualism I've never quite come to terms with, because there is absolutely *zero* use to it being there other than as a metallic form of sunblock for a thin stretch of skin below my hand. With the livestock and the garden both attended to, there are just two things left to do out here before it's time to head back inside and lock myself up for the remainder of the day and night.

The first thing is far easier than the second. I won't think about the second until I have to. Although I've done a real piss-poor job of that so far today.

There's always something therapeutic about gathering fruits, nuts, and berries. It's not hard to imagine myself a villager in an ancient civilization whose main societal function is to forage and collect resources. The truth is that I know exactly where I'm going and where to look—all the spots I hit on my route are familiar checkpoints for the Bergstrom family, and many of these trees and bushes were actually planted by them within the past fifty years and well before NDV. There are even a couple scattered trees that Hope and I planted together once upon a time, though those aren't nearly as large or bountiful yet as the others.

It's only when I'm done with this first task that I

begin to accept there's nothing left for me to do out here but the second task.

Task. It's a *task.* I fucking hate myself for even equating what's about to happen to a task, a chore, an errand.

But it is necessary. As much as I want to scream into my pillow again and curse myself for being so rigidly heartless and unemotional, I know it's the right strategy. The second I start to let my guard down again and really feel what's happening inside me today, it's all over. If I have to be a little pansy-ass bitch, I'm at least going to be a little pansy-ass bitch from inside my motherfucking queen's castle.

Yes, that's right. Curse. Swear. Use all the words you know will make you feel tough. The words you used to pull out in dive bars and bowling alleys and seedy nightclubs after too much whiskey and dancing. Too much making out and feeling each other up under sticky pub tables and strobing lights. The kind of words you'd try on for size at times to impress Hope or Hope's girlfriends to let them know you're not just another book-smart career-woman trying to beat a man at his own game. That's the kind of talk that used to get her wet right there on the dance floor, and it made you feel just as sexy and young and vibrant as the rest of them, even if you always felt like you were somehow ten years older and thirty years wiser than your peers.

It's all fun and games until I'm at the cellar door again. All thoughts and memories of drunken, oblivious, frivolous, passionate foolishness flit away like fireflies in a hurricane, and I'm left with nothing except the blank, solemn, dreadful responsibility of what I must do now.

The easiest way to bring the wheelbarrow out is to

go up the steps backwards and drag it behind me. Every time the wheel clunks to a halt another level higher, though, my breath catches in my throat and my heart skips a beat. I know there's no way I'd let the basket or its precious cargo topple over, but just the very thought of it makes my stomach turn into knots.

It's hotter now outside than it was before. The air has grown still and expectant as I weave my way along a winding path through the thick wood.

Not far up ahead is a dense thicket of bamboo that, to this day, and for all intents and purposes, makes no sense to me in this North American temperate deciduous forest environment. But because it's both unusual and unimitated in this rather uniform locale, it's also therefore special and unique. And even if I didn't find it so before Hope's passing, I certainly find it so now.

Today is not about Hope, though. Today is about Ruthie.

I bring the wheelbarrow to a stop at the edge of the bamboo thicket. Even if today is not supposed to be about Hope, it's hard to accept that when I'm seeing her grave right in front of me. Knowing that some part of her, even if it's just bones and dust and rot, is right there less than ten feet beneath the ground, is enough to bring me to my knees.

Thankfully, the wheelbarrow is also there to break my fall, and I lean on it heavily as I try with all my might to utterly blockade those thoughts and feelings that just will not stop with me today.

There's a reason I don't come out here anymore. Unless it's December the twenty-fifth—which is her birthday, because she's my forever Christmas baby—I don't like to visit. Or maybe I would *like* to visit, but I know that I can't. Because something would probably happen that's akin to what's happening right now, and that would be dangerous and nonproductive and stupid.

Despite all that, there's work to be done. I only have one task left on today's agenda, and then I can retreat back to my miserable private sanctuary and find some other way to distract myself from the terrifying reality of this new life.

I lift the shovel gingerly off the wheelbarrow and set to work. There's solace in quietude and there's solace in sweat. I wring as much as I can from both before it's too late.

When the hole is ready, I am not. There's something all too familiar about digging in this particular area of the forest. Even though it's been five years, it suddenly feels like it was just yesterday that I was standing in this same spot, with this same shovel, undertaking this same task.

Of course, back then, it was for a person, and not a dog. And it was not just for a person, it was for Hope. It was for my best friend, my soulmate, my life partner, my wife. My everything.

Of course, now it is not just for a dog, though, either. Ruthie was my dog, she was Hope's dog, she was our dog together. She was the reason we first moved in together, probably long before I would have otherwise agreed to such an arrangement.

And, as of the past five years since Hope went away and left me to fend for myself in this crazy shitstorm, Ruthie has been the one and only constant companion by my side, day in and day out, accompanying me to the chicken run and to the secret garden and to the fruit and nut trees and going everywhere inside the house with me, including sleeping with me every night beneath the covers of the bed that I'll never share with the woman who adopted her.

Had. Ruthie *had* been the one and only constant companion by my side who *did* all those things.

But she can't do any of them anymore because she's dead now, dead like her mother before her, and dead like I will be, I'm sure, soon enough. Because what's the point of any of this really if it can't be shared with someone else, even if that someone else is a four-legged animal that licks her own butthole?

Licked.

I close my eyes and dip my fingers below the body in the wheelbarrow basket. Some insane, asinine part of me wants to unwrap her and shake her awake, like somehow that might bring her back from the dead. She's fourteen years old, though. This dog lived a perfectly normal, perfectly long, perfectly happy life.

Down to my knees I go again as I lower the swaddled creature into the shallow grave. There's a sudden strong desire to peel the blanket back and look upon her one last time, but I savagely beat that impulse back like it's the most sacrilegious, profane thought in the galaxy.

Instead, I rise up and take the shovel in my hands. Before I can think about any of it any longer, I'm ferrying mounds of dirt and grass into the hole. Every time a load falls atop the soft, blanketed mass down below me, a pressure valve threatens to break loose inside my soul.

I can't stop thinking about her stupid smiling face with her tongue lolling out comically on the side of it, or her hind leg reaching up as she scratched frantically at an unseen itch on the back of a floppy ear, or the way she tilted her whole head up to howl at nothing simply because I was howling and Hope was howling and she wanted to howl, too, because she was a part of us and a member of our pack and our child.

It's no use. The tears are there all over again, the unfortunate episode, the conscious denial of that which is real and unavoidable. I pat the dirt down as best I can, but I also don't really care anymore, because what's really the point of anything ever again, anyway?

And now that I'm done, I put the shovel back in the wheelbarrow, and I grab the handles and I turn the whole thing and my whole body away from this godawful bamboo thicket, and I start walking in the opposite direction just as fast as my legs will carry me, bound and determined never to return again, not even at Christmas this time for her birthday, not for all the world. In my head, the next time I come here, I'll be a dead body myself, arriving at long last to join my two sisters in the ground.

But then I remember that I'm the last one, the Last of the Mohicans, and there's nobody left to bury me now. And that thought is easily the worst one I've had all day, and it puts a poison cherry on top of the satanic sundae I've been unwillingly swallowing for hours now with these reckless thoughts and feelings of Hope and Ruthie and of what it means to be really, truly, finally all alone.

TWO

"Come here. Come on. Get down, Ruthie. You can do it. Be a big girl now."

Hope slaps her thigh enthusiastically twice and points to the pavement.

"You can do it. Come on now."

The puppy—I have not consented to the name Ruth Bader Ginsburg for a *dog* just yet—alternates staring frantically at Hope and at the ground. I'm sure the unforgiving black surface looks a million miles away from the floorboard of the jeep.

"Come on out. Be a big girl, Ruthie. Jump down."

Hope keeps smiling and slapping her thigh while talking in a weird, singsong falsetto voice that I don't think I've ever heard her use before. It's endearing, even if it's not necessarily attractive. Christ, though… is this going to be the new normal? If so, I should probably squash it right now before it's too late.

"Maybe it just needs a little boost."

I say the words and take decisive action at the same time, scooping the small black-and-white animal and setting it down gingerly on the asphalt between us.

Hope immediately relieves me of the leash, for which I'm actually thankful.

"Please don't refer to her as an 'it.' You can call her Ruth, Ruthie, Ruth Bader Ginsburg, RBG, Your Honor, The Honorable RBG, or The Notorious RBG. But you cannot call her 'it.'"

"Are we sure about this name? I love Ruth Bader Ginsburg as much as anybody, but it almost feels like we're insulting her memory if we name a pound puppy after her."

Hope's brown eyes blaze with righteous indignation.

"First of all, she is a *rescue*, not a *pound puppy*. And second of all, what better way to honor RBG than to make her the namesake of our newest family member?"

Even the mutt is staring challengingly at me. Clearly, I'm outnumbered. This is how it starts.

"We're not going to be one of those couples that gets a 'who rescued who?' bumper sticker and dresses up their dog for Halloween. I'm laying the law down now on all of that."

Hope grins mischievously, winks at me, and starts walking.

"You can lay the law down now all you want. But I'm the one who has a Supreme Court justice on my side."

And she does. It's a small, furry, awkward little thing, but it's right there at her side already, prancing and galloping forward to keep up with Hope's long, athletic strides. And all the while, my girlfriend keeps a firm hold on the leash and fully lets loose with that high-pitched baby voice.

Terrific. Just terrific. I hit the locks on the jeep door and close it behind me.

I'm not sure if it's more funny or more annoying

that I have to jog a bit to catch up with this new dynamic duo. But am I really about to let myself get jealous of an animal?

Perhaps. We'll see how the rest of the hike goes.

"She's doing great, isn't she?"

Hope says it as I draw even with them. Based on that ridiculous voice she keeps doing, I'm pretty sure she's talking to the dog and not to me.

"You sure you're not going too fast for her? Your legs are like, six times longer than hers."

"See, you do care. I knew deep down you'd end being a big softie about this whole thing."

"Of course, I care. Just because I don't want to name our dog Ruth Bader Ginsburg doesn't make me a monster."

"Look! Did you see that?"

Hope stops dead in her tracks and points at the dog, who is looking up at me with wet brown eyes and panting furiously.

"See! She's already responding to her name."

Hope starts walking again.

"It's too late, Alex. Game over. What's done is done. Maybe you get to name the next one."

That comment necessitates an immediate laugh-snort.

"Ha! 'The next one.' I'm still not convinced about the first one."

"Well, then I guess it's a good thing you don't have to be convinced, isn't it? Never forget that I gave you three choices, and this is the one you picked. You're stuck with us now, for better or worse."

For better or worse. It's an interesting choice of words, and I wonder if she did that intentionally. Hope did indeed give me three choices; although, in my mind, they were more like ultimatums than options. Diamond, diapers, or dog. That's what she said to me. Put that way, the 'choice' was an easy one.

"Are you really that lonely already? I haven't even started residency yet."

Hope's jaw tightens.

"It's a pre-emptive strike. Call it an insurance policy for later."

"You act like I'm getting deployed for four years. It's OB-GYN, not Afghanistan."

"I'm just doing what I need to do to prepare myself. You've been very honest and very communicative with me on what I should expect and on what you're going to need from me to get through this. This is me giving you the exact same courtesy."

The puppy lunges at a squirrel off the side of the trail. Constrained by the leash and by her own youthful clumsiness, she doesn't come anywhere close before the bushy-tailed acrobat is darting up a nearby tree to safety.

"That's okay, Ruthie. Next time."

"Next time? You're not actively encouraging her to kill wildlife now, are you?"

I'm expecting Hope to fire back a quick retort, so I'm surprised when I catch her glancing over at me with what looks like a kind of glowing fondness instead.

"You're so funny, you know that? You want so badly to pretend like you don't already secretly love this cute little girl, but you just can't help yourself. It's already coming out of you in bits and pieces; a crack here, a splinter there. I guarantee you that when all is said and done, you're gonna be the one snuggling her and taking naps together on the couch. Just watch. And by the time

October rolls around? We'll see then how you feel about dressing up for Halloween. I bet you're the one who suggests a theme for all three of us."

I can't help but laugh at the absurdity of that, imagining the three of us dressed up in matching black judges' robes, and I decide to let Hope in on the joke.

"You could wear a white wig and go as Sandra Day. I could be the as-of-yet-unknown future first Black woman Supreme Court justice. Or I could just be Clarence Thomas in drag… *puke.*"

It's Hope's turn to laugh. The tension from earlier seems to have dissipated a bit.

"Nah, I'd want to be Kagan. I'm still holding out that she's secretly one of us."

"A lesbian?"

"A Swiftie."

"Of course."

Fucking Taylor Swift. Not Beyoncé, not Rihanna, not even Madonna or Britney Spears. Of all the women in the world, Hope had to pick the Whitest, straightest one to be her favorite musician and celebrity crush. The heart wants what it wants, I guess. I'm just glad it also wants me. I laugh and take hold of the free hand she's not using to hold a leash.

Speaking of the line between homos and heteros, there are three shirtless men splashing around at the edge of a small body of water just up ahead. Hope's much more familiar with these state parks than I am, but I'm pretty sure that forest pond is not exactly meant for casual swimming. It's probably not meant for humans in general.

These muscled-up bros don't seem to give a damn, though. They've all stripped down to their Polo Ralph

Lauren boxer briefs and seem much more preoccupied with wrestling and dunking each other's heads beneath the water than they are with the possibility of any leeches or snakes being in that water with them. White, obnoxious, and probably drunk, these college kids stand out like a sore thumb on steroids in an otherwise serene, quiet patch of nature.

Hope and I don't have to say a word to each other. As we pass them by, neither one of us gives the boys an ounce of the attention they so obviously, blatantly, desperately crave from the world around them.

Ruth is too new to our gang, though, and she doesn't get the memo. Maybe it's all the whooping and the splashing that makes the puppy think this must look like great fun, because the leash suddenly goes taut as she drives her way off the trail and back toward the men.

"Nah-ah. Come on, Ruthie. Keep moving."

For such a little thing, she sure is strong when she wants to be. And stubborn. The more noise the guys make, the more she wants to go join them. I can feel Hope's body tensing as she pulls against the resistance on the leash.

"Nice bitch you got there."

One of the three men smiles and nods amiably from the water. The other two finally stop wrestling and appear to take notice of us for the first time.

Hope's still struggling with the dog. We're still holding hands. I'm acutely aware of this second fact, even though I shouldn't have to be.

"Excuse me?"

The speaker scratches absentmindedly at the crotch of his briefs. His smile is radiant and friendly, and his ruddy cheeks tell me he's either very sunburnt or very drunk.

"I said, that's a nice bitch you got there. But I was talking to her."

He doesn't need to do this, but he points at Hope just to make his point clear. One of the other guys snickers.

I can feel Hope growing tenser by my side, and I'm aware at this moment that it's no longer a response to the dog.

"Come again?"

There are whole oceans separating the way I said, "Excuse me?" from the way Hope just said, "Come again?" We're technically saying the same thing, but our meanings couldn't be further apart. I want to whisper something like "easy now" or even just "Hope," but the young man speaks faster than me.

"Your bitch. Your female dog. You do know what a bitch is, don't you?"

I want to ask him how he knows our dog is female, but I also know that it's pointless to engage. Besides, I know what he really means right now, as well as what he really wants from us and wants from me, specifically. I'm not about to give him the satisfaction.

"Come on, Hope."

It's a full-on tug-of-war now with me pulling Hope and Hope pulling Ruth. Except now Hope feels like she's resisting me more than she's resisting Ruth. And that's a problem.

"Hope. Come on."

The puppy is bouncing and bounding wildly at the end of the leash, but Hope's body is solid and still. It's like trying to yank a slab of granite from a rock-face by hand. She's staring hard at the men, and her muscles are tight with coiled energy. I know that if I don't find a way to defuse and de-escalate this situation fast, I'll lose her entirely.

"It's not worth it. I promise you. Hope? Let's go."

With a swift tug, I manage to somehow dislodge her concentration just a bit, if not her actual physical orientation. She turns her head, and I see all too well the telltale mounting violence in her eyes. I know that look, and I know what it means and how dangerous it could be for us.

"Let's keep going, okay?"

It's imperative that she understands me right now. I will every unspoken thought I can into the expression I impart on her and hope that it's enough.

And it looks like it just might be after all. Her chin dips a couple times as her jaw spasms and her head nods a begrudging, cooling acceptance of what I'm communicating telepathically to her with all my focus and intention.

"Yeah. Let's."

We're on the same team now, and with our powers combined, the young pup is no match for us. There will be other swimming holes and other playtimes, Ruth. This is neither the time nor the place. You will learn. You will learn.

He calls out to us again once we're back on the path.

"You're not even gonna say thank you?"

I lift up my free hand without breaking stride. Ten years ago, I would have beat his ass by now. Five years ago, I would have at least given him the finger. But I'm thirty years old now, and I'm starting residency in two weeks, so I just send him a quick wave without looking back, and then I'm done with it.

"Fucking *dykes*."

It's not quite a knockout blow for Hope, but it's close. Her feet stop moving for a second, and I feel the heat exploding in rapid psychic bursts from her body.

From somewhere deep within the well of my life experience, I drive us forward until she's in motion again and my voice is a command without me needing to make it so.

"No."

We plow forward along the trail, and if the kids say anything else to us, it's lost behind the leaves and the gentle noise of running water. The only clearly discernible sound coming from behind us now is laughter, which is as sickening as it is unsurprising.

Hope and I just keep walking, hand in hand, dog in tow, breathing thinly out of our nostrils and wondering to ourselves who will be the first to break the silence… and wondering what will be said.

After a while, it's Hope.

"Motherfuckers."

I look over at her, less because I'm expecting her to say something else and more because I'm just making sure she's not about to turn around and go back there again.

"Those motherfuckers."

Maybe the puppy's more intuitive than I gave it credit for, because Ruth has slowed her pace a bit, and I'd swear she looks like she keeps checking in with us. Or, at least, checking in with Hope.

"I can't believe that."

"I can."

Her eyes dart over to meet mine.

"You can?"

"Absolutely."

I can tell she wants me to elaborate, and even though I really don't want to, I love her, so I will.

"It is what it is. No point in trying to change some people's minds."

"What? How can you say that?"

I sigh. This is not the first time we've had this conversation, and unfortunately, it won't be the last. Every time though, it's never easy to explain.

"My mama used to say that some people just need Jesus. You can take them to church and make them read the Bible all you want, but ultimately, it's on them to decide whether they're ever going to become a good person. And with those types of people, you just can't win. You'll drive yourself crazy trying to turn them into something they're not."

Hope is fuming, but I can see that she's at least absorbing everything I'm saying to her. Why? Because she's a good person, even if she has a short fuse.

"So, you're saying those fuckheads back there are hopeless and that only God can save them?"

"I'm saying that's what my mama would say, yes, if she were alive today. You know where I stand on God and Jesus and all that stuff."

"Yeah, but where do you stand on what just happened right now?"

Truthfully, I stand on the side of saying or doing whatever magical combination I need to do to change the subject. The sooner we can stop talking about this, the sooner we can put it behind us.

"On them calling us dykes?"

"Yes, that. And calling you a bitch. What's your stance? Not your mom's stance. What do *you* think?

How do *you* feel?"

I sigh and stare forward out along the path. My focus widens until all the scenery and features up ahead of us start to soften and blur together in my field of vision. It really is beautiful here. I can see why she likes getting outside and into nature more and more. It's a recent phase of hers that's quickly becoming a phase of ours. And now that we have a dog to take on walks with us, maybe it won't be a phase much longer. I think I'd like that, come to think of it.

"What do I think? I think I've been called worse things in my life than dyke or bitch. I know I have, actually, and it won't be the last time, either. That's something that's not going away anytime soon, so you learn to live with it as best you can. And then when it happens, you don't give those people the time of day. You don't waste your time or your energy on them, because that's what they want. And if you don't give it to them, then they can't have any power over you."

I can feel Hope's eyes searing into me still.

"That sounds like you're ignoring the problem rather than confronting it."

I sigh again.

"You wouldn't understand."

She stops walking.

"Why? Because I'm not Black?"

No, because you came from a loving family who are also so rich they have a second home, a *summer home*, in the middle of a fucking *forest*. Because you've never had to work a day in your life unless you wanted to. Because you're absolutely, breathtakingly gorgeous, and you can use your looks to your advantage, and you know it. Because your fiery temper, while not something to be trifled with, also affords you the great luxury of being able to speak your mind without a filter and to act willfully and even irrationally at times, knowing full well that others will chalk up your extreme behavior as a loveable personality quirk. Because you're not going into an extremely competitive, extremely cut-throat, extremely White-straight-male dominated profession where everyone around you either secretly or not-so-secretly is hoping you'll fail. Because you didn't grow up with religion, with Sunday school, and with guilt hanging like a heavy golden cross around your neck. Because you came out to your parents at an early age, and they accepted you for who you were and didn't try to force you into someone you were not. And yes, because you're not Black.

"Did you see their hats?"

Hope blinks.

"What?"

"Their hats. There were three hats on the ground with their clothes. All identical. All bright red with white letters."

She doesn't get it.

"I'm not changing their minds. If I try to talk to them, if I try to *fight* them, what good is that gonna do? You think they'll listen to me? You think some backwoods country cop will listen to me, will believe me, will take my side over theirs? Baby, I love you, but if you think any of that for a second, you're being naïve."

Hope bristles but doesn't say anything. She knows I'm right. Even if she doesn't want to admit it out loud, she's at least wise enough not to say anything more just for the sake of having an argument.

The rest of the hike goes by uneventfully. Hope and

I don't talk very much, and when we do, it's light, trivial, observational stuff.

As much as I'd hoped the pond incident wouldn't ruin the remainder of our nature trek, I'd be the naïve one if I really believed that, which I never did. It's absolutely possible to let go of indignation and move on from rage; we all do it each and every day of our lives. We have to, or else no one would ever get anything done. The human race wouldn't survive.

That said, it's not exactly easy.

I have to admit, though, the dog really helps. It's hard to keep festering and boiling beneath the surface with something so joyful, innocent, and whimsical around, licking at your ankles and snapping at butterflies without a care in the world.

Maybe in my next life, I'll come back as a dog. And maybe in this life, I'll come to love this one.

Ah, who am I kidding? I already do.

THREE

It's the third shriek that finally gets me out of bed and into my clothes and boots.

The first one was enough to rip me forcefully from a brutal nightmare. Awake all of a sudden, yet far from alert, my deadened brain still had enough sense to attribute the scream to my dream world. After a few moments of collecting myself and willing my thoughts to abandon their phantom tormenters, I slipped back into darkness for who knows how long.

When it happened a second time, I found myself wide-eyed and staring up into the black pit of my ceiling. Stuck somewhere between sleep paralysis and an uneasy watchfulness, I waited breathlessly for the sound to come again and confirm the worst of my fears and suspicions. But because it didn't come, I must have eventually chalked it up once again to the spectral ghosts of my subconscious and succumbed back to restless sleep.

I'm ready for the third one, though. Or, if not altogether ready, I'm somehow still expectant. No sooner does the ear-splitting wail pierce in from the night through the boarded-up bedroom window than the pads of my feet hit the floor, and just like that, I'm awake and moving.

If there's one thing my old life prepared me for, it's the ability to spring into action at a moment's notice. You could be sitting and enjoying a book or a magazine in the break room while sipping on lukewarm coffee and munching on a jelly donut one minute, and then the next minute, you're rushing to someone's bedside because their water just broke and it's your job to help them usher a brand-new human life into the world.

Do that enough times over, and it just becomes a part of your identity. Nothing can change that. Not even the end of the world, apparently.

The pale needle of my flashlight guides me softly down wooden stairs. There's more need for speed than there is cause for caution, but I'm still careful to avoid the spots on the steps where I know they'll creak. The chances of anyone hearing any of that from outside are virtually impossible after all the structural modifications I've completed on this building. But then again, I've never tested the authenticity of that belief, either.

Through the inky blackness of the empty house, my light and I find our way together to the linen closet.

First, the door.

Second, the towels.

Third, the safe.

Fourth, the weapon.

Fifth, repeat the whole process, but this time in reverse.

Deviate from a process, even and especially during times of stress and pressure, and that's when you'll make a mistake. And I can't afford to make a mistake.

I'm even more careful going down the steps into the basement for three reasons. One: these steps are older and louder than the ones connecting the second story to the ground floor. Two: these steps are far closer in proximity to the cellar door, which I firmly believe is the only real way in or out of this house and thus, the most vulnerable part of it. And three: I absolutely cannot allow myself to encounter that fucking vertigo right now, not with whatever new danger is here at hand.

Thankfully, the dizzy spells leave me alone—for now, at least. My flashlight guides me over to Jim Carrey on the bench, and I'm surprised at just how much my hands are shaking as I slip the gas mask down over my face. Maybe it's because I've never heard a sound like this before. Or maybe it's because I still haven't really figured out what my plan is.

All I know, though, is that I cannot just sit and sleep and *wait* for something to happen or not happen. Passively biding my time while some person, animal, or monster howls out there in agony is a horrifically dumb idea. Not only does it keep me in the metaphorical dark about what exactly is happening outside, but it also draws unnecessary attention to my location. If I can hear this creature's shrill screech from deep inside a well-fortified house, there's no telling how far its cry might travel through the surrounding woods.

What if it's the chickens? My heart somersaults within my chest as a wholly uninvited graphic image springs to mind of bird carcasses ripped to shreds, blood and feathers everywhere inside a ransacked coop, some fox or weasel still in there, its whiskered muzzle dripping deep crimson onto the stained floor, glowing evil eyes glaring back at me an unnatural yellow in the flashlight's gleam.

What an unimaginably awful premonition. While I

certainly don't *need* the chickens or their eggs for personal survival, losing even one of the animals would be emotionally and psychologically devastating after everything I've endured of late.

I think back to the mutilated rat I found in the garden earlier today and wonder to myself if that wretched creature's killer has now come to my sanctuary to wreak havoc on what little I have left to enjoy in this world.

The idea instills a newfound urgency to my actions, and now I can feel a tingling vengeance bubbling up inside the stove of my stomach. Sure, I'll be quiet, and I'll be quick, but if these portents prove true, I'm not sure I'll have it in me to show mercy. It may be the circle of life, but if it is, that also makes me an apex predator. And I really do like my scrambled eggs.

Of course, this is all assuming the source of the sound is animal, not human. These theories and plots are formulated on a baseless belief that what I keep hearing, even now with my ear pressed against the cold steel cellar door, is either the gruesome yowls of my dying hens or some barbaric war cry of their murderer, or murderers, in bloodlust. If the spine-tingling shrieks are man- or woman-made… well, I don't have any idea then what I'll do.

The last time I came into contact with another human being was nearly a year ago now. I was out foraging for medical supplies on an ill-advised trip to the nearest residential area, a semi-rural, semi-suburban neighborhood about forty miles west of here.

At the time, I'd believed all the houses to have been long since abandoned. And while I was right about that notion for the first three houses I visited, all it took to hastily abort my mission was hearing the distinct sound of a man's cough come from upstairs in the fourth house.

Fortunately, I'd escaped the kitchen undetected through the back door before circling back to my jeep up the street and then gunning it all the way home to the forest, eyes locked on the rearview mirror the whole way back, absolutely positive that I was being pursued.

Needless to say, I'd returned empty-handed, and I've never gone back since. Truthfully, it took me days to finally come to terms with a guarded acceptance that maybe I had indeed somehow made it back to safety without being followed. And it took me weeks not to wake up in the middle of the night in a cold sweat, certain that someone had found our haven and forced their way inside to kill me and Ruthie in order to take our place and steal our beloved bastion right out from under us.

What does a human being sound like? Certainly not like this, whatever this pitiful creature is right now outside the door that's creating such an alarm. These shrieking cries sound too animalistic, too alien, too unhuman. It has to be a beast of some kind. But what kind?

I use two keys from my necklace to remove all the locks and chains keeping me in and keeping *it* out. Ever so softly, I lay all of the metal objects down on the top step beside my booted foot, and then I reach behind me to lift the Glock from the waistband of my pants. With gun in one hand and flashlight in the other, I lean my shoulder up against the heavy surface and push.

There's a new sound now: the slow groan of the hinge as it works against the weight of the barricade camouflage on the other side of the door. Some part of my brain makes a note to remember to oil that hinge in the morning, and some other part of my brain yells at it to shut the fuck up because that's not really what's important right now, is it?

The mournful wailing is so much worse out here in the open. If there's a silver lining, it's that the sound at least provides a kind of sonic cover as I lower the cellar door back into place.

I'm almost positive now that it's coming from over by the chicken coop. Even though this is the outcome I most expected and anticipated, it still feels like I just got gut-punched and had the wind knocked out of me.

I've spent enough time exploring this surrounding area, especially living here these past five years, that I'm confident that whatever predator awaits in the shanty henhouse will be no match for me and my weapon. Even if there were wolves or bears out here, they wouldn't be able to enter the coop that easily. They'd have to force their way in, and I can already see that the small structure looks undamaged from the outside, bathed in the cool white haze of my flashlight.

Besides, there are no wolves or bears out here to begin with. I would have seen one by now, or at least seen tracks or the remnants of prey left behind. Surely, I would know if something that large stalked these woods at night. That's just common sense and cold, hard logic. Surely.

Not only is the coop undamaged from the outside, but the lock on the door is still secure. Moreover, now that I'm here, it doesn't sound like the cries are coming from inside at all. Rather, they're coming from somewhere just behind and beyond the coop. They're coming from the forest.

It's a relief that the chickens are undisturbed, but that relief is also woefully short-lived. Awful as it was to contemplate a full-fledged slaughter in the henhouse, that outcome would have at least made sense to me and represented a possibility I could fathom, even if it wasn't one I could altogether accept and move on from.

This, though. Whatever this is, this is already a thousand times worse.

Not knowing. That's what this is and why it's worse. It's *not knowing* what's happening out there in the darkness that makes me pause right now. I don't know what's out there. All I can do is hear it. I can't see it.

Then the thought occurs that while *it* can't hear me, it can probably—no, it can definitely *see* me.

Against my every instinct, I decide to switch off the flashlight beam. With a quiet click, the pale white ray is extinguished, and now it's all around me, the darkness, and I'm fully immersed in the pregnant dread of the present situation.

And still, the creature shrieks and moans and screams.

I know what pain and suffering sounds like in a human being, whether it's physical, mental, emotional, or all three. That's a familiar sound to these ears after everything I've borne witness to over the past four-and-a-half decades.

This is similar to those things but different. The pain, the terror, the agony, the fear… it's all there, but it's not human. Whatever is making these sounds just ahead of me now is not human. That cannot be human. But I do not know what it is, and that just makes it worse.

Do I turn back now? Any sane person would, even armed as I am. There's no telling what kind of monster or monstrosities lie in wait just up ahead. This whole thing could be some sort of elaborate ruse or strategy to lure me out into the woods, away from the safety and security of my home fortress.

If that was the plan all along, it's a good one. Out here in the open and in the dark, my weapon is only as useful as my eyesight and my wits, neither of which seem highly functional at the moment.

I step forward into the forest because somewhere deep down I just know that I have to. Call it curiosity, call it courage, call it due diligence, or call it moronic stupidity—it doesn't matter what you call it, because I do it all the same.

My eyes are still adjusting as best they can to the natural dark of the woods at night. Even if I thought it wise to turn my flashlight back on—and I don't think it wise—I'm not sure I'd be able to, considering just how moist my fingers and palms are. Between all the sweating and the shaking, it's a small wonder I haven't dropped both the flashlight and the gun by now.

Finally, I glimpse movement and see something rather than only hearing it. Just up ahead, some kind of frenetic mass is writhing around violently.

A twig snaps beneath my foot as I come to a sudden unexpected halt. The thing hears me now for sure, because the writhing stops instantly, along with the screeches. Everything goes still and quiet as I try not to breathe.

Ever so slowly, I lift the Glock up into the air until it's pointed roughly at where I judge the mass to be. I'm fully expecting it to either charge me or to run off in the opposite direction, but neither of those things happen. Instead, the shape remains motionless and silent. I can feel its eyes on me, waiting to register and react to whatever it is that I plan to do next.

What do I plan to do next?

If ever there was a time to shoot first and ask questions later, this is that time. This is that place. This is that world that we live in now. Those types of people finally got what they wanted, and look where it got us as a society. I hope they're happy… if there are any of those morons left.

My finger moves to the trigger. Just a little pressure, and the mystery gets solved in an instant. No more anguish. No more danger. No more threat.

And I'd be doing it a favor, whatever it is, if it's really in that much pain. Hell, maybe I could talk whatever it is into returning the favor before it shuffles off this mortal coil. We could be buddies, like the buddy system they made us use when I was just a girl growing up in school. Hand-in-hand, we could face that great bleak oblivion together. That doesn't sound so bad at all.

It's this particular train of thought that stays my trigger finger. And even though I know it's madness, even though I know it could very well be the difference between life and death, I start to raise my other arm up into the air—the one with the flashlight.

Somehow, the difference between life and death just doesn't seem that different anymore these days. Maybe that's why there's a curious, calm surrender that comes over me as I flick the switch on the plastic tube and make the light appear once more.

Two coal-black pupils swiftly contract within reflective rings of gold. At first, this is the only motion I detect in the ghostly beam. But then, there comes a deliberate twitching, slow and precise, very different than the manic thrashing from before.

There's a new sound, too, and this is also far removed from everything that preceded it. Everything that came from this spot in the woods up until now was shrill, terrifying screams and squeals of torment. This new sound is an earnest, suppliant, desperate whimper. It's a cry for help.

Somehow, an orange tabby cat has become ensnared in one of my traps. I have no idea what a domestic housecat is doing out here in the woods. I've never seen a cat out here before, and honestly, I think I would be less surprised if my flashlight had illuminated any number of other creatures in the trap. Wolves, bears, mountain lions, fucking Siberian tigers… but a kitty cat? Out here, this far away from any other dwelling or domicile, alone in the brutal wilderness? It makes no sense.

Sensical or not, a cat's what I see in front of me all the same. Seeing me seeing it, the cat begins to writhe with a bit more force, and with every jerky movement and flailing limb, it only grows more entangled.

I also swallow hard when the glow from my flashlight reveals its hind legs are both pinched and probably broken between the strong, serrated jaws of a metal trap. There's a good deal of dark, congealed liquid in the dirt below the cat that can only be blood.

This wasn't supposed to happen. While I'll admit I'm not an expert when it comes to setting traps and snares, I thought I did a decent enough job of rigging these outer defenses against intruders. Most of what I constructed came from materials I found around the

Bergstrom property or within their summer home, though some of it I scavenged from junkyards and abandoned estates at the outskirts of civilization, back in the early days when it was still Ruth and me figuring out this whole mess together.

This trap was designed to halt the progress of a man, a woman, or a large predator. Never in my wildest dreams did I imagine a domestic housecat might find itself the unfortunate victim instead. It's an unbelievable development that leaves me feeling sick to my stomach and incredibly guilty at the same time.

Slowly, cautiously, I approach the wounded animal. I'm almost positive that neither the cat nor myself wants it to move its body right now, but instincts are instincts. The closer I get to it, the more the animal grows wary and nervous of my approaching proximity. I can tell that as much as it wants someone or something to help it, there's also a good deal of distrust in this creature, and I can't say that I blame it.

"Easy, now. I'm not gonna hurt you."

The cat doesn't believe me. As the writhing and wriggling intensifies, so too does the pain, and with it, the shrieks and screams. Some primordial, animal instinct is kicking in for this poor beast, and I realize as I draw closer that it has every reason to assume I'm an enemy. After all, these are my traps. This is my gun I levelled at it. In the eyes of a mere pussycat, I must be some frightful, hulking, magnificent goddess come up from the pits of hell to whisk its soul away to perdition.

Then something strange happens. The moment I'm finally close enough to reach out and touch it, the cat goes still.

By the time I've holstered the gun back in my pants-line, it's not even blinking anymore. Those golden eyes are locked on me and on my every movement, but there's a calmness there that didn't exist before, and I hear a sound gurgle up from its throat that can only be described as beseeching.

It's never exactly easy trying to manipulate an animal's body against its will, even when you have nothing but the best of intentions for it. I'm shocked at how vividly and instantly I remember that familiar feeling from my many years as a dog mom to Ruthie. Those same thoughts percolate at the forefront of my brain, and a grim determination comes upon me as I carefully work the cat's body free from the bloody trap and tripwires.

"Easy. Easy now. I'm here to help, I promise."

I resist a comical and insane urge to reassure the cat that I'm a doctor and to let it know that he, she, or they are in great hands now that a certified medical professional is on the scene.

It takes longer than I thought it would to undo all the strings and unlock all the mechanisms holding the foot-trap together, mainly because the cat's not exactly helping me do these things, but when I finally manage to pry the trap open, I'm able to slide the cat's mangled hind legs out from the fearsome metal teeth at last.

Maybe if its legs weren't punctured, swollen, and shattered, this would be the moment that the feline scampers off into the dusky jungle, never to be seen or heard from again. But because its two back legs are utterly useless at the moment, the cat remains strangely motionless on the ground, staring up at me like it's waiting to see what happens next.

What does happen next?

All my thoughts and actions tonight were undertaken with the express belief that some malevolent force of nature, whether animal or human or supernatural, was out here in the woods, waiting to attack me at the most inopportune moment.

It's clear now that I was mistaken. If anything, I owe this cat a kind of penance for my role and responsibility in injuring it, even though that injury was unintentional.

"Don't scratch me, okay? I'm just trying to help."

I switch the flashlight off and jab it into my back pocket. Time to get creative. I slip off my t-shirt and tear the thin fabric into strips. The cat emits a low growl as I use these makeshift bandages to wrap up its hind legs and hopefully staunch some of the blood flow.

When I've done all that I can do with what I have to work with, I slide my fingers beneath its furry body. At least it doesn't *seem* like it wants to resist me. Either the fight's completely gone out of it or it's saving its strength for one last ferocious rally in the dark.

There's absolutely no reason for me to count to three out loud, not out here in the darkened woods, and not with an animal that won't understand what I'm saying or doing anyway. But old habits die hard. On three, I gingerly lift the feline up into the air and nestle its body against my chest, careful as I do this not to unnecessarily jostle its broken back legs. I'm actually surprised at how easily I'm able to keep the cat calm and cradled as I do this.

Just like that, the two of us are moving through the woods, back to the place I call home now. I keep waiting for the injured animal to try and leap out from my grasp in some kind of last-ditch escape attempt, but it never does. Shockingly, the cat seems to be sort of content in my company now. Maybe it's just exhausted from all the earlier stress, but I'd swear the animal is almost dozing off in my arms as I make my way back to the cellar door.

With one hand supporting the cat and the other on the handle, I pull the steel rectangle up into the air until it's wide enough to allow me safe passage beneath it. Somewhere in the back of my mind, I know I should be so much more careful and intentional with the logs and the pallets on the other side of the door as I lower it shut behind me. But with the cat draped across my arm and pressed up against my chest, it's hard to devote the necessary appendages to those intentions.

Some habits are impossible to break, however, as I juggle cat, keys, locks, and chains between my arms and hands in the stale dark of the basement space. It isn't easy, but I'm somehow able to loop the chains and locks back into place while still keeping the animal close against my chest. I tug on all of the cold metal just to make sure I'm not cutting any corners due to this new distraction, and it really feels like I'm not.

When I'm confident that I've sufficiently locked up behind me, I peel Jim Carrey off my head and set him down on the bench. My body wants to suck in air now that there's nothing artificial strapped to the front of my face, and I don't refuse it that desire. For at least sixty seconds or more, me and the cat just stand together in the middle of the cellar, breathing and sweating and slurping in air as I remember again what it's like to feel my own face.

I start to make my way by memory through the darkness to the foot of the basement stairs. One arm is still supporting the cat as the other pulls along the banister, and my feet find their way up the creaky wooden stairs to the first floor. Once there, we visit the linen closet to lock the Glock away in the safe, and then we slowly continue our way up to the second story.

Back where tonight's whole saga first began, I grab some old blankets from the bedroom closet, toss them on the bed, and then tenderly lay the animal down on top of them before switching the flashlight on for the first time in a long time.

It's déjà vu all over again as the cat's pupils contract within the brilliant wide saucers of its eyes. The creature certainly doesn't look pleased about suddenly having a bright light in its face, but it's also so far removed from the writhing, screaming bundle of flesh and blood that it was before out in the forest. The organism in front of me now just seems absolutely exhausted, and even when faced with the ruthless inquisition of the flashlight beam, it eventually closes its eyes and perhaps even relinquishes over to sleep.

Truthfully, I'm not that far behind it, but my work isn't done yet. I use the flashlight to locate some old medical gauze and bandaging in the bathroom cabinet. Ever so gently, I unwrap the bloodied strips that used to be my t-shirt from the cat's hind legs and replace them with something more hygienic and effective.

Eventually, I'll have to find something to use as a splint for each leg, if the cat's to have any hope of walking normally again. I might even have to re-break the legs just to set them the right way. And to do any of this with even a remote degree of precision and efficacy, I'm positive that I'll need to give it some kind of sedative and anesthetic first. I'll also need the right drugs to fight off any potential infections and to ensure the wounds all heal properly.

Come to think of it, there are quite a few things I'll need if I'm really committed to playing apocalypse veterinarian here… which I guess I think I am. And to get these things—to get any of these things—means that I'll have to go out scavenging again.

Maybe I'll be able to find what I need at one house if I'm ridiculously lucky, but more likely than not, I'll have to visit several houses to amass all the supplies necessary to get this cat fully recovered. Or I might even need to risk doing something I swore a long time ago that I'd never do: go all the way into the nearest town and try my luck at a pharmacy or grocery store.

Frankly, it all sounds like suicide. Am I willing to risk my life just to make sure an animal I don't own or even know gets the proper medical attention and treatment it needs?

A voice in my head emphatically answers yes without really even thinking about the question for too long. I'd like to think it's a reflection of my true character, or at least a glowing endorsement and further proof of how good of a person I am.

But honestly, I think it's mainly just because I'm fucking lonely now, and I've lost everything and everyone I've ever cared about.

So maybe, selfishly, if I heal this cat and take good care of it, maybe it will stay with me. Maybe it will grow to become my friend and maybe even my new companion.

Not that it could ever replace Ruthie, but there was a time when I was young that I actually considered myself to be a cat person. It was a phase, for sure, but perhaps there might still be something there.

Or perhaps I'm just finally losing it.

But hey, I still took the Hippocratic Oath. Not sure if I ever had cats or animals in mind while taking it—not sure if the Greeks did either, for that matter—but an oath's an oath.

I peel off my boots and kill the flashlight before crawling beneath the covers into bed. Tentatively, I reach out one hand until just the tips of my fingers make contact with the cat's fur. There's a short yet terrible moment where I wholeheartedly believe the animal might recoil from my touch, attack me, or completely flee the room, wounds and broken legs be damned.

But it doesn't do any of those things. In fact, it doesn't do anything at all. It just lies there and slumbers with my fingertips still nestled in its fur, and before I have time to truly consider just what this all means for me here in the present and far beyond into the future, I've fallen asleep.

FOUR

"Go away, Ruthie."

The dog cocks its head at me from the foot of the bed. Is it just my imagination, or is she giving me a look of righteous indignation?

"No one likes a third wheel."

I tap my big toe against her snout and try to gently push her muzzle the other direction. The brat resists me easily. And all the while, she sits and stares.

Hope's face is buried in my left breast. When she speaks, her lips buzz against the sensitive skin there, and it gives me goosebumps. I love it, and she knows that I love it.

"That's not true, Ruthie. Your mama loves you for you. You be who you want to be."

Ruth Bader Ginsburg wants to be a pest. Refusing to take a hint, she instead starts lightly nipping at my foot every time I bring it up against her snout. Oh shit; I've created a game out of this now. What have I done?

"You still don't think it's at all weird having her up here in bed with us, huh?"

Hope keeps her face pressed against my tit.

"This is where she sleeps."

"Yes, I'm aware of that. But I mean, isn't it weird

having her up here now?"

Hope pauses to consider.

"Why? Because we just had sex?"

"Yes. Exactly."

Now she twists her chin and cranes her neck to look up at me. Her face is still flushed. She's always beautiful, but right now, like this, she's sexy as hell. We may have to go at it again. If so, that dog has got to go.

"It's not like she was up here *while* it was happening."

"Yeah, but she was in the room still. I saw her over there in the corner, standing right next to—but not in, of course—that stupid bed I bought for her. The bed she still hasn't used once in four years, lest we forget. And Hope… she was just standing there and staring at us."

A wispy smile flickers across Hope's lips. God, I want her so bad right now. And I literally just had her. Fuck. The things this woman does to me.

"What are you telling me? That we've raised a pervert? That our daughter is a sicko who likes to watch her mommies boink?"

I laugh in spite of myself.

"I'm just saying that it was distracting, that's all. I wasn't expecting to see her there."

The smile is downright devilish now on her face. Something wicked this way comes.

"Did you lock eyes with her when you came? Because you know that's how they get you, right? Dogs can steal your soul that way."

I laugh again.

"You're the sicko. I see now where she gets it from."

Hope turns her face back to my breast, and now her

hand is stroking back and forth between my calf and my thigh. Consciously or unconsciously, the pattern keeps traveling a bit higher up on my leg each time. I'm hoping that it's conscious, though either way, it probably ends well for me.

"Me? Don't blame me. You're the one who lets her watch your smut TV with you."

"Excuse me. Love Island is not smut TV. Love Island is about survival."

Hope snorts, and the hot, wet air that escapes her mouth and nose gifts me another wave of goosebumps, along with a slight body shudder. She notices, of course, and now her hand moves with smooth but deliberate intention all the way up.

"You and your smut."

A moan escapes my throat as I relax into her.

"You and your dog."

Hope traces circles around my areola with her tongue as she brings her other hand onto me.

"She's our dog. Don't you forget it."

How could I? She's still staring up at me with those big brown eyes from the foot of the bed.

But Hope does her thing with her fingers and soon my eyes are closed anyway, and then all thoughts and concerns about the dog or about anything else for that matter are long, long gone.

———

When we've finished making love for a second time, that's when those thoughts and concerns come back.

"There's something I want to talk to you about."

Hope's face is buried in the crook of my shoulder now. She always ends up burrowing into me somehow after sex; it's only a question of where she's going to be this particular time.

"Ruh-roh, Shaggy. That doesn't sound good."

I keep stroking her hair.

"Francis pulled me into his office for an unscheduled meeting today after lunch."

Hope is silent, but only for a moment.

"Oh yeah? What did Doc Spock want?"

She started calling him that a couple years ago after they met at a Christmas party, on account of his dark, chili-bowl haircut and sharp, arcing eyebrows. I haven't been able to look at him the same way since.

"He… well, he actually wants me to take his job, believe it or not."

Maybe I should have sugarcoated it a bit better, but I've never been one to tap-dance my way around what I have to say. In truth, I'm surprised I've waited this long to bring it up. I guess I wasn't expecting Hope to sex-ambush me immediately when I got home, though, and I obviously wasn't about to tell her no, either.

She keeps her face hidden in my shoulder, so it's impossible to decipher her immediate reaction. I make sure not to stop combing my fingers through her dark, slightly sweaty hair.

"Take his job? What's he going to do?"

"He told me that he and his wife want to move out to the country. Maybe start a private practice out there or something."

There's no need to add "or something," considering he told me his plans exactly and with all the plain, simple conviction of a man who's both used to being in charge and used to facing no resistance when he makes up his mind. I'm no fan of verbal wishy-washiness either, but I'm also no fan of Hope's temper when it's directed at me.

"How funny. Did you tell him that was your plan, as well?"

As a matter of fact, I did… but Hope doesn't need to know that. It came up casually in conversation maybe a month or two ago, and at the time, I didn't think anything of it.

Francis had asked me what I was thinking about for after residency, and I told him that while I didn't have any definitive plans, my girlfriend and I were contemplating getting out of the city and moving somewhere a bit more rural and undeveloped. At the time, even I wasn't sure how realistic that plan would be, however, given the dearth of good hospitals, clinics, and just pregnant women in general out in the countryside.

If anything, his reaction had been lukewarm, maybe disappointed even. Francis made no secret of his high regard for me and my abilities around the hospital, so I interpreted the blank, slightly confused expression he'd worn that day as a poor attempt at concealing his disapproval of our plans. Never in my wildest dreams did I ever imagine he'd steal those plans for himself and his own life.

"I did not. It didn't seem relevant."

Now Hope turns to look up at me from my shoulder crook.

"Hmm. Why would it not be relevant?"

Her expression is almost—*almost*—as vacant and unassuming as Francis' was that day. But I also know Hope a million times better than I know my chief resident. Somewhere down beneath that carefully constructed veneer, a timebomb just started ticking. It's now my job to figure out which color wire I need to snip before it goes off and blows me up to smithereens.

Let's try gentle reason first.

"He didn't ask me what my plans for the future were." Even though he had. "He told me what his plans for the present are, and how those plans affect me. He told me that the job is mine if I want it, and that there's no one else he'd rather have replace him."

She brings herself up to a seating position.

"Well, that's nice. I'm sure that was very flattering."

Guess the green wire didn't work. I regard her with guarded caution, the way a cat watches a dog for its behavior before arching its back or taking flight.

"It was. Not a surprise, but still nice to hear out loud."

"What did you tell him?"

She seems to want me to rip the Band-Aid off. That's what I want too, so I might as well give it a go and see what happens. Red wire, please be the one.

"I told him that I want it, but that I'd have to talk to you first, obviously. And he understood."

Hope's face is unreadable.

"He understood."

"Yes."

"Well. Good on him."

Without preamble, she spins, kicks her legs out over the side of the bed, and stands. Ruth and I both watch her closely as Hope starts swiftly retrieving her discarded clothes from the ground, slipping items back on and over her body as she goes. She moves about this whole process in hyper-focused silence, and even a stranger off the street would pick up that she's inwardly steaming right now.

It seems that I've already run out of wires. Explosion is inevitable. Ruh-roh, Shaggy.

"Where are you going?"

"I'm getting dressed."

"I can see that. But are you going somewhere?"

"Apparently, I'm not going anywhere."

We're almost to the big boom now. Less than ten seconds left, probably, at best. This is the scene in the movie where the heroine realizes the bomb is going off regardless and that it's just a matter of getting it someplace where it will cause the least amount of destruction and casualties.

"I'd prefer we actually talk about this first instead of just giving in to our emotions."

She straightens with one sock in her hand and one on her foot to shoot me a wrathful look that speaks volumes about her present emotional state.

"Oh, yeah? Well, I'd prefer you actually talk to me first instead of just making rash decisions for the both of us."

It's important that I remain calm, cool, and collected. She wants me to fight fire with fire, but I know I won't win that way. Not with Hope, of all people.

"No one has made any decisions, rash or otherwise. Nothing has been settled. This is what I wanted to talk to you about."

She sits down on the carpet to yank the other sock on and then pulls her shoes out from under the bed.

"What's the point?"

"What's the point? The point is that I'm trying to have a conversation with you about this, but it doesn't seem like you're very interested."

"Marvelous work, Dr. Washington. Your powers of perception astound me."

Boy, things are getting ugly fast. I knew there was a chance she'd fly off the handle like this, but I'm shocked it's happening this quickly, especially after all the sex. Usually, she's at her most docile and agreeable after orgasm.

"I don't understand why you're reacting this way."

"How did you think I'd react?"

"I thought we'd at least be able to talk about this first and examine it from all angles."

She stands, now fully dressed.

"What's the point? Seriously, Alex, what's the point? You told him yes."

"I told him I wanted it. I never told him yes."

"Oh, come on. It's the same thing. It's the same fucking thing, either way. You told him you wanted it, and you told him you'd talk to me, but why should we even bother talking about it? You, me, Francis… we all know that you're gonna say yes and take the job, so let's just save ourselves the fucking trouble for once, okay?"

Ka-boom.

"Can you please just sit back down so we can talk about this?"

"No, I think I'm good. I think I'll stand. Actually, I think I'll go for a walk. Might as well enjoy the sensation of free will for as long as I still have it, right?"

She practically spits that at me before striding out of the room. I clamber up to follow her, though Ruth beats me off the bed and out the door. By the time I've made it into the living room and Ruth has caught all the way up to her, Hope already has her keys and her hand on the front doorknob.

"Can we just stay and talk about this? Please?"

I get neither a verbal response nor even a backward glance in my direction. She whips the door open, pushes an all-too-eager Ruth back with one foot, and then disappears out into the hallway, slamming the door shut behind her. Ruth and I stand and stare after Hope, both of us left with our heads and our hearts spinning in the violent froth of her wake.

When she returns about an hour later, I'm ready for her.

The lights are dimmed. Every candle we own has been gathered, consolidated, and lit in the living room. CNN is muted on the TV. There's a meager but colorful bouquet of flowers resting in a glass vase on the coffee table (there are also some broken stems and missing plants in a nearby community garden, which I still don't feel great about, even though it was an emergency). If the air smells like brownies, it's because they're fresh-baked and staying warm in the oven. I've even got *folklore* by T. Swift playing on repeat from the stereo system, because I know it's her favorite album.

Hope takes only a second or two to register all of this when she opens the door, pausing ever so briefly with a twelve-pack of Miller Lite balanced in her arms, before she steps inside, turns the lock, sets the beer down, and crouches low to receive her customary canine greeting. Even after four years of bonding and growing closer than I ever imagined we would, I know who RBG views as the unquestioned alpha in our household. I'm just grateful she likes me well enough to rest her head in my lap occasionally and watch TV together when Hope's not home.

After those two lovebirds have done their usual song-and-dance routine at the front door—Hope gushes even more than usual since she left Ruthie behind on her walk—they move into the living room in tandem. Hope brings the box of beer over and sets it down on the coffee table. Normally, I might be inclined to ask her not to do that in case the cans sweat through the thin cardboard onto the tabletop, but I know better than to self-sabotage like that.

She opens the box, grabs a brew, and then picks one of our two armchairs to sit down in. I would have been shocked if she'd plopped down next to me on the couch, anyway, and really, I'm just relieved she didn't beeline for the bedroom. Mildly optimistic, I seize my opportunity while I can and move quickly into the kitchen.

The brownies are only the tip of the iceberg. I scoop vanilla ice cream on top of the warm dessert bars in a pair of ceramic serving bowls—heaping noticeably more into Hope's bowl than my own, of course—before drizzling the whole sugary sensation with chocolate syrup. Two spoons and two maraschino cherries later, I'm finally ready for my return to the living room.

Hope sips her beer and coos nonsense as she pets the furry beast on her lap. Ruth Bader Ginsburg looks for all the world like she's already fallen back asleep.

Ever so gingerly, I set her bowl and spoon down on the table in front of Hope before setting my own down and taking my place back on the couch. One of Ruthie's eyes open and she licks her lips, but she's well-trained enough, by Hope, not to bum-rush the table. She knows that if she's good and acts as if she doesn't care, Mama will likely give her some ice cream anyway, sans chocolate.

At first, I'm not convinced Hope's going to take it. I'm not even convinced she notices it's there, because she just keeps petting Ruthie and mumbling baby-talk into her ear.

Finally, though, after about thirty agonizing seconds of suspense where all I can do is wait patiently to see what happens next, Hope leans back in her chair away from the dog in her lap and swivels her attention onto me. It's the first time we've made eye contact since she opened the front door.

"This is nice. What is all this? Penance?"

I give her a tepid smile.

"Romance."

She raises an eyebrow.

"Romance? That's a bold move."

"Go big or go home, right?"

"Or go big in your own home."

She drinks in all the candles everywhere before zeroing in on the vase.

"Where'd you get the flowers?"

"Don't worry about it."

Again, Hope raises an eyebrow.

"Uh-huh."

There's a moment of silence where Hope regards the flowers, and I regard Hope with the same degree of cautious curiosity, and then she speaks again.

"You're really pulling out all the stops, aren't you?"

"I am."

"Even Taylor."

"Even Taylor."

She crosses her arms over her chest and waits. I don't let her wait long.

"Look, Hope. I'm so sorry for how everything happened earlier. That wasn't what I had planned at all. In my mind, we were going to talk about everything over dinner and decide together on whatever we wanted to do next. I think—and I'm obviously not mad about this at all—but I think I was just surprised and knocked off course by the sex and the way we just hopped to it like that the moment I walked through the door."

"Sorry, not sorry."

"Neither am I, believe me. That was so nice. *So* nice. And then I went and fucked it up and ruined all the good vibes. I'm sorry for that. I—I kept telling you that *you need to calm down*, when in reality, I should have just let you *shake it off* so you wouldn't have to leave and then come back to *say look what you made me do*. But before you tell me that *we are never ever getting back together*, let me tell you that *you belong with me*. And whether that's here in the city or out in the country or even in another country or on another planet, I love you, I'll go anywhere with you, I'll do anything for you, just don't be mad at me, because I love you so, so much, okay?"

Hope either is soaking it all in or letting me squirm. I can't tell which, so I clasp my hands together and give her my very best don't-be-mad, love-me-again, Ruthie-style puppy dog eyes.

"That was a good speech. Very clever. How many times did you practice it?"

"It's all I did while the brownies were in the oven. That's after I collected all the candles and stole the flowers from the community garden, of course."

Hope gasps melodramatically.

"You did not!"

"I did. I'm a bad girl."

Time to push the envelope just a bit. I slide off the couch and close the short distance between us on my hands and knees. Tentatively, I wrap my hands around her calves, and to my immense relief, Hope lets me.

"You see? There's nothing I wouldn't do for you, even if it means becoming a common criminal."

Hope leans over the dog in her lap as her face floats down closer to mine. Things may be turning a corner here finally.

"I should turn you in. *I knew you were trouble.*"

Slowly, seductively—I hope—I tilt my head back on my neck. She's so close now I can practically taste her. I close my eyes and lean upward until I feel her lips press against mine and then her hands grasp the back of my head as she pulls me even higher and deeper into a kiss that lets me know she loves me right back just as much as I love her.

When we finally break apart, she's smiling mischievously.

"Did you get that last one?"

"Get that last one?"

"*I knew you were trouble.* Yes? No? Maybe so?"

I have no idea what she's talking about, and she must see it on my face, because hers erupts in laughter.

"Oh, don't worry about it. That just makes your speech before even sweeter."

"Speaking of sweet, you should try some of your ice cream. It's probably all melted by now."

I attempt to turn and grab the bowl off the table,

but Hope stops me. She moves her hands down from the back of my head until they're resting under my chin on either side of my neck. Her expression grows suddenly serious.

"Now it's your turn to listen to me, okay?"

Why am I so nervous again? I have to remind myself that we were literally just making out a few seconds ago and that everything should be good between us.

"Okay."

Hope's face remains stoic.

"I thought long and hard about this on my walk. I even talked it out with the cashier at 7-Eleven just to get his take on it. He agrees, by the way, for what it's worth."

"Agrees with what?"

"Agrees that you need to take this job—take Doc Spock's old job and stay here. And I need to stay right here with you."

"Hope–"

"No, it's your turn to listen, remember? I'm serious about this. This is a great opportunity for you right now, coming straight out of residency and already having something lined up to make for a smooth, seamless transition. You already know all the staff there, you're familiar with everyone, you're comfortable there. Realistically, it's the best-case scenario that could have happened. And I'm not gonna be an asshole and ruin that for you."

"But what about you?"

"What *about* me? I'm fine. And I'm not just saying that to be some kind of martyr housewife, either. They love me down at the nursery."

"But *you* don't love *it*."

"And you know what? That's okay for now. You're

about to be the primary breadwinner in this household anyway. I don't hate my job, and most days, I actually don't mind it at all. What's important is that I have my dog and I have my girlfriend and I have this nice home with all these beautiful candles and these beautiful stolen flowers and this delicious ice cream brownie soup, and I love each and every one of those things. That's what makes me happy, and that's what's really important."

"But you hate the city. And if I tell Francis yes, that means you're stuck here."

"*When* you tell Francis yes, it means that *we're* stuck here. But listen, the country's not going anywhere. People stay in places or move to places they don't want to be in all the time, but they do it for work or for love. You can stay here for work, I can stay here for love, and then some day, when the time is right, I have no doubt in my mind we'll escape this shitty urban cesspool once and for all to go live somewhere green and pretty and safe. Just you, me, Ruthie, and maybe a kid or two… or three… or four."

I don't know if I've ever loved Hope more than I do at this moment. What I do know is that I've never loved someone as much as I love her, and I never will.

"Marry me."

She freezes.

"What?"

"Marry me."

It's actually absurd how right and how perfect this feels to me right now. I'm even down on my knees already. How insane is that? This is how it's supposed to be. Just like this, like we are right now in this moment. This is how it happens. Because of course. It was meant to be like this. Always.

"Don't play with me right now."

"I'm not playing with you."

Hope's eyes glisten as I reach up to take her hands in mine.

"Hope Deborah Bergstrom, will you marry me?"

Another bomb goes off inside her, but this one is of an entirely different kind.

First, Hope's breathing changes, then her face, and then her body, and soon she's doing something in between crying, laughing, smiling, and hyperventilating all at once. Ruth senses the muscles coming to life beneath her in the chair and jumps down to get clear just in time. Meanwhile, Hope is stammering, choking, and shaking all over now as tears roll freely down her cheeks, which glow bright pink even in the dim candlelight.

"Yes… yes, of course, yes."

She tumbles forward out of the chair, and I envelop her in my arms.

We're kissing again, and now I think I'm crying too, which is rare for me, but certainly warranted, even if it's surprising. Everything inside and outside of me is vibrating. Hope smells and tastes and feels like perfection.

There's nowhere else I'd rather be than here and now in this moment. There's no one else I'd rather be with in this moment, and also for the rest of my life and for my next life and for eternity.

She is my everything. I can never lose her. I never will.

FIVE

This is a bad idea.

That's the fatalistic refrain playing over and over again in my head like the chorus of some godawful 90s bubblegum pop song. Even in the dark of night, even with only the low beam headlights on, even keeping my speed below thirty miles an hour and sticking strictly to backwoods country roads, this is still such a bad idea.

The last time I tried to do what I'm doing now, it cost me more than just gas and time. Many sleepless, paranoid nights followed that eventful excursion into civilization. I swore to myself then that until or unless it was absolutely crucial and necessary for me to gather more supplies or equipment, I would avoid ever going back.

It's hard to justify this risk as being crucial and necessary. After five years of living alone in the woods, there isn't a whole lot I don't know how to do for myself. Sure, there are things you can't find organically out in mother nature that make it so much easier to survive—batteries, propane, gasoline, bullets—but many of those things are contingent on a style of life that I've also tried hard to evolve from.

Batteries and propane are only needed if you want

to see in the dark or cook easily. Gasoline is only needed if you have to drive somewhere that you can't walk. Bullets are only needed if you have to kill something or someone.

I've learned to see better without light than ever before, to memorize where I put things, and to remember what paths I need to traverse inside the house and outside on the grounds at night. I've learned to live without ninety-nine percent of the modern conveniences and normalcies that defined my pre-NDV life in the name of conserving vehicle fuel. Most importantly, I've learned that if I stay within a one-mile perimeter of my forest safe haven, I theoretically should have little need ever for more ammunition… though I also know that's far from a guarantee.

It's been so long since I even went for a drive. My palms are sweating profusely on the steering wheel, and as much as I know that's a byproduct of my mental and emotional state right now on this fool's errand, it could also be a testament to how rusty I am operating the jeep.

Frankly, I wasn't convinced the engine would start when I put one of my six necklace keys into the ignition and turned. Then again, I wasn't convinced the jeep would still be there to begin with, either.

But the jeep was there, the engine did start, and now I'm out here again on the open road, getting farther and farther away from safety by the minute and by the mile. And all of this for an injured little pussycat that's not even mine.

Waking up fifteen hours ago, I had every intention to take the cat outside and turn it loose. The rational, reasonable part of my survivor's brain had finally overruled the nonsensical, idiotic part that fantasized about this unlikely creature becoming a new home companion. I'd made up my mind to carry it out past all my traps and snares, give it a little water, set it down in a leafy clearing somewhere presumably safe from immediate danger, and then just turn around and walk away.

Those plans were promptly smashed to smithereens, however, the moment I woke up and discovered the feline curled up asleep between my legs with its head resting against my calf. The finishing touch had come when I cupped my hand around the back of its neck… and the cat started purring.

So here I am.

If memory serves—and it had better—I shouldn't be too far out now. Up until this point, everything has been inky, green-black streaks jetting past the jeep windows on all sides. Soon enough, however, that will change. An abandoned shack here, a decrepit silo there, a rusted old truck torn apart for spare parts. These are the telltale signs I'm looking for that will indicate I'm getting close.

There's still time to turn back. Just because I've come all this way and I've used up a good portion of what little fuel supply I have left doesn't mean I'm locked into this mission. As much as I consider myself to be the type of person who doesn't start a project unless I know I can finish it, this is different. This isn't giving up on a bad book or setting out to do twenty pushups and stopping at seventeen.

I dip my speed a bit at the first sight of something distinguishable from the surrounding darkness just up ahead. It's a large mass well off the road to my right that glows softly in the reflective gaze of the low beams.

Just to be on the safe side, I bring the jeep to a quiet crawl and reach across to the passenger seat. Keeping my eyes glued on the approaching shape, I let my fingers find the cold metal of the Glock and draw it over so it's close at hand and ready in case I need it.

The topographical anomaly reveals itself to be an overturned jeep that is the exact same model and color as my jeep. How ominously poetic. There are muddy, swerving tire tracks where the vehicle presumably lost control before it caromed off the dirt road, toppled over, and came to a crashing rest amidst the dense forest underbrush.

About fifteen yards of space remains between the two jeeps when I bring mine to a stop. I knew I'd have to make some tough judgment calls on this trip, but I wasn't expecting to make them this early before I even got to the outskirts.

There's a part of me that that wants to pull off the road behind this wreck and scavenge for potential resources. And then there's another part of me that wants to just floor it and get the hell out of dodge before it's too late. Which part do I listen to?

I decide to creep up a bit closer so I can get a better gauge of the situation. Even from here, though, there's not much more I can see in the dim diffusion of the low beams. The upturned vehicle is too far off the road and too nestled in with branches and leaves to really get a strong read on it. All I can tell for sure is that no one has stripped the tires yet, since all four remain oddly pointed up in the air.

Possibilities swirl inside my head.

If this was an accident, the driver and any passengers could be inside the cabin still. They could be injured, they could be dead, or they could be armed. If this was an accident, the driver and any passengers could have also crawled out from inside and gone off; and if so, how long ago was that, and when might I expect them back?

If this was *intentional*, the tires would be stripped, and there'd be more signs of looting around the vehicle itself. That is, unless this was intentionally left as bait designed to tempt someone like myself into stopping.

"Christ."

Decisions, decisions…

The one thing I shouldn't do above all others is just sit here doing nothing and wasting time. Ultimately, it's somehow the cat that makes up my mind for me. While I still have no intention of making these foraging adventures a routine occurrence in my life, I also had no intention of caring for another pet after RBG died, and look where I am now. The safe choice might be to carry on, but the smart choice is to try and take what I can— particularly the gas.

Everything needs to be done quickly. I pull off the road and nose up right behind the upside-down jeep, one hand on the steering wheel and the other holding the gun tight in my lap. Delicately, quietly, I put the gear shift in reverse and check my mirrors, ready at a second's notice to take my foot off the brake and slam the accelerator if need be. I've already slumped down low in my seat as well, giving any potential snipers as difficult of a shot as I can while still doing my best to maintain my own three-hundred-and-sixty-degree sightlines.

When I'm ready, I cut the ignition and slip the key necklace back overhead and down the front of my shirt.

One Mississippi.

Two Mississippi.

Three Mississippi.

Four Mississippi.

Smooth and silent like a snake in water, I slip the door latch and slide my body down out from the seat until I'm crouched low beside the front left wheel. I give it four more Mississippis, and then I reach my non-gun hand back behind the driver seat and fumble around until I find the hose, the plastic jug, and my old frenemy Jim Carrey. Four more Mississippis elapse as I tug the mask on over my face, and then I'm in action, always careful where I put my feet, always watchful where I put my eyes.

Now would be the time to take a shot if I were them. That's what I'm thinking as I waddle over to the overturned jeep, breathing heavily into the sweaty apparatus, my thighs low to the ground. The closer I can keep my body to other bodies of metal, the better. Unless, of course, they're on this side of me. If that's the case, I'm a sitting duck no matter what I do.

There doesn't seem to be anyone out there, though. Or if there is, they're holding their trigger finger… for now.

Next question is whether there's anybody still inside. My neck curves forward as I steal a glance through the shattered remnants of a broken window, fully expecting to find myself face-to-face with either a topsy-turvy dead body or the barrel of a gun.

I find neither. There's a whole lot of broken glass and twisted metal, but no immediate signs of life or death.

Well, that's not entirely true, since the sight of blood is unmistakable even in the scant lighting. It's all over the steering wheel, the dashboard, the seatbelts, the chairs. To my immense relief, however, it looks like it's dried and hardened in all the places I'm seeing it, stains and painful reminders of some grisly tragedy that feels a bit less tragic to me now that I know it's not fresh. I feel guilty for having that thought, but I have it all the same.

No bullets, bullet holes, or casings, though. I'm no forensic scientist, but it sure doesn't look like this was an ambush or some kind of premeditated strike.

For all intents and purposes, it looks like what it ought to look like: an accident. Some poor unfortunate motorist, or motorists, did something dumb like fall asleep at the wheel or overcorrect during bad weather conditions, and then calamity struck. The vehicle veered, flipped, and crashed, and its survivor or survivors slithered out to safety and elected to abandon it before further misfortune arrived.

I've seen enough. It's time to finish what I came out here to do and then get back on the road. After popping the gas door open, I slide the plastic hose down all the way until it finds the inner reservoir. Glock still in hand, I pull my mask up high onto my forehead, lift the other end of the hose to my lips, and start to suck.

It's been a while since I've done this, and I'm surprised at how quickly and easily the pungent liquid finds its way down the channel into my mouth. Immediately, I move the end of the tube into the jug and spit out the gasoline as quietly as possible. My eyes, throat, and nostrils burn at the taste and at the smell, but I refuse to cough. I'm confident that I'm alone out here, but there's no point in challenging that notion unnecessarily.

Siphoning is a slow process, but at least it's a quiet

one. So long as no one is truly out here moving in on me, I'm pleased with my decision-making. Even as committed as I am to being carless, you never know when you'll need a vehicle that runs in a life-or-death emergency. The gas tank in the jeep was almost empty before. This impromptu pit-stop should be profitable enough to cover at least one or two more trips in the future.

When I'm confident that I've drained the jeep of all its fuel, I search around beneath the seats, in the glove compartment, and in the back for anything else that might be useful. It's a bizarre exercise, considering I'm working against gravity the whole time, and in the end, it's not nearly as rewarding as I'd hoped. Most of what I find is really just refuse, junk, and personal effects, but I do stumble across two containers of water hidden inside the spare wheel cover on the back of the jeep. Those, along with the wheel itself, instantly elevate this exercise into an incredibly beneficial raid.

I debate whether to strip the other four tires as well, but ultimately decide to leave them. The biggest factor in my choice is time, since I feel like I've already spent a good amount of it getting the gasoline, the spare, the waters, and really just staking out the terrain throughout this process. I know full well those tires might not be here when I come back this way, but that's all right. My jeep already has a spare, and now I have two. And while there's no such thing as having too much of anything nowadays, I still feel like it's time I move on.

I'm riding a kind of high as I roll into the outskirts of civilization. It's a curious sensation only because it's new—or at least it feels that way. I know I've experienced this feeling before in my life, of course, but it's just been so long. There's a buzzing, vibrating, rolling lightness in my chest, and I'm downright shocked when I look up into the rearview mirror and see my mouth doing something I haven't seen it do in weeks, if not months.

Smiling. That's what that is. I'm smiling right now. I feel like I'm… like I'm actually happy. If only for a minute, if only until something hard happens, and reality sets back in.

But for now, for this precious moment or two or three or however long it might last before I spoil it, I'm kind of, sort of happy. I don't know if it's being out on the road driving again, the thrill of my haul from that wreck, having something alive waiting for me back at home, or maybe it's just that I accidentally ingested a bit too much gasoline, but whatever it is, I feel good right now in my brain.

It stays with me all the way to the first house. Even though it's been nearly a year—I think?—the memories come flying back like it was only yesterday. I remember scouting and surveying this whole neighborhood for a solid hour, slowly, quietly taking it all in and assessing what potential dangers lurked behind these impressive stone facades.

Eventually, I'd settled on this one as my initial foraging target, and it hadn't disappointed. Large, sprawling, and somewhat removed from the other houses on this wide serpentine loop of a street, the home had been devoid of people but filled with treasures.

It wasn't until I'd visited that fourth house that I had heard the man cough. While I can't fathom a world in which he'd still be alive and/or still be living in that particular place, I'm also not about to check up on him to see if he's cleared out. With any luck, I'll find this first house to be just as generous and magical tonight as it was back then, and maybe I won't even need to visit any others.

In fact, I'll make a point to get creative if need be. I'm going to set a personal goal for myself to get anything and everything I need for my furry little patient back home right here and now at this first stop. If the house doesn't have my top choice of supplies, I'll make do with my second choice. I'm a resourceful individual, and I'm sure that the cat isn't too picky.

Obviously, I'll visit as many homes as I need to in this neighborhood to find what I absolutely have to have, but I'm manifesting that it will all be right here. I've had a rough go of everything lately, but my luck feels like it's finally changing. Let's keep riding this high until it runs out.

The first thing I do is sweep the street with my vision for any signs of life, movement, or change. There's a delicate balance between taking the requisite amount of time to be cautious (and to stay alive) versus wasting time and putting oneself in otherwise avoidable danger. After five years of being on my own in this godforsaken country, though, I think I've gotten a pretty good handle on knowing which is which.

With the coast clear, I turn the jeep off the paved road and climb up the sidewalk and then onto the lawn. It's a short, slow, muddy drive up to the side of the house, and I continue as far back as the outer walls will let me until my lights bounce back at the windshield from a high, wooden backyard fence.

Yes, this is exactly how I remember it. I'm not completely concealed from the street, but I'm far enough removed that you'd be hard-pressed to notice the jeep tucked into this far corner where the house meets the fence. Especially at this time of night, and with the dark hue of the vehicle itself, you'd probably need to be coming at just the right angle down the street and with the headlights turned up high to spot my ride.

And in that scenario, I'd either see you, hear you, or both, and well before you'd have a chance to surprise me. I'd have time to flee, and even if I somehow didn't, I'd have time to hide and then time to fight. And if you tried to raid or jack my jeep while I'm still in here, I'd pick you off from a window. That's what the Glock is for. I still have plenty of rounds left.

The gun isn't the only thing I'll need to take with me. I also grab Jim Carrey, my backpack, and a crowbar from behind the passenger seat. The primary purpose of the crowbar is to help me get inside, of course, but its secondary purpose is to serve as insurance for any close, unexpected encounters where I might not have time to draw my firearm or aim properly before I shoot.

Masked, prepared, and primed, I kill the engine and loop the keys back around my neck, and now I'm closing the door silently behind me and padding quickly through the wet grass to get a running start on the fence. My momentum carries me halfway up into the air until my palms catch the rough wooden posts, and then I use my inertia, back, and biceps to hoist the rest of me up and over the top.

There's a voice in the back of my head that wants to let me know this felt easier a year ago than it does right now, but I dismiss that voice the same way I dismiss those nagging thoughts and fears that show up uninvited on sleepless nights to whisper how much weaker, slower, and older I've become.

We're not going down that dark, miserable path tonight, and certainly not here and now. There's work to be done, and I'm not ready to relinquish the dopamine high of my adrenaline just yet—not even when the hard ground sends shockwaves up my shins as I drop to the backyard turf, and especially not even when there's a momentary spell of dizziness and disorientation.

I shake it off violently with a couple quick jerks of my head, and then I'm moving once again through the cool night air across the moist lawn and up the wooden porch steps to the back door.

A year ago, this door was locked but not reinforced or boarded up when I broke in, and nobody was in the house. Tonight, it looks like it's been repaired since I took the crowbar to it, though curiously, the knob turns, and the door opens easily when I try it.

I'm not exactly sure how I feel about the back door being unlocked and repaired. If someone had truly taken up shelter here, they'd have done a better job barricading this entrance. Unless, of course, this is their main way in and out of the house themselves.

That's a possibility, I suppose, but an unlikely one. Surely no one makes a habit of scaling that fence every time they want to get anywhere? And did the front door look boarded up? It didn't—I remember now that it looked like a normal front door from the outside when I was scoping out the situation earlier from the street.

The most likely explanation is that someone was here long enough to repair the back door but not long enough to actually board it up and establish a permanent residence. That's the interpretation I'm going with, though I still draw the gun from my waistline just to be on the safe side as I slip through the crack across the threshold and close the door softly behind me.

The key to staying alive in the outside world is staying undetected, and the key to staying undetected is giving off as little light and sound as possible. To that end, I resist digging into my backpack for the flashlight. Yes, I want to conserve the batteries for as long as possible—although batteries are certainly on my shopping list this evening if I can find them.

More importantly, though, I don't need anyone to see a bright flashlight beam lancing across the windows from outside. As much as I want to believe this whole neighborhood is utterly deserted, I don't know if that's true. A lot can change in the span of a year. There's no need to create my own miniature searchlight in here.

Darkness is a friend, darkness is safe, and darkness is life. Would it be nice if Jim Carrey came equipped with night vision? Of course. It would also be nice if I didn't have to wear Jim Carrey in the first place for fear of catching a lethal respiratory virus. Maybe if I could just see in the dark the same way my feline friend does back at home…

Thinking of her—or of him? I realize I have yet to check the cat's sex—reminds me of what I came here to do. My eyes have adjusted long enough being inside and away from the moon and starlight. Let's get back to it.

The trick is to look in all the same places a thief would look. Where once a person might have hidden their money, their jewels, their priceless family heirlooms, that's where a person now hides their medicine, their weapons, their water.

Who knows how many individuals or how many families have set up temporary residence in this house since the world went to shit? But with each hostile takeover and changing of the guard, it's up to the new tenant to locate all the hidden stashes of the former tenant. Inevitably—because people are innately good at hiding things and innately bad at finding them—some of those stashes go undiscovered and get unknowingly left behind.

That's how I've learned to forage and plunder: with my brain. Stay smart, stay safe, stay alive.

It really is that simple, but it was still shocking to see just how many idiots went straight back to the towns and cities they had previously fled from to try and gather supplies, and well after it was already too late. Grocery stores, pharmacies, shopping malls. These places all became the settings of one great big boneheaded bloodbath.

The rookie mistake that so many people made when all of this started was to do what they saw people do in the movies. Well, that, and then to only listen to what they wanted to hear from the news they wanted to watch on TV. Throw in a blatant disregard for science and common sense, then combine that stupidity with a mindless, cult-like devotion to a charismatic politician who thinks he's a deity but who's really a bombastic imbecile, and this is exactly what happens.

A virus no one wants to call Covid-28 gets named Niger Delta Virus or NDV for short, then gets nicknamed the Africa Virus by our president, and then gets re-nicknamed the Black Virus or the Black People Virus by our fellow Americans.

First, it's panic-buying and veiled racism. Then, it's panic-shooting and blatant racism. Soon, it's also blatant sexism, classism, favoritism, ableism, homophobia, xenophobia, transphobia. Every -ism and phobia there is rears its ugly head after a while if you're hateful and afraid, until everyone who has an opinion also has a gun, and then all bets are off.

Smart people sensed a breaking point was on the horizon and got out of there while there was still time. I am a smart person, but in this respect, I was dumber than dumb. My selflessness turned to selfishness right before my eyes until it cost me everything.

No, stay on the high. Keep moving, keep searching, keep positive. Guilt is a fucking soul-sucker with no endgame. I don't have time for that. Ain't nobody got time for that. Now, what is that one from? I can't remember anything anymore…

Never mind. Stay focused in the present. Reach into the corners of these kitchen cabinets. Check under the oven. Feel beneath the refrigerator, along the sides and near the back where it's pushed up against the kitchen wall. Never mind the wires, the spiders, the cuts, and the dust. Where would I hide my most valuable resources?

There might be a safe somewhere, but that will do me no good. A closed safe is a locked safe, and the only person who would know the combination is undeniably dead. And an open safe is an empty safe.

What else, though? I'm trying to remember what I found here last time. If you've been in one country farmhouse in the middle of the pitch-black night, you've been in all of them. I've certainly been in a few over the years. Plus, it's been nearly a year since I've been in any.

That's interesting. There's a lock on the door to my right in the hallway that leads out of the kitchen toward the second-story stairs. I don't remember coming across any locked doors the last time I was here in this neighborhood, even if it was a while ago.

Really, there are only two possibilities here. If this were a horror movie, someone would put a lock on this door to keep something evil or terrible on the other side from coming into the rest of the house. But because this isn't a horror movie, someone would put a lock on this door to keep something valuable on the other side away from anyone coming into the rest of the house.

Hello, Ms. Crowbar, it's your time to shine.

Surprisingly, the lock busts within a matter of seconds and under very minimal pressure. The only downside to how easily it comes off is that I'm not at all expecting it to happen that quickly, and there's a thud as the metal falls and hits the floorboards next to my feet.

I wait in silence to see if anything happens. This has been my only mistake so far tonight. I wait to see if I will pay for it, Glock in one hand, crowbar in the other, trying to breathe normally and to maintain my tenuous hold on that flaky, wispy high from before.

After twenty Mississippis, I'm as satisfied as I'm going to get. My gun hand turns the knob, and ever so slowly and ever so softly, I open the door.

If the rest of the house was dark, it doesn't seem so now, compared to this new vacuous space before me.

Space. That's what this reminds me of, actually. Outer space.

I could reach my arm out and not be surprised if I struck nothing or if I struck solid matter. It could be a brick wall in front of me or an endless corridor. I have absolutely no idea what I'm looking at through my mask right now.

Begrudgingly, I slide my backpack off one shoulder so I can twist it around and trade the crowbar for a flashlight. Dangerous as it might be, I'm not sure I have any other choice. This locked door easily represents my most promising lead in the house so far. I owe it to myself and to the injured cat waiting for me at home to fully check it out.

It's times like these that I wish I were an octopus. One arm for the gun, one arm for the crowbar, one arm for the flashlight. Still wish I had that night-vision, too. Maybe if I'm exceptionally lucky, there will be some night-vision goggles or something equally as cool and useful in this room waiting for me when the light comes on.

When it does, I realize it's not a room at all. It's a flight of stairs leading down into a basement.

Once again, I'm reminded of every horror film I've ever seen. Whatever you do, don't go in the basement. If you have to go down there, at least don't go alone. And if you have to do that, too, well then sure as shit turn the lights on and don't go down with just a flashlight in the darkness.

What choice do I have, though? Even if I wanted to risk turning on the lights, there are no lights to turn on. The people we put in power failed us, and then the people who powered us failed us.

I get an eerie, déjà vu-like feeling as I descend the steps into the cellar. Even though I've never been here before—not on this staircase or in the basement of this house, or at least not that I can remember, and certainly not after breaking a lock—it's an uncanny feeling of familiarity that I chalk up to the daily ritual I have of going down my own flight of stairs at home into the cellar, willing my brain and my body not to lose control, not to get anxious, not to get dizzy, not to get old. Those are the mantras that cycle through my head as I step off the last stair and onto the cement floor.

Mantras. Fucking mantras. I told myself I was done with all that, and I am. If there was a brief moment of vertigo or weakness, it was only a flashback. I'm fine now. Everything is fine.

Actually, everything is better than fine. Everything is gloriously good. The high is back and better than ever, because lo and behold, the very first thing my flashlight beam picks up in this room is a shelving unit tucked into the far corner that is positively *littered* with drugs.

And not just drugs. Miraculously, I spot medical tools and supplies I never thought I'd see again. Scalpels, syringes, scissors, sutures, bandages, gauze. It's an improbable smorgasbord of kitty-stitching supplies.

I can't help myself; I actually run across the short distance separating me from this tower of treasures. In the pale needle of light, I can make out the names of so many old friends from my past life as a doctor. For one transcendental moment, I'm not standing in a stranger's basement scavenging for pills in a global pandemic, I'm standing in a hospital pharmacy staring at medicine in a normal world and in a normal time. The moment is so surreal and so powerful that I get lost in it for a second.

But only for a second. Even though everything's turning up roses tonight, I know how quickly that can change, and I'm not about to wait for it to happen. Hurriedly, I start scooping all the plastic vials and containers off the shelves and into my backpack with my forearms, working as quickly and as quietly as I can with both hands full.

It doesn't take long before the shelves are empty, and my backpack is full. Still reeling from my unbelievably good fortune, I zip it all up and hoist it onto my shoulders. All told, I have now accumulated a whole backpack's worth of drugs, two water bottles, a replenished tank of gas, and a spare tire on tonight's expedition. There's no point in pushing my luck trying to find batteries, bullets, or anything else on my wish list. I've gathered all of this, and I only had to visit one house and one abandoned car wreck on the side of the road. That's unbelievably lucky.

I turn around just in time to see the butt of a rifle come flying in fast, and then there's a cracking sound before everything goes black.

"I still want a ring, though."

My vision swims as the world rings round and round, round and round. I must have had too much to drink or else I've been drugged. Someone forced me to take all those pills I found in the basement of that house.

"Just because I said yes doesn't mean I don't want a ring."

I know that voice. But how? How can that be possible?

There, there in the swaying, shifting, shimmering gloom, she's standing there in front of me, and I'm down low. Am I on one knee? No, I'm in a chair.

No, that's not right either. I'm on the floor. I think I'm lying crumpled on my side on the floor.

"You're not off the hook yet, Dr. Washington."

Nobody calls me Dr. Washington. Nobody even knows my name anymore.

"I do. Alexandra Washington, will you be my bride?"

There's a shadow there that I know, so I reach for it, but I can't. My hands won't move like I want them to. Something's wrong with my wrists.

"This is perfect. Everything is perfect. But you're still on the hook. You know that, right?"

"What?"

"Mama wants a rock."

"What?"

Darkness…

"…crazy bitch keeps muttering to herself. Talking in her sleep."

"Well, wake her the fuck up, then. We gotta go."

There's an incessant snapping sound until finally a hand materializes, and then a body, tall and looming, forms around it. As my eyelids flicker, I glimpse the hard, inhuman face, and my blood freezes over as I process the magnitude of what it means to have this monster staring down at me. There's also a second monster in a mask not far behind the first one, and both have their focus squarely leveled at my body on the ground.

My *body* on the *ground*. I am down on the ground. That much isn't a dream; that much is real.

"Wakey-wakey, nigger lady."

It's the first monster, the one closest to me.

"*Theeeeeere* she is. She's waking up now."

There's a jagged line running down the front of my

vision. At first, I assume the worst and fully believe they've torn one of my corneas. But blinking causes me no discomfort and my eyes don't feel like they're in any pain. My forehead hurts, but it's a steady drum of pain, rather than anything splintering or incapacitating.

It's Jim Carrey. They split the mask, my mask, with the butt of a rifle. That's what happened before everything went dark, and that's how all this happened. I can see it even now, even through this cracked and broken facemask: the rifle, leaning up against a wall in the corner, illuminated ever so meekly from the ghastly cast of my fallen flashlight.

More snapping sounds as the hand appears again and clicks in front of me.

"Right here, nigger, right here."

I zero in on the hand, the arm, the body, the head.

"That's right. She sees me now, all right."

Yes, I do. That, I do.

The one closest to me stops snapping long enough to lean down and brandish a wicked-looking knife.

"Hey-o. Welcome back to the land of the living, dark chocolate."

I need to do something… but I can't. My hands strain against something behind my back. There's something wrong with my wrists.

"Uh-oh, SpaghettiOs. Looks like you're in a bit of a pickle, aren't you now, Black Virus?"

They've tied my wrists together with some kind of rope or cord, but the idiots haven't done a very good job of it. It's all too easy to wiggle my hands back and forth against one another behind my back, and if I can do that, I may well be able to jimmy both hands completely free of the bonds with enough time. I just need to buy myself some of it first.

"Hey… hey, listen. Is this your place? I didn't know anybody lived here, I promise. That's my mistake and I'm sorry for it."

The two gas-masked men exchange a quick glance at one another before the one closest to me squats down on his hamstrings to draw his face closer.

"You… dumb… cunt."

He presses the knife up close against my chest.

"You think we live here? We're just passing through. Same as you."

The tip of the blade touches my collarbone as I work my wrists back and forth behind me ever so slowly. He tugs the knife down against the neck of my shirt to expose more of my keyring necklace, my cleavage, or both. Even from behind the sweaty plastic of his visor, I can see the man's beady black eyes roving down there.

The cheap rope they've used is just about to break; I can feel it. Just a little more time, and I'll have both hands free. I have no idea where my Glock is, but I can see my backpack over against the wall next to the rifle. All I need is the element of surprise—knock the first guy with the knife back on his ass, then make a run for the rifle and hope I make it there before the second guy does.

"You… you don't live here?"

The man in front of me shakes his head and wheezes into his mask. I think he's laughing.

"Is this bitch deaf or dumb or both?"

His buddy behind him also starts to laugh, but then abruptly stops and clutches at his throat. There's a strange, abnormally long moment where I don't know what he's doing, even though something clearly is happening with him. And then, all at once, I understand.

Somehow, something sharp and shiny has found its way through the neck of the second man. Two hands grasp at the foreign protrusion in a slow, shocked attempt to either investigate it or remove it somehow from being there. And then the man is falling to his knees and toppling over onto his side, and now the blood is flowing outward in every direction as he frantically strives in vain to stop the last great flood of his lifeforce from escaping him.

By now, the first man has followed my gaze and turned himself all the way around. If he's shocked to see his companion bleeding out on the floor before his eyes, I have no way of knowing it, since I can't see his face and he doesn't make a sound.

Where once the second figure stood, there's now a third masked man, short, thin, and heavily tattooed on both arms. His knife is stained black and dripping on the floor.

This new stranger wastes no time in rushing forward at the first man. A scuffle ensues as the first man manages to dodge the blade swipe and wrestle back against this unknown presence.

If ever I had an opportunity, that opportunity is now. I push and pull at the flimsy ropes harder than I've ever pushed and pulled anything before in my whole life. All the while, from the narrow slits of my eyes behind the crack in my mask, I try to keep watch and mentally prepare myself for any possible ending as these two beings grapple with one another and with their knives.

In an alternate universe, maybe I would have wondered who I'm supposed to be rooting for between them. Now, I only hope they kill each other so I can make my escape in peace.

Lovely as that idea is, however, it is not meant to be. The first man, the one who loves to snap his fingers and call me the 'n' word, manages to knock the third man down to his knees. Before you can say the word Mississippi, he has his knife buried in the other man's side. The third man lets out a gurgling sound from behind his mask as he realizes what it feels like and what it means to have a knife in your side.

It's at this exact moment that the ropes finally fall to the ground, and with a start, I realize that I'm free, so I rush over to the rifle in the corner. By the time I have my hands on the gun and I've turned around, the first man is closing fast upon me with the knife. I level the rifle at him and pull the trigger, and there's a deafening blast that knocks him skyward and backward into the air until he lands in a heap on the ground.

And then there is silence. I stand with the rifle pressed firm against my shoulder, waiting and ready for him to get up and present a renewed threat.

But he doesn't. The man lies on the ground in a crumpled pile of clothing that is completely still, and as I hold my breath with my finger on the trigger, I notice the dark pool of liquid as it begins to ooze out from his form.

What threat is left? There's the first man, who I just shot square in the chest with this rifle. There's the second man, who got a knife stuck through his throat. And there's the third man, who came in out of nowhere to dispatch the second man and make a run at the first man, and who now lies still on the basement floor in a puddle of blood.

Could there be more of them upstairs? Surely, they

would have come down here by now when they heard all the sounds of a struggle. If nothing else, the sound of the rifle going off would have brought them down here.

If there's no one else, though, I should get moving myself. I'd like to think that being down here in the basement probably muffled most of the gunshot sound from escaping the house as a whole, but you never know. Besides, I'm only just barely removed from either being raped or killed myself. Probably both.

There's no time to waste processing what just happened, though. At least not here. Once I'm back in the woods and back home behind my reinforced walls, boarded-up windows, and locked doors, that's when I can allow myself whatever mental and emotional exploration I need to do. But only once I'm safe. Right here, right now, I am anything but safe.

Hurriedly, I gather up my belongings from around the room. Midway through this process, I'm surprised to feel a kind of solemn satisfaction bubbling up within my chest. Frankly, it borders on pride. My original belongings: the backpack, the Glock, the crowbar, and the flashlight, are all once more back in my possession. Now, though, I also have a rifle and a bag full of medicine. Somehow, the catalog of spoils I've accrued keeps on growing.

I need a new mask, though. Jim Carrey and I have been through too much together for me to just casually discard him—especially down here in a tomb with these monsters. I'll bring him home with the hopes that I might repair him. But just to be on the safe side, I should definitely confiscate these three gas masks too. It's not as if their owners will be needing them anymore.

As long as I'm grabbing their masks, I may as well

check for other items of interest. I need to be quick about it—I've already encountered three more human beings than I planned to encounter tonight—but I'd be a fool not to at least see what each dead man has on him.

I'd also be a fool to just walk up and start looting without ensuring first that each dead man is, in fact, a dead man. Disrespectful and distasteful as it may be to kick a man while he's down (and dead), that's exactly what I do with the first man.

Unpleasant memories of the 'n' word, the 'c' word, and really just all the words that came out of this man's mouth start to re-emerge for me, along with the way he dragged his knife down against my shirt collar. The kicks quickly become a hell of a lot more brutal than they need to be, and I'm not mad about it. Justice is served.

He's definitely not alive. I check for a pulse just to make sure, and when his expiration is confirmed, I relieve him of the knife and of the leather sheath he presumably kept it in on his belt. I check his pockets— empty—before peeling off his gas mask. The bloated, bearded face on the other side might have been ugly in life, but it's downright repulsive in death.

I resist the urge to start kicking again. He's got the kind of face that just begs to be kicked.

The second man is more profitable than the first. He has a flashlight, some more of the not-very-good rope, a pocketknife, a bottle of aspirin, a canteen of water, a set of keys, and his mask, of course. I'm starting to run out of room in my backpack.

I go to kick the third man when my leg freezes in the air.

No… it couldn't be. There's no way…

But there's also no denying the sight of the man's

chest as it ticks up and down, up and down. This person is *still alive somehow*. Despite the gaping wound in his side and the lagoon of blood haloing out around him on the basement floor, he's still holding on somehow.

If this were the first man, I'd leave him down here alone to die a slow and painful death. I'd probably do the same for the second man as well. But the third man… the third man killed the second one, and he probably would have killed the first one, too, if he hadn't gotten stabbed.

So, what does that mean?

The answer comes quickly and easily: it means he deserves to be put out of his misery. As if providing an answer of its own, the rifle seems to float up at my side until my finger finds the trigger, and now I'm aiming down at the man's head.

If not for this man, who knows what would have happened. I was doing a decent job of stalling and buying myself time to work at the ropes behind my back as the first man lobbed his ignorant prejudice at me.

Could I have broken free in time before they did whatever they had planned to do to me? I'm not so sure anymore. The first man only had a knife, but he had it pressed right there at my chest. Even with the element of surprise and with my hands suddenly free, I probably would have had to roll backward away from him to create some space before trying to either fight back or run away.

Plus, the second man wasn't far away. Assuming I did somehow get the jump on them both and break free of my bonds in time, could I have really evaded both men long enough to make it to the rifle?

Impossible. I would have been shot dead before I

made it halfway across the room.

The thought dawns on me that this tattooed stranger probably saved my life. Actually, there's no 'probably' about it. He did save my life.

Why am I hesitating? I've now been in this basement far longer than is safe. Just shoot the guy and get it over with. Don't make him suffer needlessly, especially not after how he helped you.

"Fuck."

I'm still hesitating. He's still breathing. My finger is on the trigger, but for some stupid, asinine reason, I just can't seem to pull it.

"Fuck."

What am I waiting for? Am I really feeling pity right now for this complete and utter stranger who I know absolutely nothing about?

On the one hand, yes, he 'saved' me, I suppose you could say. Or at least that's what it looked like he was trying to do before he failed.

On the other hand, I really have no proof that's what he was doing. Plus, he failed. So, there's that.

The right thing to do would be to shoot him. Make it quick and painless. Whoever he is and whatever he's done, he deserves that much, at least, for what he did here tonight, intentionally or not, successfully or not. It's the right thing to do.

Or the right thing to do is to try and help him.

"Fuck."

That new thought, that new idea, has been knocking at the door in the back of my brain for a while now, actually. It was faint at first, when I was still getting over the shock of realizing the man was alive. But the more time I've wasted standing here like an idiot with the gun in the air, the louder that knocking has become. And now, against all my better judgment, I've opened up the door to finally face what's on the other side.

What is on the other side? What would 'helping him' even look like?

Of course, that's an easy question to answer for a woman with over two decades of medical experience and training. I know *exactly* what I'd need to do if I wanted to help this man try to survive this injury, gruesome as it is. The harder question is answering whether I *want* to help him in that way, and the hardest question is answering *why* I should help him at all.

Because he saved you.

"Fuck."

Assuming I did decide to help him and was successful in saving his life, what then? What do I do with him?

If I do this, if I help this man and try to save his life, I'm not doing it here. I'll stop the bleeding and take care of the life-threatening conditions here if need be, but I'm not sticking around in this miserable place to nurse him back to health.

This is even dumber than the whole business with the cat. Lest I forget, I've already got one patient waiting for me back at home. At least if that patient ends up being a foe instead of a friend, it's fine. Because a cat's just a fucking cat.

But if this patient ends up being a foe instead of a friend? It's a fucking man. Plus he'd be there, with me, in my home. He'd know where my safe haven is. Even if I took care of him until he was completely healed, what would happen then? I couldn't just turn him loose out the cellar door and wish him good fortune on the rest of his life. I'd have to blindfold him and take him far away somewhere and just leave him out there.

And at that point, wouldn't the whole thing have been a great big waste of time? He'd probably end up dead anyway. And I'd be out whatever resources I'd shared with him up until that point that I could have been using for myself.

That settles it. He can't come with me. It just doesn't make sense. It's a decision that would be made based off emotion rather than logic, and that's not how I operate. That's the kind of thinking that will get you killed.

I'll leave him here, then. Let fate or God or fuck-all decide what happens to him. He's not my responsibility anyway. This isn't some hospital charge under my care and supervision. His life isn't in my hands.

Although, it is…

"Fuck."

Fine. I won't shoot him, but I won't let him bleed out, either. I'll tend to his wound quickly, and if it looks like he's a goner anyway, then I'll leave him be.

And if it looks like it will require more time, more effort, or more supplies than I have with me now, I'll leave him in that scenario, too. But if I can help him in a timely, practical, efficient fashion, I will do that now. I guess I owe him that much.

A heavy sigh escapes my lips as I work to stem the blood flow and stitch up the wound. This process is made all the more tedious by the pitiful white halo of flashlight illumination I'm forced to work within. Slowly but surely, I labor with practiced precision at saving this stranger's life the way he saved mine.

At long last, I finish. My hands are caked in blood, so I decide to use just the smallest amount of water from the second man's canteen to rinse them as best I can. Mostly, I just drag them back and forth across the floor, smearing long stains into the concrete.

Time to go. Actually, the time to go has long since passed. I'm way overdue to make my exit from this awful basement. Awful, yes, because of what happened here with these men, but also still somehow kind of sublime because of everything I found and gathered down here. Christmas came early.

I'm halfway up the steps with my bulging backpack weighing me down like Santa Claus's sack of toys when I hear the cough.

This one, from this person, sounds nothing like the man's cough I heard a year ago in that other house. That cough was free and unencumbered, though distant. This one is the cough of a man fighting through injury and struggling to breathe normally through a gas mask, and it comes from just a few yards away.

I shake my head, close my eyes for a second, and then take another step up the staircase. The coughing continues—harsh, metallic, relentless.

My head turns of its own accord, and I take in the sight of him lying there alone in a pool of his own blood, flanked on both sides by dead men. Men he either killed or tried to kill. Men who would have otherwise killed me if not for his timely intervention.

There's nothing more I can do. I climb the remainder of the stairs as quietly as I can, trying with all my might to shut out the sound of the man down in the basement struggling to breathe. Struggling to stay alive.

Out the back door, up the fence, along the side of the house, and into the jeep I go, tossing the heavy sack behind me as I close the door. I have the car key fished out from my necklace ring and halfway up to the steering wheel when I hesitate.

Why, oh why, is this so goddamn difficult for me to do? Is it Ruthie's fault? My dog dies, and suddenly I'm a basket-case of emotions that needs to tend to every injured cat and man I encounter? What the fuck is going on with me?

Out of the jeep, along the side of the house, up the fence, and in the back door I go once again.

Since when did I allow my heart to overrule my brain? I don't want to blame my dead dog, but I don't know what else could do this to me after all this time.

He's still coughing as I make my way down the basement stairs. At least something is happening inside him still, though. I guess that's a good thing, considering I'm about to do the dumbest thing I've maybe ever done in my entire life.

What a sight it must be to see me walking this bloodied figure out the front door of the house into the brisk night air. He was difficult enough to get up the stairs, even considering he's not a particularly large guy and I had both of my arms free for the challenge. By the time I reached the top, I knew there was no way I could get him up and over the backyard fence.

Instead, we're boldly marching out here together where anyone could potentially see us without difficulty. Even double-armed, with the Glock in one hand and the rifle wedged between our bodies, it's a ridiculously risky and probably suicidal move to come right out down the front walkway into the open, especially with the man's dead weight dragging against my side and slowing me down.

Mercifully, we encounter no problems on the

painfully slow slog to the jeep. When I finally reach the passenger side of the vehicle, I pop the door open for him. Already suppressing feelings of revulsion and regret, I help lift his dirty, bloodied body into the passenger seat, and once he's clear, I shut the door behind him.

Keeping my eyes peeled in every direction, and with both hands now fully engaged with their respective weapons, I do a full three-hundred-sixty-degree rotation around the jeep, ready and waiting for any kind of surprise attack to materialize.

There's a dull ache now at the top of my skull from where the butt of the rifle made contact, and it reminds me that I'm never in the clear, not even when I think I am. If they were going to pick me off, though, the time to have done it would have been while I had my hands full with the body.

It's time to go. Whether I've sealed my fate or not by bringing aboard this unintended extra cargo, my fingers do not hesitate this time when they find the key and bring it into the ignition.

As I reverse the jeep out from the fence across the lawn and back onto the road, I see it for the first time: a bright yellow Hummer parked right at the end of this neighborhood street.

That canary behemoth was definitely not there when I drove in. If there was another exit or a road to get out of here in a different direction, I would take it, but there's not. Part of the reason I originally came here a year ago was *because* there was only one way in or out.

I slump low in my seat and rest the end of the rifle along the open passenger side window. Maybe it's fucked up, but the thought crosses my mind that the man I've brought with me might very well serve as a human shield if I'm fired upon as we pass this Hummer. I'm not wishing it on him, obviously, but if it goes down that way, it goes down that way. At least I'll know I was right to get him out of that basement and bring him along with me this far.

My eyes follow the length of the rifle out the window, and my finger is on the trigger as we draw level with the hood of the Hummer. I give the jeep just a bit more gas at this point so our speed changes quickly in the event that someone's tracking us from inside it. The cabin looks empty, though, as we roll on past, and I don't glimpse any sudden movements or changes in or around the machine, which is good.

I'm still tucked low in my seat as we fully clear the other vehicle. Even in the dusky aura of my brake lights and the ambient glow cast off from the jeep's low beams, I can make out two giant bumper stickers on the back of the metal monstrosity, as well as a large sticker decal on the rear window, all from my view of the passenger side mirror. The writing on the bumper stickers is a bit too small to make out clearly, but I see enough letters, colors, and symbols to put together what they say based off all these context clues.

'STAND FOR THE FLAG, KNEEL FOR THE CROSS' is one bumper sticker. The other is a Roman numeral III that's circled in stars.

Both classic. Why am I not surprised? The make and model of the car already screams out: "Look at me! I hate the environment!" These stickers add to that exclamation: "I also hate gays and want to shoot people!"

The worst by far, though, is the large sticker decal

on the window, because there's absolutely no mistaking it for what it means. In an otherwise solid black tinted glass rectangle, the owner of this vehicle has pasted an oversized sticker that shows a raised white fist in the center of a white hangman's noose.

A part of me wants to stop—not so I can loot this car for supplies, but so I can slit the tires and maybe break the windows for good measure. I'm positive this must be the mode of transport for those two good old boys lying dead in the basement of that house.

I keep on driving, though. Those bigots are long gone now. Someone else will come along to loot or commandeer the Hummer... though it won't be easy, since I'm pretty sure I have the keys to it in my backpack.

Mainly, I keep going, though, because I now have not one, but two charges under my care and supervision. Evidently, you can take the woman out of the hospital, but you can't take the hospital out of the woman. Here I go again, listening to my heart instead of my head.

How did you let it come to this, Alex? How did we get here?

SIX

"How is this happening right now? Is this real life?"

I want to answer my wife. More than anything, I want to let her know that no, this is not real life. This is only a bad dream, and together, we can wake ourselves up from it.

But that's not reality. The events unfolding on the large television screen in our living room are surreal, for sure. There's no doubt in my mind that I never in a million years would have imagined I'd be seeing the types of things I'm seeing on my screen today.

Then again, who would have ever expected to see Confederate flags flying around the U.S. Capitol over one hundred and fifty years after the Civil War ended?

If that could happen seven years ago, then it makes perfect sense that this kind of deplorable madness could happen today.

After spending three years as chief resident in a major metropolitan hospital, I can truthfully say there's not a whole lot that surprises me anymore. I've seen all manner of events and occurrences that defy conventional logic and understanding.

Whether you believe in the miracles of modern medicine or the miracles of a higher power, there's no denying the shared commonality between these supposedly opposing viewpoints: miracles. As crazy as these things may seem at first glance, they still somehow happen, which keeps you constantly on your toes and re-evaluating exactly what you think is possible.

This—this chaos—this carnage we're witnessing on the screen… it just doesn't seem possible. The images and sounds being captured and streamed to us live from the comfort of our own living room just don't seem real. I'd sooner believe we're watching a summer blockbuster on Netflix than live news coverage on MSNBC, but this is where we're at right now as a country. This is what happens when society breaks down and splinters apart right before your eyes.

"Alex?"

I turn to look at Hope, who has quickly gone from nestled in the crook of my shoulder to sitting bolt upright next to me on the sofa.

"Huh?"

"I said, how is this happening right now? Can you believe this?"

Both of those questions seem rhetorical to me, but I know they're in earnest coming from Hope, so I give her an answer.

"It's crazy, that's for sure."

Is it, though? What's crazy is that this country re-elected this man in the first place four years ago.

For that matter, it's crazy he was ever put in office to begin with. A reality TV star, failed businessman, sexual deviant, and xenophobic bully? Sure, sounds like the perfect candidate to represent the party of wholesome White American Christians.

Can I *believe* that all of this would happen, though?

Absolutely. Nothing surprises me anymore.

"My fellow Americans. I want to speak to you tonight about the troubling events of the past week…"

The President of the United States of America certainly *looks* troubled, I'll give him that. There's a bleak, weathered expression worn on his face that comes across as weary and sincere. He grips both sides of a podium that bears the great seal and peers directly into the camera after a lengthy sigh.

"I want to be clear: I unequivocally condemn the violence that we saw last week. Violence and vandalism have absolutely no place in our country and no place in our movement."

The news feed smash-cuts to footage from various cities around the nation as the leader of the free world continues his live press conference.

In San Francisco, Chinatown burns as masked marauders hurl Molotov cocktails into local eateries and businesses, none of which have signs that are in English.

In downtown Chicago, the camera operator pans up an alley wall to reveal gigantic, spray-painted writing that reads 'SEND THEM BACK.'

In Atlanta, rows upon rows of police officers in full-on militaristic riot gear advance ever forward behind plastic shields and unmarked uniforms that conveniently conceal their names and identities, occasionally firing smoke grenades, tear gas, or rubber bullets into a crowd of peaceful protesters that by and large share my skin color.

In Dallas, beleaguered hospital workers in scrubs and face masks silently hold the line outside of medical facilities as 'patriots' brandish megaphones and crude cardboard signs proclaiming LIBERTY OVER

DEATH' and 'GOD'S JUDGMENT IS UPON US.'

"No true supporter of mine could ever threaten or harass their fellow Americans."

More footage of Americans threatening and harassing their fellow Americans then follows.

An Islamic mosque in Ohio burns as rioters, not firefighters, form a protective ring around it. Mourners lay out candles and photographs of children outside a Connecticut elementary school, site of the latest mass shooting that will fail to either move or motivate the necessary political interest to rethink gun control laws. An oversized effigy of Dr. Anthony Fauci is burned at the stake outside the National Institute of Allergy and Infectious Diseases in Maryland.

From sea to shining sea, urban neighborhoods, Planned Parenthood clinics, and LGBTQ+ centers are ravaged, ransacked, and razed.

"Today, I am calling on all Americans to overcome the passions of the moment and join together as one American people. Let us choose to move forward united for the good of our families, our communities, and our country. Thank you. God bless you, and God bless America."

Hope mutes the TV.

"This is insane."

"This is only what they can show on TV. Imagine everything that's happening that they're *not* showing us right now."

Ruth Bader Ginsburg meticulously cleans her own butthole between us. I watch her do her thing and wonder what it must be like to be a dog. Is there bliss in ignorance? Is simplicity really best?

"I think..."

Hope trails off for a second or two before continuing.

"I think we should get out of here."

How does the dog know she's clean enough? Is there some kind of inner biological mechanism that lets her know when she's done?

"Did you hear what I said?"

"What?"

"I said I think we should get out of here."

There's a split-screen on the television. To the left, the director of the CDC addresses the media. On the right, image after image appears of mass gravesites around the country. Below all of this is a black-and-white banner that boldly proclaims a death toll number so high it seems like a mistake. Surely, someone added a few extra zeroes and commas in there on accident.

At least, that's what the non-doctor part of me would think in an alternate universe to this one. The real me in the real here and the real now isn't the least bit surprised by the figure on the screen. Saddened by it? Sure. Disappointed by it? Obviously. But surprised by it? Definitely not.

"Are you listening to me right now?"

I turn to her.

"Of course, I am."

"Well, then, what do you think?"

"About what?"

Her mouth twitches with annoyance.

"About getting out of here."

I'm not following.

"Sorry, babe. Out of where?"

"Out of here. Out of town. Out of the city."

Hope's face is grave.

RBG has finally come to rest between us, thanks to whatever mysterious inner or outer force of nature there is that clued her in to stop licking because it's all good down there now, thank you very much.

"What are you talking about?"

She points at the screen impatiently with the remote control.

"Are you seeing what I'm seeing?"

I follow her gesture to the screen. It's more of the same: more political talking heads, more shallow graves, more gas masks and hazmat suits, more dismal statistics that don't seem like actual numbers.

"I guess I'm not following you right now."

Hope's expression borders on incredulity.

"How can you not be following me right now?"

She stands up and points the remote at the TV again.

"Are you seeing the same thing I'm seeing? This is *it*."

Again, I connect the dots between her arm and the television console with my eyes. And again, I fail to mentally connect the dots she's trying to show me.

"What do you mean?"

"What do I *mean?* I mean, this is *it*. This is really happening. It's happening right now in front of us."

"What is the 'it' you keep referring to?"

Hope's face is turning pink.

"Really? Seriously?"

My palms turn toward the sky.

"I don't know what you're talking about."

"This is *it*, Alex! Shit is… breaking down!"

She starts to pace.

"I'm serious! Look at that number on the screen.

Look at that… no, seriously, look at that right now!"

I turn to look at what she wants to show me. The mass gravesite images have stopped on the right-hand side of the split-screen. In their place is a new video feed taken from a distance via drone or helicopter of a sea of people, maybe several thousand, surging against barricades and security officers stationed outside a government building. The words 'live' and 'insurrectionists' are amongst those typed out on the screen.

Hope's body is shaking all over.

"That's less than thirty minutes away from here! Just think about that for a second, will you?"

She's not wrong. I'm almost positive that the building on the screen right now is our city courthouse, which is only a few blocks away from my hospital. I walk past that building sometimes on my breaks.

"That's right around the corner from the hospital."

Hope is exasperated.

"I know it is! That's my point!"

She returns to the sofa.

"Alex… this is *it*. I'm not trying to scare you, but this is really happening. It's happening right now, from coast to coast, and all around the world, too, for that matter. I know you're more up-to-date with all the NDV stuff than I am, obviously, but look at what's happening right now."

She sets the remote down on the coffee table, her expression dire.

"We have to get out of here."

As soon as I smile, I know I've made a mistake.

"Where do you… where do you think we should go?"

"We'll go to my parents' place. Not the condo; the summer house. Out in the woods. Out in the wilderness. Far away from all this shit and all these lunatics."

Every marriage has its sticky subjects—those discussion topics that are better off left alone. Hope knows that this is one of them.

"I thought we agreed to give this current setup five years minimum before making any major decisions. Did we not?"

Her jaw drops.

"*Yeah*, but we agreed to that in a world that wasn't falling apart. Wouldn't you say that the situation has changed since then?"

"Certainly. I'm not an idiot, Hope. Everything you're seeing, I'm seeing too. In fact, I'm seeing it firsthand on a daily basis."

"I know you are! That's why I'm surprised you're not totally on board with this right now. You know better than anyone what this virus is capable of doing to people… and what's it capable of making people do to each other. Don't you think it's time we do something about it ourselves?"

Gently, I lean forward to take her hand, and she lets me.

"Baby, I am doing something about it. My whole ward, we're on the frontlines now. Our whole focus is on doing whatever it takes to help save lives and stop the spread."

Hope's hand is trembling.

"And listen, that is amazing that you have been doing that and helping to transition your team in the midst of all this insanity, but Alex… this is *it*. This is different. This isn't just opening up your beds and bringing in ventilators. Look at that building on TV."

There's not much to look at anymore. Where once there was an elegant city courthouse, now there is only black smoke and swirling flames on the screen. It's stunning and frighteningly incomprehensible to see firsthand how quickly fire can change the physical makeup of a *building,* a familiar landmark I've walked by hundreds of times before. Now, it will never be the same again. Assuming it even survives in any capacity at all.

"That could have been your hospital. That very well *could be* your hospital any day now."

Hope reaches until she's caught my chin in her hand and turned me back to face her.

"I can't wait until that happens. And make no mistake, it will happen. It's just a matter of time."

She takes both my hands in hers on the couch.

"Please."

My thumbs slide across the skin on her hands as I really absorb for the first time the full extent of her concern on this subject. I wish I would have picked up on it sooner, because it's painfully clear to me now just how worked up she is from everything that's happening out there in the world.

"Hope… this isn't something we can run from. This disease… this virus… it may be worse in the cities right now, but not for long. Especially the way we're reacting as a country right now. It's only a matter of time before it's just as bad in the rural areas as it is in the urban ones."

"But it's still a matter of time, which means there's still time. If we leave now, we can even try and stock up on everything before everyone else does. Don't you want to get a head start on this while we still can?"

She's completely taken the bait and started running

with it. Hook, line, sinker. Everything.

"I still don't know what 'this' is. You keep referring to 'it' and 'this' like I'm supposed to know what you're talking about right now, but I don't. I'm sorry, but I'm not following you."

"I don't…"

Hope pauses to take a big breath in, then sighs with frustration.

"I'm not trying to be overdramatic here, but this," she points at the TV, "this is not normal. Everything that's happening right now in the world is not just another hardship we have to overcome as a people or as society or whatever. This isn't just news coverage or current events… this is *it*, Alex. I don't think there's any coming back from this. This is how it starts."

"How what starts?"

"The end."

Again, I can't help myself or stop myself from smiling ever so slightly, even though I know it's a mistake.

"The end of what?"

She hesitates, so I continue.

"The world?"

Hope's forehead crinkles.

"I… I don't know. Maybe."

I bury my smile as quickly as I can. It's not quick enough.

"Smile and laugh all you want. I don't think there's anything funny about this at all."

My smile is long gone now.

"Neither do I, just so we're clear. Don't forget that I'm right there, up close and personal, with all of this madness and pain that you're seeing on the TV at home.

I'm working my ass to the bone every single day to try and slow down that growing number you see at the bottom of the screen."

"Well, then, why aren't you taking this seriously?"

I pull my hands free.

"Excuse me? I'm a doctor. No one takes this more seriously than me."

Hope grabs my hands right back.

"I know you are. No one takes this more seriously than you. So, take it seriously, then. Alex… it's out of control. They're not just hitting random buildings anymore; they're targeting the pharmaceutical companies and the research facilities that are working on a vaccine. Think about that for a second. Most of these people—they don't believe in science. They think this is some kind of plague sent down by God to wipe out all the sinners. And they think it's their job to help Him do it."

RBG watches us both carefully. Intuitive creature that she is, our dog seems to have picked up on the mood change here on the sofa. She stares up at the interlocked hands above her snout with gleaming eyes.

"It's not safe for us here. They're intentionally targeting the cities. Transmission rates are *obviously* going to be higher in the more heavily concentrated areas, but they don't want to hear that or look at it that way. All they care about is that this pandemic finally gives them an excuse to come out of the woodwork and terrorize the same people that their politicians and their news anchors have been demonizing to them on a daily basis for years. Do you know what they're calling it now? NDV?"

"The Africa Virus."

"The *Black People* Virus."

I hadn't heard that yet, although it doesn't take a quantum leap of the imagination or intellect to understand how and why this situation has devolved to that new low.

"All it takes is one racist asshole with a gun. And in this country, there are millions of them running around right now. The bad cops look the other way, and the good ones are overrun. Things are getting worse, not better. These people aren't worried about the police or about the pandemic; they're energized by all the chaos, because this is an opportunity for them. This is the perfect opportunity for all their hatred and bigotry and prejudice to truly come out of the shadows so they can rise up and give in to it all."

"I don't disagree with you. But you're forgetting the most important aspect here."

Hope looks at me expectantly.

"People are still dying, Hope. This virus isn't discriminating based on skin color or on where a person lives. It's taking lives on both sides and on all sides. And unless I do something—unless we all do something—to try and stop it, it won't matter who you voted for in the last election. What's most important right now is that we fight back against the common enemy, not against each other."

"What's most important right now is *us*. You, me. Ruthie. We're what's most important. And we're in danger here. All of us. But you, especially."

She cups my cheek.

"I love you. I don't want to lose you."

"You're not going to."

Hope stares hard into me.

"Please. Please, Alex. Trust me. Believe me on this one. We're all each other has left."

The stillness and heaviness of the moment crystallizes and then cracks like a bone snapping in my chest as I reach up and lay my hand over hers against my face.

"I… can't. I love you, too, but I can't just up and leave. Not now, not in the midst of all this, not when I'm at my most needed."

"What about my needs?"

Hope's eyes glisten and it breaks my heart to see.

"I swore an oath. This… this is bigger than me. I'm sorry, Hope, but… it's bigger than us, even. If you really believe that this is the end of the world… then this is how I save it. This is how we save it. By saving as many lives, as many human lives—Black, Brown, White, whatever—as we can."

I can feel Hope's fingers trembling beneath mine atop my cheek. She takes in a breath and bats her eyelashes a couple times before forcing a smile out on me.

"Okay."

Her face changes slowly. There's a sort of settling that occurs as the skin around her lips, nostrils, and neck twitches and then goes smooth. Where once there was a threat of rain, Hope's eyes are now dry and clear.

Of course, I'm not convinced by any of this.

"Okay?"

She nods, and now her fingers are caressing my cheek.

"Okay."

"Really? You're not going to storm out of here?"

That at least earns me a slight but sad smile from

her.

"No, I don't think I am."

Hope studies me.

"I've made my position clear. But so have you. I actually completely understand where you're coming from and why you feel like you have an obligation to stay."

She spots the apprehensive expression growing on my face and cuts me off before I can interject.

"I do! I really do, Alex. And I admire you for it, actually. You've always had such a… a dutifulness about you, and a stubborn commitment to doing what you truly think and feel is right at all times. I love that about you, and I would never, ever, in a million years want you to compromise those values. They're what make you you. I wouldn't be able to live with myself if I ever asked you to change."

She sounds sincere, but it's also not like Hope to pivot this quickly—especially not on something this big. Usually, she'd allow her emotions to work her up into a frenzy, and then all hell would break loose until we finally found a common ground. Or else she'd need to take a break from it all and go for a walk or a run just to get a breath of fresh air. Truth be told, she's every bit as stubborn as I am, only she comes with three times the temper.

But none of that is on display now… and that's what worries me.

"You're really okay, then? Okay with me staying and seeing this through until it's all over, and until we can get back to normalcy once again?"

Hope dips her chin into a quick, curt nod, and again, flashes me her sweetest smile. It still comes across just a bit mournful to me, though, as if she's consciously swallowing something bitter… or resigning herself to her fate. My stomach twists.

"I'm okay with *us* staying and seeing this through until it's all over. There is no 'I,' 'me,' 'my,' or 'you' anymore, silly. For better or worse, till death do us part, remember?"

"I remember."

Her smile flits away along with her hand, and now she's up on her feet again and moving away from the sofa and into the kitchen.

As is expected, RBG trails close behind. No matter how close that dog and I have gotten over the past seven years, there's no denying who she sees as alpha.

"Well, now that that's settled, I suppose it's time we pop open some of the stronger stuff and talk about that other great big fucking elephant in the room."

I watch her dig a bottle of whiskey out from our liquor cabinet.

"And what elephant is that?"

Hope slams the bottle on top of the island counter, turns, pinches a couple tumbler glasses out from a cupboard, spins around, and begins to pour an obscenely generous portion of the spirit into each glass. All the while, there's a bright, manic light dancing in her eyeballs.

She lasers them onto me from across the room. The expression on her face is quintessential Hope: fight me or fuck me. And as always, the problem is that it's nearly impossible to tell the difference.

"A healthy marriage is all about compromise, right? Give and take. Making sacrifices to appease the other person. I showed you that I'm willing to go against my gut and my better judgment because I trust you, I love you, and ultimately, I want you to be happy. And if staying here in the middle of this fucked-up city to battle this fucked-up virus in the midst of this truly fucked-up situation gives your life purpose, then I want to help give you that, as well."

Hope crosses back to the sofa and hands me one of the drinks. I'm not sure which of the two I dread more: the heavy pour of straight liquor or whatever it is she's about to dump on me.

She purposefully keeps me in suspense as we clink glasses and each take a sip. The whiskey burns all the way down, but it's still not as red-hot as the wicked grin this woman wears right now in front of me.

"And if raising a child here in the middle of this truly fucked-up situation will give *my* life purpose—and believe me, Alex, it most certainly will—then I trust you'll do the right thing, too, and you'll give me that, won't you?"

I cough as the whiskey comes back up my throat.

It's going to be a long, long night.

SEVEN

"Hellooooo? Helloooooooooooo?! Is anyone out there? *Hellooooooooooooooooo?!*"

At first, the voice exists only in my dreams. There's no clear identity behind it or logical explanation for why it's even there in the first place. I don't recognize it, but then again, sometimes dreams aren't very recognizable to begin with. It's just another strange, nonsensical anomaly being processed alongside a whole series of strange, nonsensical anomalies whipped up by a brain with too much time on its hands and not nearly enough emotional anchors left in this life to keep it tethered to reality.

When the voice finally tears me from my dreams and makes itself known as a real, conscious, waking thing, I sit bolt upright in bed, alert as I've ever been and wary as I need to be. The last time this happened, it took several tries to finally get myself up and into action. I'd like to think my response time is better now, and that the sound I'm reacting to has only just recently begun.

Still, it disappoints me to fathom a world where I'm sleeping through these kinds of alarms to begin with.

First, it was the cat screeching. That took me several tries to finally divorce myself from chalking it all up to dreams and nocturnal fantasies. I would have hoped that I'd learned my lesson from that episode and that I'm more sensitive, receptive, and reactive now than I was back then. That's the hope, at least, and the expectation I have for myself.

If this man's voice has been screaming out into the night for minutes or even hours now, and I've been dead to the world asleep and assuming it's all just a nightmare or a dream? That would be worrisome. I can't accept that for myself, because that would mean I'm slipping. And I can't afford to slip.

These feelings of dread and concern are at least slightly mitigated by the surprise and delight I get from realizing the cat is following me down the stairs.

One of the simple and rare newfound joys of my daily existence has been sharing my bed again with another warm-blooded creature that has both a heartbeat and, presumably, a soul. That joy has also increased exponentially as I've borne witness to the cat's speedy recovery from the injuries it suffered in my tripwires and traps. It's one thing to have a front-row seat to the powers of healing and rehabilitation; it's another thing to also feel the pride and satisfaction that comes from knowing you are solely responsible for that progress.

But this—this is a new type of happiness I experience, noticing the cat for the first time as it limps its way down the steps behind me. Not only does this mean the cat feels strong enough to accompany me on such a journey; it also means the cat *wants* to accompany me on such a journey. We are continuing to bond and grow closer.

I'm unexpectedly touched by this, and I have to stop

and turn at the base of the stairs, reach down, and stroke it below its chin.

Perhaps it's time I name you. Perhaps it's time we make this official, you and I.

"Hellooooooooooooooooooooooo?!"

His voice startles me and breaks me from the momentary trance I found myself in.

What was it that I was just doing? A lapse in judgment, perhaps, to get caught up in my own emotions and to forget about the task at hand. As nice as it may be to finally have a new friend—my brain stuffs back the words 'a new reason for living'—there's important work to be done here.

1-2-2-5-9-1. I put the Glock behind me in the waistband of my sweatpants, lock the safe, and make my way to the door that leads down to the cellar. Even from up here—and even when he's not yelling and making an awful racket—I can still hear him down there: breathing, coughing, and shaking around against his constraints, I'll bet.

Still, this is a first. I realize it all of a sudden, and I'm surprised I didn't think of it before while I was still upstairs in bed, or even just now down at the linen closet getting the gun. Up until now, I've never heard his voice… because I've never heard him speak. Because he never has. Until now.

This is big. What's about to happen isn't just another day or another part of the weird new routine I've adopted for myself these past few days or weeks or months or however long it's been now since I started taking care of my two patients. The cat has never followed me down the stairs, and the man has never made anything other than painful, unintelligible moaning sounds. This is all uncharted territory for me tonight.

I glance down in the darkness just to see if the cat's still nearby, and it is. It's not exactly easy to see here without light, but I'm pretty sure she's staring up at me. In my head, she's asking me if I'm ready for what comes next. It's a good question that I don't know the answer to right away.

Together, we make our way down the steps into the basement. I find my way by memory to the bench, grab the flashlight, aim it where I know he is, and flick on the switch.

He's been silent ever since I opened the door. Probably because he heard me coming down the stairs. Who knows what he believes is about to happen right now? I wonder where he thinks he is and what kind of trouble he thinks he's found himself in.

Given that there's a loose pillowcase with airholes torn into it that's draped over his head and duct-taped around his shoulders—and given that he's been sequestered down here in absolute pitch blackness ever since I brought him back, save for the occasional bit of light that must come in when I open the cellar door to go outside or come back in each day—he has quite literally been left in the dark this whole time.

He also has been bound to a basement support pole by tape, rope, and chains. Unlike those idiots back in that other basement with their piss-poor rope and their even more piss-poor job of tying me up with it, I made damn sure that my charge wasn't going anywhere. Not on my watch.

I say 'charge' because words like 'captive' and 'prisoner' understandably don't sit well with me. While this man was indeed brought here against his will, it was still done with good reason, as he absolutely would have died if it weren't for my timely intervention.

And though I'm sure he's not exactly thrilled to awaken now finding himself sitting in the dark on a cold floor, propped up and tightly bound to a pole and with a bag over his head, at least I gave him some airholes to breathe through. I also removed his gas mask just as soon as I knew it was safe to do so after confirming that not one, not two, but three NDV rapid tests all came back negative.

I can't decide if the tableau in front of me belongs to a horror or a comedy. Seeing a man tied to a pole with a pillowcase over his head can either be terrifying or ridiculous depending on your mood, his mood, and just the general mood of the setting itself. Surrounded by the unforgiving dark and with only the narrow, pale beam of the flashlight making him visible, I decide this scene definitely ventures more into scary movie territory than zany parody or send-up.

Everything is so quiet down here without his screaming. The cat is zeroed in on him at my side, and the only discernible sound now that I've stopped moving along the basement floor is the intermittent ragged breathing that comes from inside the pillowcase. He still sounds like he's got a way to go before he'll be fully recovered from his knife wound.

Speaking of which, now's as good a time as any to check the injury to make sure it's still healing properly.

Of course, this is also the first time I've been down here that he's been truly, fully conscious—conscious enough to string words together and to question the exact nature of his situation. I can either wait till he passes out again and try to check up on him then, or I can actually engage with him now.

Weirdly, I might be better off doing it here and now while he's conscious. At least then we're both conscious of each other's consciousness.

If I try to come back another time when I think he's asleep, how will I truly know that's the case? I could always drug him just to be sure, but sooner or later, I'm going to have to talk to this guy and find out who he is and what I plan to do with him.

It was only a matter of time before this day arrived. Or this night. Whatever.

I knew this was what was going to happen eventually when I made up my mind to bring him back here to my safe haven in the first place. There's no going back now. The only way out at this point would be to kill him, and that wouldn't make any sense, given all the time, energy, and resources I've already invested in bringing him back to life.

I keep shining the light on him. He keeps breathing erratically beneath the pillowcase. The cat keeps watching him from her sentry position at my side.

I think it's time I give her a name; I think she deserves it at this point.

"Hello?"

It's the first time he's spoken since I opened the basement door. His voice is softer and yet hoarser now than it was before. Maybe he *has* been screaming all alone in the darkness down here for longer than I thought.

What do I say to him? I've already made up my mind that I need to treat him like an enemy first before I can remotely even consider the possibility of treating him like a neutral party. And even if and when I do decide the coast is clear enough to elevate his standing in my estimation to that level, I'm not sure I'll take the pillowcase or the chains off. There's still just too much at stake here and too little I know about who this man is, what he represents, and where this relationship could potentially go or not go in the future.

"I know you're there. Can you… can you please just tell me what's going on?"

His voice breaks toward the end of his question.

Something new, something desperate and perhaps even a bit pathetic and plaintive sounds in his speaking tone now. Is his chest heaving up and down because he's having a difficult time breathing still, or because he's getting himself worked up emotionally? Could he be fighting back a sob right now? Is that even possible for a man this outwardly intimidating, a man who ran a knife through another man's neck without so much as a second's hesitation?

"Please… please don't hurt me. I… I have a family…"

Something is definitely happening to this man. Whereas before his voice came bellowing all the way from the basement, through a door, past the ground floor, and up to the second story to wake me up from a fitful sleep in my bedroom, now that voice can barely muster up enough breath, sound, and strength to connect with me, and I'm standing right here not twelve feet away from it.

I can't tell for sure because of the pillowcase, of course, but it seems like he might actually be crying now.

"My name is Brett Taylor. My wife… my wife's name is Victoria Taylor. Vicki. We… we're gonna have a baby. She's eight months pregnant. I know that you don't know who I am… and that none of this probably means anything to you. But please… I beg you… please just let me go. Let me go… so that I can take care of them. She doesn't know where I am or what happened to me… I… I don't know, either, and I don't have to know… I never have to know. Just please… please, let me go back to her… let me go back to my wife and my baby… please…"

Even strapped tightly to the pole by two rolls of duct tape, a spool of utility rope, twenty feet of chain-link, and an old bicycle U-lock I found in a crawl space down here, it's clear this man is visibly trembling as he wrestles for control over his emotions. He has no idea who I am or what I want with him, but it seems he's decided to push all his chips into the middle of the table, lay his cards down, and go for broke.

Already, I can feel the mechanisms spinning inside my brain as they work overtime to try and help me formulate a plan of action for what I will do next.

On the one hand, here is a man not far removed from a grisly puncture wound to his side. Though it's healed nicely and thus far escaped infection and any major setbacks, he's still very much on the mend, given the limited supply of medication and equipment I have at my disposal to work with.

This man most certainly saved my life, whether intentionally or not. And now it looks like he's weeping from beneath a dirty, holey pillowcase as his body flexes and strains against multiple lines of constraints that I've orchestrated to keep him firmly in place. Not as my prisoner or as my captive, though—as my charge. It's important that I maintain that mental distinction for myself.

On the other hand, I have absolutely no way of validating or verifying that anything he's said so far or anything he plans to say in the future is true.

Having a wife out there waiting for him is convenient. Having a pregnant wife—eight months pregnant, to be exact—is even more convenient. There's obviously no possible way he could know about me or my history as an OB-GYN, but if he had to get himself captured, tied to a pole, and telling some sad sob story to his captor, he sure picked the perfect captor to tell this particular sob story to. God, I have to stop saying the word 'captor', though.

"Please... don't kill me..."

I can, at least, put that fear to rest. While there are a great many things I'm still figuring out about this man and what I plan to do with him, killing him is nowhere on my radar.

"I am not going to kill you... provided you cooperate."

Those three final words get tacked on well after the first seven are spoken, but I don't regret them. Whether everything he's saying is true or a lie—and whether he's a decent human being or not—he still needs to understand right from the get-go that I'm the one with all the power in this situation. The sooner that sinks in on his end, the better. For both of us.

Even still, it's hard not to take pity on this figure, slumped down and shaking against a basement pole. There are stains on the ground around him, some of which are blood and some of which I can only imagine are urine and feces. It's also clear he's been trying to break free from his bonds by the wear and tear I can see on his clothes beneath all the ropes and chains.

I've done my best to help move nutrition and sustenance in and out of his body to keep him alive while he's been unconscious, but it's also not that easy to do any of that without the modern conveniences of a hospital, technology, or a staff. Needless to say, there are odors and stains down here around this poor man that are better off left uninvestigated.

But just as soon as I make a mental note to do a deep clean of this basement floor after he's gone, I'm reminded how nebulous that phrase 'after he's gone' really is. What does that mean? When, and in what fashion, does his leaving from here actually occur?

"Of course. I… I'll do whatever you want. Just… just please… please don't hurt me…"

He's definitely crying.

Because of my job—or my old job, I mean, back when jobs were still a thing—I've unfortunately experienced the aftermath of more miscarriages and personal human tragedies than any normal person has a right to. Even with my track record being as sterling as it is… or was, rather.

Anyway, I know what it sounds like when a man breaks down and fully lets loose with the waterworks. It's unusual, and it's unpleasant, but it's powerful stuff. And this is it, there's no doubt about it. Brett Taylor is now sobbing, slobbering, and sniffling beneath the pillowcase.

Still… I have to establish boundaries. There need to be rules and laws for him and I to coexist, for however long that may be. Just as he needs to fear me and understand on a primal level that I hold his heart in my hand, I need him to also learn right here and right now that this yelling and screaming at the top of his lungs will not fly… whether he's blindfolded and bound or not.

"No more yelling. Do you understand? If you yell out like that again, I will gag you. I don't want to, but I will."

The pillowcase tries to nod a bit as Brett struggles to regain his composure.

"I… I'm sorry. I'm so sorry about that. I… you have to understand… I didn't know. I still don't know. Where I am, who you are, what you want with me… I don't know what happened. All I can remember is pain… and darkness… I had to cry out, just to see if anybody was there… and I can't tell you how happy it made me, whoever you are, just to see a light again… and just to hear a voice again…"

The cat is suddenly feeling very bold. Slowly, silently, confidently, it traverses the space that separates us from the hooded man on the floor, only stopping finally when it's maybe four feet away from him.

I have half a mind to call it back. But what would I call it? I've only just decided I should name it, and it will probably take weeks before it recognizes the name I give it. Even then, it's a cat. There are never any guarantees with cats.

The cat and its name are not my priorities right now, though, I remind myself. This man, this stranger I've locked up in my basement with no definitive plan of action or strategy for the foreseeable future, this is my priority right now.

"No more yelling, though. It's too dangerous. You understand?"

Again, the pillowcase dips up and down.

"Absolutely. No more yelling. I'll be quiet, I

promise."

There's a moment where I just watch the cat as it completes a methodical semicircle around the man, its luminous cat-eyes glued to his figure the whole time, observing and plotting in some ancient animalistic fashion I wish I knew how to replicate today.

And then, just like that, it takes off into the corner and darts out of sight.

Instinctively, my hand follows it with the flashlight, sweeping the beam across the room and away from my charge to try and keep up with my feline companion. But wherever she went, she's no longer visible. I can't hear her, either. My flashlight sways from side to side where last it detected movement, but everything is dark and still over there now.

Maybe she saw a cockroach or a rat. Whatever it is that distracted her from the task at hand—whatever that task at hand may be—it's probably a good thing. One less roach or rodent in this house could only be a welcome development.

The man is still trembling slightly when I bring the flashlight beam back to rest on his slumped figure in front of me.

"Can… can I ask you a question, please?"

I'm still just a little unnerved by the cat's sudden, unexplained disappearance, but I remind myself that everything is still well within my grasp and control. Not only am I the one holding the flashlight; I'm also the one with the gun. This person has neither one of those things. Plus, this person is shackled to a basement support pole. Cat or no cat, I have nothing to fear in this scenario.

"Go ahead."

"Are you the woman I saved? The woman they had tied up in that basement?"

My mouth goes dry. Again, there's no way of knowing if what he's saying right now is true. He could be lying through his teeth about all of this.

That being said, it's certainly not a bad sign that he seems to remember what happened to him and to me down in the basement of that other house. Moreover, hearing him admit out loud in his own words and with his own voice that he was actively trying to save me can't help but register a sense of massive relief within me.

Again, though, there's no proof. Although I don't know how I could prove it, even if I wanted to. All I have to work with are the facts of what happened down there, what he's saying to me right now, and what I'm thinking and feeling about what he has to say.

So, what do I think and how do I feel about what he has to say? Ah, yes. That's the million-dollar question now, isn't it?

"I am."

What's the point in lying to him? There's no sense in concealing my identity. What even is my identity anymore? It's been years since I heard another human being call me by my name. This isn't my house. I don't have a social security number or a bank account or an email address. No one does.

"Does that mean you killed him?"

There's a second or two where I don't know who he means, and then I remember. The last thing Brett Taylor probably remembers is getting stabbed in his side with a knife. He said himself that all he remembers is pain… and darkness. For all he knows, he's still in that basement.

Come to think of it, why was he in that basement to begin with?

"Why were you down there?"

I realize I've unintentionally revealed to him we're no longer in that basement by using the word 'there' instead of 'here.'

Does it matter, though? So as not to think about it any longer, I press on. I've got to get out of my own head.

"Down in the basement of that house at the end of that neighborhood. Why did you come down there? What brought you there?"

Brett seems to be getting a better hold of himself. His speech is less choppy now, though his voice still sounds strained and tired beneath the cotton.

"I went there to get supplies. Vicki—my wife—I told you she's just about ready to have a baby. I'd been there before, to that house, maybe a few months ago… I don't how long… for supplies. No one was there, so I thought maybe I'd get lucky again, and I'd be all alone."

You and me both, Brett. I guess the moral of the story is it's just not safe to hit the same place twice, even if it seemed safe and absolutely bountiful the first go-around. Too much can change, no matter how little or how long a time it's been since you were there last.

"I wasn't expecting anyone to be there. But then I heard a voice coming from the basement, and I realized someone else was in there with me."

"Why did you go down? Why didn't you flee?"

All it took was a cough to send me scurrying out the door from that other house a year ago and back to safety. Maybe in a normal world and in normal times you might call that cowardice, but not in this world and these times.

That's called survival.

Being overly cautious, intuitively aware, and highly reactive to your surroundings is how you stay alive today. Why in the world would this man come charging down the stairs toward another human voice? It doesn't make sense to me.

"Everything's different now with the baby. Maybe if it was still just me and Vicki, I would have run. But I knew if there were voices down there, that meant there was probably also going to be supplies down there, too. It's where I'd keep my most precious things if it were me. So, I knew I had to get down there and that I had to get whatever I could from the basement, because I knew that's where it all was."

Brett's body has finally stopped shaking in the dim white spotlight I have him trapped in.

"So, you came down into that basement—without a gun—knowing there was someone down there already, maybe multiple people down there already, just to see what kind of supplies you could find for your pregnant wife?"

"Absolutely. Without a doubt. Wouldn't you?"

He can't see me right now, which is probably a good thing, since I'm convinced my face must read like a great big flashing billboard. This electric jolt of sorrow, remorse, and of pure, blistering *loss* just rips through me without warning and without mercy. It's enough to cause my knees to buckle, but I steady myself in time as I force the avalanche of thoughts, emotions, and memories back into the furthest, deepest, darkest recesses of my mind.

Not here. Not now. As a matter of fact, not ever again.

I can't go there and do this—do that—to myself again. Especially not with everything that's changed. I'm not alone here anymore. I can't just wallow in the guilt until it withers me up from the inside out and I fade away to nothing.

"Yes. Yes, I would."

Of course, I would. I would have done anything for my wife. I *should* have done anything for my wife.

But I didn't. I didn't do the one thing she asked of me... the one thing that mattered most... and now I... now I...

"Good."

This man is still here in my house. Not my house, though... *her* house...

"Good. You get it, then. We would do anything for the ones we love. Are you... are you alone here?"

That snaps me out of it.

"What?"

"Are you alone here? Wherever we are right now?"

"Why would you ask me that?"

Brett tries to shift in his slumped but seated position and then lets out a low groan of pain when he fails. It can't be comfortable being forced to stay like that for so long, but at the moment, I also don't care all that much.

"I didn't mean anything by it. I just... you sounded like you might have someone, too. Someone you'd do anything for. Maybe a husband?"

"A wife."

I blurt it out and glare at him, this stranger in my house, in her house, in our house.

Go ahead. Say the wrong thing. Give me a fucking reason to drag you back to that other basement with those other bastards and put you right back where I found you. Just say the word, say any of the words, and I'll leave you for dead for real this time.

For the first time tonight, I wish I could see his face right now. I'd know right away just by looking in his eyes. That would be enough to tell me everything I need to know.

Brett finally ends his pause.

"I'm sorry. That was wrong of me to assume. Is she here right now?"

"She's dead. Why do you keep asking me these kinds of questions?"

He pauses again, but this one is shorter.

"I'm sorry. Really… I'm not trying to offend. I'm so sorry for your loss."

"I am, too. But why are you asking me about her?"

"I just… I just… I guess I'm just trying to get to know you, I suppose?"

He laughs. Brett laughs, awkwardly, gently, beneath the pillowcase.

"I don't know. I don't know why I'm here, or what happened to me. I don't know what you have planned for me. I know that I can't see much of anything, which is intentional, and I get it. I also know you've got me nice and tight here against some kind of metal pole or something, which, again, I get. I guess I'm just trying to figure out what comes next, you know? I feel like, based off what I did for you back there in that house, I guess I don't understand why you've got me locked up like this—"

"I *saved your life*, Brett."

Spit flies from my mouth through the dust motes that float in the air, all of it illuminated ghoulishly by the flashlight's gleam.

"That's what happened. You got yourself stabbed in the side, and I stitched you up and saved your life. You'd be dead right now if I'd left you there."

"And I am so, *so* deeply grateful that you did that for me. Listen… I… I didn't know that until now. You have to remember, I don't know anything.

"The last thing I remember, I'm sticking my knife through one guy's neck and charging at the other guy while you're still tied up on the floor, and then I feel this… this searing, awful, incredible pain in my side, and then *poof*… everything goes dark. I didn't know you saved me. I… I wondered if I was even still alive, or if this was hell or something. You have to believe me… I didn't know anything. I still don't know anything.

"But if you saved me, if you saved my life like I saved yours back there, then I want to thank you. I am so incredibly thankful you did that. You saved my life, so my wife, Vicki, doesn't have to raise our baby alone. You did a wonderful thing for us, and I am forever in your debt. If there's anything we can do to repay you, please, you just let me know. Anything at all. You've got it."

It's hard not to smirk. This man sounds sincere, but what he's saying is ludicrous if you stop and really think about it.

What in the world does he have right now to offer me? He's strapped to a pole in my basement with a pillowcase taped over his head. Clearly, there's not a whole lot he can give me in his present situation.

I've already gone through what little belongings he had on his person. Truth be told, the man he killed was more valuable and useful to me in terms of physical goods, supplies, and loot.

Of course, this is all working off the assumption of the present scenario alone. Tied up in my basement, Brett Taylor represents a great many things, and none of them are positives. He's a living liability, he's another mouth to feed, and he's a 'money pit' when it comes to resources, supplies, time, and energy. Anyone with half a brain would say I'm better off without him. They'd also say that I have less than half a brain for bringing him back here in the first place.

Again, though, this is all based on the present, and on what he is to me, here and now: a prisoner—no, a *charge*—of mine recovering from an injury he suffered while possibly trying to free me.

I won't say 'rescue me' because saying as much would be giving him too much credit, given the stupidity of his actions in coming down the stairs knowingly without a gun to begin with and then getting himself wounded in a failed attempt to take on and take down two other men.

Though the fact remains that, whatever his intentions were that night, he did come down those stairs, he did attack those men, and he did—whether inadvertently or not—help aid in my escape. I certainly don't owe him my life, and even if I did, I've obviously repaid that debt in its entirety by saving his life in return. I'm the one who stemmed the blood flow, stitched him up, brought him back here, and nursed him back to life. We're even.

Now that he's here though, what could he represent? Bound and bagged, he's a liability and a drain. If I were to let him go, however, could he make good on his word? Exactly what *could* he do to repay me?

'Anything at all.' That's what he said. If there's

anything he can do, anything he and his wife can do—
Vicki—just let him know. Anything at all.

There are two of them, Brett and Vicki Taylor. They're a package deal, two for one, that have somehow managed to beat the odds and survive this long without either one of them succumbing to NDV or to other people.

More than that, Vicki's pregnant. Brett's been out gathering supplies for not only the both of them, for two people, but for a third person that's incoming as well.

For all I know, they're sitting on a whole hoard of food, water, and supplies somewhere that would put my forest fortress here to shame. Maybe they have they have more than just chicken eggs, nuts, and berries to eat each day. Maybe they have enough fuel and enough batteries that they don't need to try to learn to see in the dark for half their lives.

"Where do you live, Brett?"

"What?"

"Where do you and Vicki live? Do the two of you have something permanent, or are you just always on the move?"

He pauses briefly.

"We… we do have a place. We haven't been there long, but it's a good enough spot for us for now. Nobody's come through, and we've managed to secure it from the outside. It's actually not even a house, believe it or not. It's an old, abandoned ranger station out in the middle of a state park. There's obviously not a whole lot of space inside, but it's all the space outside around it that really made us stop and give it a shot."

Smart. It's a smart decision, I'll give them that. Not that I have any way of knowing this, but I imagine people still flock to the cities in droves searching for some mythical, undiscovered utopian paradise, like an army surplus store that hasn't been picked over or a magical grocery store with self-replenishing food stocks, running water, electricity, and machine gun turrets surrounding the perimeter.

Why do I imagine this? Because people are creatures of habit, because people are stupid, and because people are afraid.

Hope was right about the country. She saw the writing on the wall long before I did, and she knew that if we wanted to survive, we'd need to find someplace remote, hidden, and fortifiable.

No doubt, a ranger station out in the desolate wilderness of a state park, far away from civilization and well off the beaten trail, would have been a satisfactory option for her and for us if her family summer home wasn't also in the picture. She'd approve of the Taylors' decision if she were here right now, I'll bet. Hope always did love her state parks.

"We… we actually have more than enough food and water there for the both of us. I'd say we have enough, easily, to last us another couple months, even with the baby on the way. I know there's no such thing as having too much of anything, but if there's something you need… something you're low on here, or just something you want even, anything at all, really, we could give it to you. We would happily give it to you, considering everything you've done for me and how you saved my life. It would be the least we could do. And it would make us happy."

How much is more than enough? I have an impressive stockpile of resources that I've hidden around this home in various places, but still, I'm not sure I'd refer to any of it as 'more than enough.' Like he just said, there's no such thing as more than enough.

He's probably lying. Chained to a pole in a puddle of his own dried blood and wastes with a cloth over his head, there's no denying that Brett Taylor is undoubtedly a desperate man. It stands to reason he'll say whatever it takes to get himself free of this predicament he's found himself in. That's what I would do, anyway. It's what anyone with sense would try and do to stay alive in this type of situation.

The ranger station, the state park, the overabundance of food and water. Only his eight-months-pregnant wife left behind to guard it. I'll bet. I'd probably roll right up into an ambush if I took him there. He'd direct me along some deserted country road and then give two or three of his buddies a signal and they'd spray me from the treetops. All just to get their hands on another vehicle, get one of their own guys back, and rid the world of another person that shares neither their general viewpoint nor their general genetic makeup.

Easy now, Alex. He's not one of *them*. Think about it. He's someone who *killed* one of them. He even tried to kill two of them.

Would he have killed me, though? If he'd been able to overpower both of those men in the basement, would he have really come over, bent down, and used his knife to cut my ropes? Or would he have come over, bent down, and used his knife to cut my throat?

What would I have done, though, had our roles been reversed? If I was desperate enough to knowingly take on two men all by myself, and all in the name of procuring the resources I needed to provide for my wife and my unborn child, would I have stopped to free Brett Taylor then, if he was the one tied up by those men on the ground? Would I have killed him just to be safe and just to ensure he wouldn't come after me, assuming he found a way to eventually free himself the way I did?

The more I think about it, the more I can't blame Brett for doing anything that he did back in that basement. 'Without a doubt,' he said. He went down there to do what he did without fear and without hesitation because it's what he had to do. For his wife. For his baby.

"Miss?"

Brett's voice is hesitant, meek, unassuming.

"Yes?"

"Well… what do you think? Does that sound good? If you take me back there, back to my wife and our baby, you can have whatever you want. Take as much of anything as you need. It's the least we can do. Please… I just want to see her again. That's all I want in the world. She's… she's all I have left. Please."

Something tickles my ankle.

When I look down, it's the cat. She's back from wherever she's been this whole time… and she's *filthy*. Even in the dim glow of the flashlight, I can see what looks like sawdust all over her red-orange coat. As she gazes up at me with those reflective saucer eyes, I notice she's even got some of it in her whiskers and in the soft fuzz around her muzzle. I reach down and pluck a whole woodchip free from the space between her shoulder blades.

Just what have you gotten into down here, my friend? Where have you been this whole time? What have you been doing?

"Miss?"

"Stop calling me 'miss.' My name is Alex, okay?"

And just like that, I've given him my name. There wasn't even a decision I had to make or anything. It just came out of me. For the first time in years, I've introduced myself and told another human being what my first name is. Does this mean I have an identity again? Am I a real, live human being again?

"Alex. Nice. It's nice to meet you, Alex. I'm Brett. But you knew that already, didn't you?"

He laughs again. It's just as peculiar seeing for the second time a man chained to a post with a pillowcase over his head laugh as it was seeing it happen the first time.

"Listen to me, *Brett*, and listen carefully. If we do this… if I decide to take you back to your wife… and to let you go… we do this completely my way and on my terms. This isn't your show anymore. Whatever happened before between you and me, we're even now. You saved my life, and I saved yours. You understand me?"

"Absolutely."

"I don't owe you anything. If I decide to take you out of here and to take you back to your wife, it's not because I'm doing you a favor or because I'm repaying one. It's because that's what's best for both of us. I didn't bring you back here to hold you hostage. I brought you back here so I could heal you and give you the proper medical treatment you needed to survive, while doing so in the safety and security of my own home."

"I understand, and again—"

"No, don't talk, just listen. If we get out there—out

to this park you're talking about—and there's no cabin or ranger station or whatever it is, I will kill you. If there's no pregnant woman out there waiting for you or her name isn't Vicki, I will kill you. If anything at all happens between us leaving here and us getting there that isn't *exactly* the way you've described it to me, I will kill you. Make no mistake, Brett Taylor, I have killed men before. I have killed more men than just the one who tried to kill you. Now you may talk. Do you understand me perfectly?"

"Perfectly."

"Good. Then this is how it's going to work. You're going to spend the rest of the night down here and you're not going to make a peep. I don't want to hear you breathe. You can sleep or not sleep; it doesn't make a damn bit of difference to me. In the morning, I'm going to do all the things I normally do in the morning. I'm going to do all the things I normally do all day. If you need to eat, drink, or use the bathroom, I will help you do those things, but I want you to remember that I will be armed the whole time, and you will not be. You still following me?"

"I am."

"When dusk falls, I'll come for you. I am going to administer a heavy dose of medication that will knock you unconscious. Only when I am absolutely sure that you are totally unconscious—and I know what totally unconscious is because I spent twenty years as a doctor—only then will I undo these restraints and move you to my vehicle. Even then, I want your unconscious brain to remember that I will be armed the whole time, and you will not be. Once we're both in the vehicle, I will restrain you once again. I will drive us far enough away from here, and then when I revive you and finally take that pillowcase off your head, you will guide me the rest of the way back to where you and your wife have been staying. When we arrive, you will call to her from inside my vehicle. I will keep one gun on you and one gun on her. If anything happens that I don't like, both guns will fire. I want to make sure you're still listening. Brett?"

"I'm listening, I promise."

"On the way there, you're going to give me an exact inventory of everything you have. Then, once we arrive, I'm going to tell Vicki Taylor exactly what I want her to bring me. Once she has brought out everything I've asked for and put it all in my vehicle, then, and only then, will she be allowed to take you out of my vehicle. I will drive away from the both of you, and when I've put a short but safe enough distance between us, I will throw the key for the lock on your restraints out the driver side window, and that will be that. We will never see each other again. I will go my own way and you will go yours. You and your wife will make no attempt to ever find me, and I will forget all about the ranger station in the state park. And that's it. That's how all this is going to happen. That's how all this ends."

There's a momentary silence. Again, I find myself wishing I could look him in the eyes, just to see what's there, to try and gauge what he's thinking about everything he's heard.

"Do you have any questions?"

He tries to shake his head, stops, and emits another low grown of pain. You'd think he would have learned by now, but I guess this guy's not the brightest bulb on the Christmas tree.

"No. No questions. Just… thank you, again. Thank you for this. For all that you've done for me, but especially for this."

"Brett. I want this to work out just as much as you do. But believe me when I say this: just because I gave you back your life doesn't mean I won't take it right back away from you."

For a second, I think I see something shiny glint out from one of the crudely torn airholes in the pillowcase. Was that an eyeball peeking out or was it just my imagination? Either way, it's gone just as quickly as it came.

"Don't worry. I'll do everything you ask of me. I don't want to die again. I'm not ready yet."

EIGHT

How is this happening right now?

The high-pitched metallic wail of an alarm keeps droning from the speakers in the ceilings and out down the hallways. Rapid footsteps get louder and then softer as people hurtle by the open doorway, running away from or toward something, I'm not exactly sure. I really don't remember anymore.

Occasionally, the footstep sounds will stop abruptly outside the door—but only for a second or two—and a panicked voice will reach out to me with words that I know should mean more to me than they actually do right now.

Sometimes it's "Dr. Washington, you've got to get out of here!"

Or it's "They're coming, we have to go!"

And once, it's even "Alex, you need to leave her!"

That's the only one that gets me to look up from the side of the bed. When I do, I slowly recognize the sweat-streaked, utterly petrified face staring back at me through a protective mask and plastic face shield as one that belongs to Amy Chin, my best maternity nurse and quite possibly my best friend. Or at least my best work friend.

"What?"

Amy is exasperated but also terrified. She keeps glancing backward in both directions from the doorframe.

"There's nothing more you can do for her. Save yourself!"

My jaw drops open, but before I can respond or react, Amy is gone. She takes off in a frenzied sprint, and now she's just another one of the endless pairs of footsteps coming and going down the hallway, getting softer and softer as she runs off like everyone else. They all blur and blend together after a while. Even Amy.

But not you. You're not like all these others, running around like chickens with their heads cut off, screaming and sobbing and calling out for each other or for God to help them.

You'd think these people would be better prepared for an emergency, given what they all do for a living. Every single one of them has experienced profound trauma to the most heightened degree; it's just a part of the job. It actually *is* the job.

Even if you were awake right now, you wouldn't be like them. Knowing you, you'd probably want to stand your ground and take on the idiots coming here yourself. You'd grab a scalpel in one hand and a hypodermic needle in the other, or maybe you'd just rip a fire extinguisher off the wall and use it as a makeshift club. Anything you've seen before in an action movie, that's what you'd suggest we try doing right about now.

But instead, you can't do any of those things, because you've got all these fucking wires and all these fucking tubes running through you. And it's all my fucking fault.

There's a sound of glass shattering outside. I'm vaguely aware of what I think must be gunfire. It's simultaneously much louder and also much less obtrusive than I ever thought it was going to be.

Actually, everything feels less obtrusive to me now that I'm here with you, right where I should be, and right where I should have been all along.

Where I should have been all along.

That's a painful phrase to chew on and digest, but it's just the tip of the iceberg when it comes to my own penance and self-flagellation. I have no doubt in my mind that I will spend the rest of my life chipping away at that iceberg, only I'll be using a small salad fork instead of a pickaxe. And the demons and the ghosts of my godawful guilt will put me in the cold, black water around it, with my mouth bobbing just above the surface, as I whittle away in vain at the colossal floating mountain of my shame.

Maybe I should just drown, then. That might be easier. I might not have to even do it myself; the way things are going outside, they might make this easy on me. Maybe they'll come tearing up the elevators or the stairs, guns blazing, and put a bullet in the back of my skull before I ever realize what's hit me.

Is that too easy, though? Do I deserve that kind of swift exit, stage left?

I'm not convinced my conscience would allow it. Now, if they take me hostage and torture me for a century or two, perhaps then I'd start to make some kind of small amends for the sins I've committed these past two years.

Everything could have been different if only I'd listened to you back then. You warned me; you knew this was coming, all of this, and you told me so to my face. I had every opportunity to take you seriously, and I didn't. And because I didn't, now you've left me. It's all my fucking fault.

Someone lets out a bloodcurdling scream from outside, probably somewhere in the staff parking lot area. After all my years helping women navigate through childbirth, these ears have become fairly accustomed to screams. Not that a scream ever grows on you or even becomes a sound you can just tune out, but it becomes something you can tolerate after you've heard enough of them regularly in all their varying frequencies and pitches.

This one is different, though, I must admit. There is a stark contrast between what it sounds like to usher in new life versus what it feels like to have your own life ushered out for you. It snaps me out of the past and thrusts me back into the present long enough to send a rippling shudder through my body.

Fear. It's fear I feel right now.

For the first time since it became obvious they were coming for the hospital, I am afraid. Up until this point, I didn't have a stance on the situation unfolding fast around me. Now, as I hear and really register what a different kind of scream sounds like and what it means for the screamer, my position solidifies. I suddenly realize with a calm, cool clarity that I do not want to die… even if I deserve to die for what I've done.

But then… what do I do… with her?

Hope lies prostrate in the narrow hospital bed, guarded on one side by me and flanked on the other side by a towering, wheeled mass of cords, tubes, screens, bags, and fluids. Her face is turned away from me and angled into the ventilator. She has been on life support for twelve days now. Though no one until today has actually said it out loud, I know that every other person working in this maternity-ward-turned-NDV-ward-turned-morgue has shared in Amy Chin's belief that there's nothing more I can do for her. Truthfully, my medical brain has known that, too, this whole time.

When she slipped into unconsciousness, stopped being able to breathe on her own, and started suffering open rebellion from multiple vital organs in her body, I knew our time was up. If she wasn't my wife and this wasn't my hospital, they would have let her die over a week ago in order to give someone else with a better fighting chance the bed, the machines, the resources, and the attention.

Add that bit of knowledge to the growing heap of guilt I'll carry like an iron yoke around my neck for the rest of my miserable life.

If my mama were alive today, she'd still have faith. Of all the women I've ever known, she is probably the only one who would have completely, unequivocally had my back throughout this ordeal. She would have stuffed a Bible under Hope's right hand and stuck a cross in Hope's left hand, but still, she never in a million years would have doubted the healing power of the Lord to come save the day at the eleventh hour. My mama would have spent every last second praying for a miracle.

Of course, my mama also died from stage four lung cancer, and she never smoked a day in her life, so there's that.

Tires squeal from somewhere down below outside the small hospital room window. It's impossible to tell if that's someone I know making a last-ditch effort to escape or someone I don't know making a concerted effort to get here faster. I could stand up and check the window, but either way, I know what the message is: my time is running out.

Hope's time has already run out. I've prolonged her time artificially and against her will—yet another log to throw on the bonfire of my betrayal. I know this for a fact because we both made it clear to one another in no uncertain terms long, long ago that neither one of us had any desire to ever be kept alive medically and mechanically.

And yet, when her lungs started to fill up with mucus and debris, and the decision was made to hook her up, I already knew then that I would both put her on and keep her on life support for as long as I had to if that's what it eventually came to.

When it eventually came to that, I didn't feel guilty for lying to her and breaking our promise to one another. No, I felt guilty for not listening to her two years ago when she told me that this would happen.

Hope tried to tell me that this was 'the end,' as she called it. It didn't matter then, and it doesn't matter now, that *her end* actually comes at the hands of the worst-possible variant strain of NDV, rather than at the hands of redneck wannabe rebels, racists, and thugs.

What matters is that this, this right here in front of me, this moment, this decision I've already made, this end she predicted… none of it had to happen. If I'd only listened to her back then and left the city, maybe she never would have gotten infected to begin with.

It's impossible to know for sure, of course, and too much of my brain and my soul is hard-wired for reason, logic, and science to truly believe we would have been impervious to this plague had we fled to her summer house out in the woods when she wanted us to. The virus doesn't discriminate. NDV doesn't pull up short at the far edge of civilization, turn around, and go back home.

Still, though… I wonder. I wonder how much time we might have had and how long we could have made it work, just her and me and Ruthie, out there on our own together. With enough of a head-start and the proper amount of planning, we may have been able to stave off her 'end' after all. We may have been able to ride out this disease and weather the storm of domestic insurgency.

But now, I'll never know. Instead, I will get to spend the rest of my life wondering. That is my punishment.

No, that is just the tip of my punishment iceberg, actually. The ultimate punishment is knowing that no matter how big and how painful my punishment iceberg ever gets, the guilt iceberg will always be larger. And that one will never go away.

All right. It's time. It's past time, actually. I knew this day would come. I've put it off long enough.

Everything feels wrong about how it's happening right now. Even beyond the what-ifs of the choices we made—particularly the one choice I made that she accepted simply because she loves me for me—this current scene just doesn't feel right. If this really was meant to happen this way, and there was no other alternative trajectory, at the very least, she should have her friends nearby. She should have RBG on her lap. Her parents should have been spared from this pandemic just long enough so that they could stand here with me, hold her hands, and say something.

I should say something.

No, I *should have* said something. That is the difference.

If I had said something, if I had listened, if I had let go of my own foolish need to play the heroine and do the right thing and do my job, none of this would have happened. I wouldn't need to stand here dumbly with the whole world crumbling around us, unable to open my mouth and unsure of how I'm supposed to tell you goodbye.

"I'm sorry."

What is the deepest, darkest circle of hell again? Who is it reserved for?

Traitors, I believe. Treacherous betrayers and liars and phonies.

That's where I'll go. 'I'm sorry'? Really? That's the best I can do?

"I'm so, so sorry."

At least cry. I should be crying right now.

If I had a heart, if I wasn't just this great, big, soulless automaton, I would be sobbing. This is my wife. My soulmate. The love of my life is lying here in front of me, dying, dead already, dead for days now, and it's all my fucking fault, and I can't even muster up a single tear for her?

I hate myself. I fucking loathe what I have done.

From below, more shouts and more gunfire. It's getting closer now. For all I know, it's actually coming from inside the building now rather than from outside the window. All sound and sensory awareness is distorted in the wake of this ear-splitting, incessant alarm that keeps endlessly cycling through the speakers everywhere.

It's too late. I want to tell the person who pressed

whatever button makes that whining warning happen that it's far too late for that.

There were so many chances to change paths. We blew it. I blew it. None of us took it seriously enough. We all just stood around with our collective thumb up our own ass, shouting our outrage into the cyber void of social media, doing nothing of substance and nothing of actual physical agency until it was far too late. Now it doesn't matter anymore. It's just too damn late.

Though I can't give Hope the tears, words, or time that she deserves, I can at least give her the one thing I should have given her two years ago: action. All she wanted was for me to take action before it was too late. I failed her then. I will not fail her now.

Quickly and quietly, I move with a renewed purpose out of Hope's room and into the hallway. No one is nearby, thankfully, and there's no sign or sound of other human beings anywhere. All of my coworkers are gone.

There's a stretcher in a large storage room halfway down the hall. I become another one of those pairs of footsteps running down the tiles, only I'm decidedly running toward something rather than running away from something. Those others, my coworkers and friends, they all only wanted to save their own skins.

'Save yourself!' That was Amy Chin, one of the nicest, most selfless people I think I've ever met. When it really comes down to it, self-preservation trumps everything else, apparently.

Not that I blame them. Their loved ones aren't here. Some were maybe only trying to save themselves, but most were probably fleeing to wherever their homes and their families are.

Once I have the stretcher in tow, I cross back out

into the hallway and jog toward Hope's room. So far, so good. No one in sight, and no new sounds, either. Just that same automated alarm siren, over and over and over again.

By the time I reach her doorway, I've already decided that I cannot hesitate with what I'm about to do. Stopping to think about the consequences of my actions could get us both killed, and I've also already decided that as much as I deserve to die, I am not ready to die just yet. When and where that time comes, it will not be here, and it will not be at the hands of the people coming in from outside. They don't deserve that satisfaction.

As I move around to the far side of her bed near the window, I can't help myself—I steal a look through the glass.

Three stories below me, there are men with assault rifles congregating in the hospital staff parking lot. Some of them wear masks, but many of them are too stupid for that, even. Normally, I'd experience a complex and contradictory sense of both profound pity and sadistic glee at witnessing such a sight, but there's no time for that now. All that matters in this moment is that they're here, but that it also looks like most of them are still outside.

Importantly, however: so is my car. I can see the jeep from here. The men aren't anywhere near it, but it's well within the range of their automatic weapons if I'm seen. I'll need to remember that when I make a run for it.

This has to happen first, though.

No hesitation. Remember that she's already dead. She died nearly two weeks ago. Selfishly, I've been forcing her to cling on against her will. What I have to do now is what I should have done then.

No hesitation. Be a woman of action. Give her that much, at least. Do it now, live, and spend the rest of your days paying for this moment until you die, and then pay for it some more in the afterlife, assuming there is one.

I try not to think as I remove the tubes, the wires, the tape, the mask.

Be a blank slate, a brick wall, a cold, indifferent bitch. Be that iceberg you'll be stabbing and picking at for all of eternity. You couldn't cry before or say anything better than 'I'm sorry.' Don't start up now when she needs you to keep it together. It's too late. You're still just too goddamn late. For everything.

Ignore the new sound the monitor makes as the line flattens. Ignore the pounding of your own heart as you try desperately to forget how we got here. Ignore those terrible thoughts ramrodding your brain, beating down upon your body, and reminding you in their grating, growing chorus that you are actually, finally doing it now. With every simple physical action, you are literally killing your life partner.

Focus on the alarm wail. It was all you could hear before, and now you've already forgotten it. How quickly, how easily, how soullessly we forget.

You did this. This is all your fault.

I slap myself hard across the face, swallow a sob, and lift Hope's lifeless body out of the hospital bed and onto the stretcher. As smoothly as I can, I tuck her limbs between the rails, release the brake, and then we're on the move together, rolling out of the room and down the long hallway toward the elevator.

If it were just me, I'd take the stairs, but it's not just me. It will be just me from now on forever and ever, though, because that's what I have done. But for now, and for just a little bit longer, it's still us. Sort of.

As we wait for the '4' to light up and the doors to open, I realize I should have checked the window again one last time before doing this. There's nothing that says these metal doors won't open to reveal a person or several people on the other side. If that happens and they do reveal exactly that, chances are the faces I'll see won't be familiar to me. Chances are that will spell the end of my suffering after all, like it or not.

I do not want to die yet. Whatever else happens, whatever I must still endure, I cannot forget this. I do not want to die yet.

Taking a page out of Hope's book—or out of what I believe her book would have been, were it still being written—I grab the closest thing in sight: a fire extinguisher on the wall. Who knows what good this will do me once we're outside, but at least while we're inside—and especially while we're getting into an elevator that may already be occupied—this might actually work even better than a gun.

The light switches off the '2' and onto the '3' as I hoist the hard metal cylinder up from my side with both hands. I position it so the butt of the extinguisher is facing toward the elevator doors and so that I have both arms and all my strength coiled and at the ready. If there is a face on the other side, it is getting smashed in. If there are multiple faces, hopefully I'll be fast enough to hit them all and to capitalize on some general shock and surprise.

For that matter, hopefully my reflexes are good enough that I'll be able to pull back if I need to, so I don't accidentally hurt or kill somebody that I know.

Let's just actually hope that there's no one on the other side at all. How about that?

There isn't. The doors open after the '4' lights up, and I let out my breath for the first time in forever.

There's no time to waste, though. I can't breathe a sigh of relief just yet. We have to go.

It's the longest, slowest, most brutal elevator ride of my life down to the ground floor. I force myself not to look at her and not to think about anything other than getting to the jeep in the parking lot. That's all that matters right now. Everything else can come after. Nothing else matters but this.

Again, I loft the fire extinguisher in front of me to prepare myself for whatever appears on the other side of these doors when the elevator finally stops moving. There can be no hesitation. Hesitate, and that's it. That's the end for me. Struck down ignobly by a punk in a 'FAMILY OVER FAGS' t-shirt who will later regale his cronies with the story of how he slew some random Black lesbian doctor trying to escape with her dead patient wife.

That cannot happen. I cannot hesitate.

The doors open. There's no one there. But my God, this place is unrecognizable.

Emergency strobe lights flash methodically in every direction. If the siren alarm sound was a screaming eagle on the fourth floor, it's a shrieking harpy down here. The floors are strewn with all manner of hastily discarded items: papers, file folders, clipboards, stethoscopes, lab coats, trays.

No one is here. There are no doctors roaming the hallways, no nurses working behind the kiosk counter, no security guard protecting the entrance from the threats outside. They're all gone. Hopefully. Otherwise, they're dead or taken prisoner. And more than likely, that would just mean dead.

Briefly, I debate whether it's wise or idiotic to scout out my path ahead to the parking lot. There's something to be said for making damn sure the coast is clear before speeding right along, but I also know that the longer I linger, the less likely it is I make it out of here alive.

It's already a small wonder I've made it this far—back and forth along the fourth-floor hallway, in and out of Hope's room, into the elevator, and out of the elevator into the lobby—without getting caught and shot dead.

I ultimately decide to risk it, but not before unhooking the hose on the fire extinguisher first and taking a quick glance at the pictorial directions on the attached paper tag. Pull the pin, release the lock, and squeeze the lever.

While it's true the extinguisher could have proven itself useful in close quarters as a bludgeoning device, the idea that it might come in handy as a ranged 'weapon' is ludicrous. But what else can I do? I can't throw the whole thing at someone with a gun, and I don't have time to search for anything else.

We follow the flashing lights along a hallway littered with debris and abandoned belongings. At the end of this hallway are a pair of double doors that lead out to the far end of the employee parking lot. I've specifically come this way to put as much distance between us and where that group of armed men are standing—or at least where I hope they're still standing. I'm also banking on them either entering the hospital through the main entrance at the other end or on them not entering the hospital at all.

I have no idea what their primary objective is in being here. It could be just to scare and terrorize, it could be to commandeer space or supplies, or it could be to take hostages and/or kill some healthcare workers just for sport. Whatever their true mission is, I'm not about to stick around and find out.

Now that we're here at the doors, it's time for stealth. Everything else was some rough combination of stealth, speed, initiative, and instinct. This next part calls strictly for stealth and initiative. I must be as courageous and as quiet as humanly possible, especially since I won't be going alone.

I back into one of the doors ever so softly, poking it open just wide enough that I can stick my head out and sweep my vision both ways. There's not a whole lot I can see immediately other than parked cars. My ears don't pick up on any conversation either, though it'd be hard to do that anyway with all the noise from the alarm, which is not only blasting inside the hallway we've just come down, but also outside along the external walls of the building as well.

I pilot the front two wheels of the stretcher across the metal threshold and then the back two wheels, stopping just before it's completely clear of the opened door. Gently, I pull the end of the stretcher free and then take hold of the door, guiding it back toward the frame until it closes without a sound.

If only I had four arms and four eyes, I could keep a three-hundred-and-sixty-degree watch while simultaneously propelling the stretcher across the pavement and keeping the silly little fire extinguisher nozzle primed for combat as well. With but two eyes and two arms, I'll have to make do with pushing the stretcher but keeping the extinguisher close at hand on top of it and keeping my head on a swivel.

Multiple times, I think I hear something or someone, only to jerk my face in that direction and come up empty.

Relief is never there, though. Just more anxious hallucination. The thought that turning my head to the left is exposing me to some new threat on the right. Constant phantom sensations of being watched, being yelled at, being told to stop, being snuck up on, being aimed at, being fired upon.

If time slowed to a sadistic crawl in the elevator before, it freezes entirely out here in the blistering parking lot. A merciless sun blazes down upon the back of my neck as I try not to let my hands get sweaty and lose their grip on the stretcher rail. My eyes see waves that aren't there shimmering just above the blacktop. None of these cars look familiar. Even worse, none of them are mine.

I can't stop turning my head around to check behind me, but every time I do, I shave off another split-second I know that I'll need in just a bit to escape with my life. It's impossible to stop, though. All my senses are in uproar. Everything is baked in the heat from the sun and a cloudless sky where God has abandoned us to our own destruction. My vision keeps faltering as my ears slowly give themselves over to the siren's wail. I'll never hear again, and that's okay.

Just let me get out of here. Please. Someone, anyone. Let me get out of here.

And then it's there; the black jeep comes out of hiding behind a massively long and tall pickup truck. I have to blink to make certain it's not just another mirage, a trick of the mind playing with what little is left of my heart.

But sure enough, it's my jeep. It's our jeep.

I can scarcely believe it, but I do not stop. The second I stop to marvel at how I've made it this far, that's when I know they'll get me. I cannot let my guard down.

Who knows where I plan to go if I make it out of here alive—is this happening only here or is it happening at our house, too?—but I tell myself not to go there yet. The only place I need to go right now is to the other side of the jeep, the side furthest from where I judge the people to be.

It's a sad, sloppy, disrespectful affair getting Hope off the stretcher and into the back seat. In a normal world, this would all be so different. There would be a process—a painful one, but a process nonetheless—to transport her to a morgue. She'd be treated with dignity, grace, and care, rather than getting pushed and pulled into the back seat of a car like she's just a cumbersome bit of cargo. But this is no longer a normal world.

I close the door behind her as gently as I can before booking it around the front of the jeep and clambering into the driver's seat. One last hurried lighthouse-scan in every direction just to make sure no one is running up on me, and then I start the engine. It's the most noise I've probably made thus far, and I know it.

Time to let go of the stealth and initiative, though. It's all about speed and pure instinct now.

Throwing the gear in reverse, I hit the gas pedal a bit harder than I planned to, and we go lurching backward in a rush. My stomach churns as I hear Hope's limp body roll up against the back of my seat, and it takes every ounce of self-restraint not to look in the rearview mirror to check on her.

Instead, I put the car in drive, spin the wheel, and take it just a bit easier with the gas this time as we glide forward past the rows of other vehicles toward the back exit of the lot. We're nearly there—the open street in front of us is maybe forty yards away—when I see him.

A very young man, probably in his late teens or early twenties, comes sprinting into view from out of nowhere to take up position right smack-dab in the middle of the open gate. There's a look of genuine surprise on his face, and I feel like I can watch his mind work as he takes in the approaching vehicle and realizes it's not one that he recognizes.

He lifts both arms up in front of his body, and I realize far too late that he's holding a gun between his hands, and that he means to use it on us. I stab my foot against the pedal and shove it to the floor, then lean back in my seat—like somehow that will save me from the rain of bullets he plans to fire through the windshield— and hold my breath as the distance that separates us suddenly becomes nonexistent.

There's a fleeting moment where we lock eyes, and then it's followed by a horrible sound as his body smashes into the front end of the jeep, rolls up the windshield, along the metal top, and flies off the back. Some crazy instinct stops me from stopping or taking my foot off the gas. I just keep driving forward breathlessly until we hit the street, and then I yank the steering wheel to the side, tires squeal, and the jeep feels like it might just tip and roll over. But we don't, and now we're barreling down the road past the hospital and leaving it all behind.

Every other second, I check the mirrors to see if anyone is chasing us on foot or in vehicles of their own, but it doesn't look like anyone is.

Still, I take no chances. Like it's some kind of action movie or video game, I zip the car into hard turn after hard turn, arbitrarily taking lefts and rights onto random residential streets, weaving and speeding with no clear direction or purpose other than to lose the imaginary pursuers closing in behind us.

Who knows how long I've been doing this when I finally realize where I am, and I spill out onto a major street that I know will take us all the way home. Even though I'm unfamiliar with the state of traffic on this street at this time of day, since I'd usually be at work, it seems eerily deserted for such a typically busy passageway. In the mornings and in the evenings, this is bumper-to-bumper traffic. Right now, this four-lane road is virtually empty; I count maybe two cars that pass me by on the other side in the span of a minute. There seems to be no one else headed in my direction.

I'm still checking the mirrors, and I don't plan to stop until I get home. I might not ever stop checking the mirrors, actually, and looking behind me wherever I go now for the rest of my life.

The only thing that gives me some small modicum of hope is that, realistically, I'm not worth following. Despite all the crisis and adrenaline, the logical, rational, practical doctor part of my brain will not be denied. Politely, it reminds me that those men back there didn't come to the hospital for me or for Hope. No doubt, they won't be pleased to find one of their own has been hit—*killed?*—by a car, but there will be no revenge crusade or massive woman-hunt taken on my behalf.

And the police? I'm not sure the police exist anymore. If they do, I imagine they have bigger problems on their hands right now.

That thought is further reinforced by the sights and scenes I witness on the journey home. Scattered trees are aflame on either side of the road. Sometimes, so are businesses and houses. The blue sky buzzes with swarms of police helicopters, news helicopters, drones, and the occasional flyover from what looks like, sounds like, and even *feels* like military aircraft.

But I do not dare keep my eyes upturned for long, because soon, what this road lacks in other vehicles, it more than makes up for in *people*. At first, it's just the occasional ragtag lawbreaker that's out jaywalking or running where they shouldn't be. But then I see more people running, and I realize from their expressions and the sweat stains on their clothing that they are actually running from something, whatever that may be, and that it appears many of them must not have a functioning car, bike, or some other more practical mode of transportation at their disposal.

More and more of them appear in front of me… and not all of them are headed this same direction. Some are running the opposite way, and worse yet, some are running toward me and my vehicle.

I stifle a scream the first time one of these people comes out of nowhere and flings themselves at the side of the jeep, clawing at the door handle and shouting obscenities before I accelerate. The would-be carjacker stumbles, falls, and gets left behind, but I nearly hit a family of four while watching this happen in my rear-view mirror.

Hope was right. She was right about everything. The city is lost. This is the worst possible place we could be right now. I have to get home so I can get Ruthie if I can.

If I can. I love that dog, she's all I have left now, and she's all alone, so I will try to make it back to her unless it becomes too dangerous.

I mean… it already is, though. Too dangerous. This is madness out here.

There's a group of skinheads with machetes—*machetes*—standing in a line outside the entrance to a popular convenience store on my right. They eye me—maybe with menace or maybe with envy—as I try to drive even faster.

What is my plan?

My plan is to go home.

That's such a bad plan. I might not even have somewhere to go home to anymore. For all I know, our house might be just like one of these other houses I drive by—the ones that are all engulfed in flames.

But still, I have to try. What else is there to do, anyway? Where else can I go?

Hope wanted us to go to her family's summer home. It seemed like a joke the first time she suggested it, and then it seemed like an overreaction when it became crystal-clear that she wasn't joking.

As it turned out, she was absolutely right. About everything. About all of this.

If that's where she thought we'd be safe, then it's worth a shot. I've been too late on everything else; I might be too late on this, as well. This civil unrest logically seems like it should be centered in the cities and the urban areas, but you never know.

Enough. Enough spinning my wheels pointlessly—both metaphorically, and also literally as I drive out here without a firm plan in place. I just saw maybe two dozen soldiers and a tank—*a tank*—heading off down a quiet suburban street that I passed by.

There is no part of me that wants to know what they are doing there and why they have come. Enough is enough.

I will go home. If I have a home to go to. There, I will gather my dog, Hope's keys to the summer home, and anything else that I think is important and that I can't live without. Even though, right now, there isn't much I can think of that I can't live without.

The one and only thing that comes to mind is already with me in the car. And though I have her with me, I don't really have her with me, of course. Though I risked my life to commit a daring rescue operation to bring her to safety, I didn't really, because she was already beyond saving.

I have spent my entire adult life caring for pregnant people and helping human beings bring more human beings into this world. Yet in the span of the last hour, maybe less, I have brought about the end of one human being's life… and maybe two.

What does that make me? A murderer? A sinner?

These are not new words, thoughts, or concepts. What difference does it make when it happened? I murdered my best friend, my soulmate, my lover, my partner, my wife. Whether it was today or twelve days ago or two years ago. I did this. The world is burning right now because I have brought hell to Earth through my actions. Through my neglect, my arrogance, and my selfishness.

Except I'm not the one who pays the price. Hope is.

Finally, *finally*, the tears come like a tempest.

NINE

It's time for Mr. Brett Taylor to wake up.

Although the key is in the ignition, the engine's off. Is that stupid? Perhaps. It certainly adds an extra second or two to any escape attempt, should I find the sudden need to get the jeep in motion and drive out of this wooded thicket and back out onto the country road. And there's no denying that an extra second or two could absolutely represent the difference between life or death.

On the flip side, gas is gas. Next to food, water, and shelter, I can't think of a more precious commodity left to human beings on Earth. Even with the added fuel I siphoned from that overturned wreck the other night, the gas tank is only about a quarter full. Maybe even a bit less.

Ultimately, I've decided it's more important to me to conserve the gasoline than it is to keep the car running in case of emergency. Besides, at least it's quieter this way. With the car running, anyone could theoretically hear it from a distance while on foot. But with no engine humming, you'd pretty much have to walk right into the jeep to discover it… and that's what I've got guns for.

The Glock rests in the cupholder between the driver

and passenger seats, while I have the rifle positioned on the driver-side windowsill doorframe with the barrel sticking out into the woods and angled toward the road we came in on.

In the back seat, Brett Taylor slumbers under the effects of a powerful anesthetic. Occasionally, he'll mumble something unintelligible, but mainly all I hear is light, ragged snoring from back there. Given the dosage of the drug I put in his system, his ongoing recovery from the puncture wound to his side, and the gas mask I slipped over his head in place of the pillowcase, I can't say I altogether blame him, either.

I made sure to wait until after the injection ran its course to swap out his headgear. That was also after I made damn sure he was fully asleep, too. I may have given him a couple quick kicks, but they were soft, and in no way, shape, or form resembled the kicks I bestowed on those other two men back in that basement. My intention in the two scenarios obviously could not have been more different.

Brett is NDV-negative—I know this because I administered three separate rapid tests when I first brought him into my home, and because I also gave him another pair at two different times earlier today. I'm also NDV-negative—I gave myself a test the same night I brought him back after my interactions with those men in the basement—but it's still a general rule for me that I don't go anywhere outside without a mask on. I've decided to extend that rule to cover Brett as well, because I'm a good person.

Maybe if we'd had the proper time to develop and distribute a vaccine to society, this rule wouldn't apply, but the anti-vaxxer extremists and anti-common-sense 'freedom' fighters saw to that when they burned down all the research facilities and slaughtered all the scientists and healthcare workers.

Though to be fair, if they hadn't done all that, and if an effective vaccine actually had been rolled out en masse and in time, Brett and I might not be in this situation to begin with.

At any rate, the mask he's wearing belongs to him, anyway. Sadly, the mask that I'm wearing isn't my old friend Jim Carrey, who proved to be beyond repair after that asshole cracked the visor when he knocked me out.

For sentimental reasons, I've decided to hold onto him, since you never know when you might stumble across the right kind of materials needed to make the repairs after all. I even have half a mind to include some items for that very purpose when I give my list to Brett and Vicki Taylor. For now, though, I sport one of the confiscated masks that belonged to my attackers in the basement. Even after a thorough disinfecting, sanitizing, and deodorizing, this thing feels unclean over my face. Every inhalation, I'm reminded of where it came from, and it's difficult to tell whether the stale, stinking, rotten air I'm breathing in is just my imagination or if I actually didn't do a good enough job in eradicating the former owner's stench from it.

Either way, it's time for Brett to wake up. We've been here long enough, and I'm starting to get antsy. I turn around in my seat to size him up.

Even with his slight frame and modest body composition, he's deceptively heavier than you'd think. Either that, or maybe I'm just not as strong as I thought I was. Dragging him up the stairs of that house from the basement to the ground floor and then all the way out to the jeep—especially with him essentially being dead weight, not to mention slippery from sweat and dried blood—had to have been the most grueling physical exercise I've gotten in years. It's also a minor miracle the dizziness spells didn't set in during the midst of all that.

Getting him up out of my basement and out to the jeep tonight was no picnic, either, although this time, I was lucky enough to utilize a two-wheeled dolly once I got him up to the first floor. After all, you never know what random supplies or equipment you might need down the road. I was certainly grateful this evening that I had the foresight and presence of mind to nab that dolly on a raiding mission years ago, even when at the time I wasn't sure what I'd ever use it for.

Though neither tall nor muscular, Brett's body seems oversized in certain random places that don't make sense to me. His legs, particularly his thighs, are massive, as evidenced by how tight his dirty work jeans get around the muscles in that area. The boots on his feet also seem abnormally large to me, though I'll admit I am perhaps one of the least qualified individuals left on the planet to know what is normal or abnormal in the area of men's footwear.

Brett's hands are calloused, and his fingernails are long and filthy. He definitely strikes me as someone who knows how to swing an axe and use a shovel.

The tattoos are also a defining feature of his body. I made a point of examining them carefully while treating him in my basement, and I'd be lying if I didn't find the sheer volume of them more than a bit excessive and unnecessary. It's not that I have anything personally against tattoos or those who have tattoos, though I'll admit I never really understood how self-vandalism became a fad and skin mutilation a fashion statement.

More importantly, though, the tattoo inspection had to occur because I needed to make sure there was nothing incriminating emblazoned permanently on him. I'd imagine the reason most people get tattoos is to have some form of visual, artistic representation of meaningful concepts, people, places, or organizations etched onto their body. Either that, or maybe they simply like the look of them.

In Brett's case, it was imperative that I find nothing distasteful in the patchwork canvas of ink on his arms—distasteful meaning 'hateful' in this case, not literally art that leaves a bad taste in my mouth and that I find disgusting or dislikable, which I indeed found most of his tattoos to be.

Thankfully, though, the tattoos were weird, obnoxious, of poor quality at times, and genuinely head-scratching and tacky most of the time, but they were not hateful. I even checked beneath the t-shirt and inspected his torso, thinking it might make sense to better conceal your more deplorable preferences back when normal society was still a thing and tattoo shops still existed.

No swastikas, no SS bolts, no othala runes, no iron, blood drop, or burning crosses, no Confederate flags, no raised white fists, and no nooses.

I saw enough between his neck and his navel to negate the need for looking below the belt. If he's littered with hate symbols beneath his jeans, so be it, because I was more than satisfied with the search I conducted. Besides, one of the tattoos was the word 'VICKI' stenciled in big red letters over his heart. To be clear, I think this tattoo is absolutely ridiculous and a terrible cliché, but in retrospect, at least it helps corroborate his story.

Interestingly, I have no idea what color Brett's eyes are. In my company, he has always had either a mask or a pillowcase drawn down over his face to either protect him from the virus or to protect and preserve the identity of my safe house from him. Those rare instances in which I had to swap out his headgear, I've always made sure he was unconscious, and he was unconscious from his injury when I first brought him back, so his eyes have always been closed during those brief moments.

I do know that he's bald, though he has a thick beard that nearly travels all the way down a stocky neck to meet up with his chest hair. His body hair is black, and that's the predominant color in his beard, though there's also quite a lot of brown, red, grey, and even white in there as well. He sweats a lot, and he doesn't smell that great, but then again, I'm sure I don't smell that great, either. I've forgotten what a shower would even feel like.

I'll go easy on him at first, I decide spontaneously.

"Brett. Brett, wake up."

I'd describe the level of my voice right now as being 'a loud whisper.' Truthfully, I'd be shocked if it worked, but again, I've decided to start with the nice and easy stuff first.

When it's clear that it hasn't worked, I twist a little further around in my seat so that I can reach back and give him a small shove in the chest. His body absorbs the impact and barely seems to move at all.

Granted, he's not only strapped in with a seatbelt. He also has his arms wrapped close to his sides by chains that travel around his back, chest, and biceps several times before dead-ending in the bicycle U-lock positioned between his shoulder blades. His wrists are bound together, first with rope and then with a full roll of duct tape over that rope that also manages to totally constrain and conceal his hands and fingers, making it look like he's got one big bulky grey knob instead of two fists.

I give him a couple small shoves just to make sure before pulling the rifle in from the windowsill. He'll never believe that I tried to do this the easy way first with just my voice and my hands. Oh well.

With a concertedly gentle but firm effort, I angle the butt of the rifle toward his stomach and give it a quick, decisive smack, like I'm stamping out a cockroach that I'm afraid might bolt or fly away if I miss.

Brett comes to in a hurry, coughing and sputtering as his chest rocks forward and over his stomach protectively, only to be met by the seatbelt and chains. I have no doubt in my mind he's bewildered right now, as his last clear memory was likely getting the injection while he was still locked up and tied to the basement pole.

"I tried saying your name and shaking you myself, but you just weren't waking up."

He's still making an awful succession of sounds behind his gas mask. I'm surprised to discover I actually feel sorry for him, even though it had to be done.

"I apologize for that. I'm sure it didn't feel too good."

Brett's really struggling to gain his composure back. Doubtless, he's also probably confused mentally as to where he is, who I am, and what we're doing. That was some powerful anesthesia I gave him, after all, so he's very likely dazed and still cloudy up there in his head.

"Are you all right?"

He's able to nod slightly despite the rollicking convulsions. At least his head and neck aren't restrained anymore like they were in the basement against the support pole.

I wait as patiently as I can until he finally grows quiet and still again, and then I speak.

"Do you know where we are?"

It's sort of a trick question, since there's really no possible way he'd know where we are. I drove us out about twenty minutes away from my house in the woods and picked a secluded area off a dirt country road to take a turn. From there, I found a spot in the trees where the jeep could hopefully go unnoticed until Brett woke up. Not that I expect anyone to even use this road anymore anyway. But you never know.

There's no way that Brett knows this area, but he still takes a few seconds to pivot his head in both directions and give it a real try. It's hard for me not to sigh with impatience, but I did ask him a question, and he seems intent on answering me truthfully.

"I don't."

His voice is hoarser than it was yesterday. I wonder if that's grogginess or if it's still just his body trying to recuperate.

"In about ten or twelve miles, this road dead-ends into a larger road called River Crossing. Are you familiar with that one?"

Brett instantly nods his head, which is a relief.

"Yes."

"Good. When we get to River Crossing, the lake will be due east of us. Do you know which way we'll need to turn on River Crossing to get to your state park?"

He pauses for a moment to think before answering.

"Right. We'll need to take a right."

"You're sure?"

"Yes. I'm sure."

These masks make it impossible to read faces. Here is yet another moment where I'd love to have any extra added information I could get from simply analyzing his facial expression.

It is what it is, though. I'll have to take him at his word.

"Okay, then. This is what's going to happen now. I'm going to start the car, we're going to take it slow, and we're going to drive up this road until we hit River Crossing. When we get there, we'll take a right, and then you're going to navigate me the rest of the way to your place. You understand the plan?"

"I do."

The key on my necklace is halfway up to the ignition when I turn back around.

"Just a reminder. Anything funny, anything strange, anything I don't like or that doesn't add up… I won't hesitate. I'll turn us around, I'll find a safe place, I'll kill you, I'll dump your body, and then I'll head back to my house alone. No skin off my back. I don't need any of your supplies, and I don't need to keep you alive. This mission, this is all about wrapping up loose ends and doing what's best for the both of us. I want it to go smoothly, and I don't want anyone to get hurt. But remember, I can wrap up loose ends just as easily with a bullet as I can by taking you home. Remember that. Okay?"

Brett nods solemnly.

"Absolutely. Believe me, I love my wife. We'll do anything you ask of us. Nothing bad is going to happen. Trust me."

It's the only choice I have. That, or kill him. And I've already decided I'm not going to do that unless he makes me.

Onward, then.

We drive in silence with the low beams on along the country road. I know this area well, and I know there's nothing out here. No forest homes, no farms, no campgrounds, nothing. Just pure, unadulterated nature with a thin, brown snake of a dirt road weaving its way through it all.

In another life, this would have been a wonderful place to explore together with Hope. Most of our adventures hiking in the woods happened relatively close to her family's summer home. She always wanted to venture out further into the wilderness and the great unknown, but I was usually the wet blanket who stymied those ideas with my concerns about getting lost, getting injured, or getting eaten by the local wildlife.

If I could do it all over again, I would have kept my mouth shut and my eyes open, and I'm sure we could have had a magical time together. I would have said yes more often and wouldn't have let my work or my practicality stand in the way of her adventurous spirit. She was good for me that way; she pushed me out of my comfort zone, constantly.

Her love for nature—both plants and animals—was something that gradually rubbed off on me the more time we spent together. Maybe if we'd had even longer, I could have morphed into the type of person who suggests taking spontaneous treks out to the middle of nowhere in the name of charting mesmerizing new frontiers and feeding our souls directly from Mother Nature's kitchen.

If I could do it all over again. In another life. If we'd had longer.

River Crossing is similarly abandoned. Back in the day—back when there was a day, and a night, and time, and people, and order—this was a semi-busy road. Nothing like a freeway or a city street, even, but it certainly didn't go unused. Hope and I took it a few times together, but I know she grew up using it all the time in the summers with her family and friends.

As a child, she'd come along this way in the back of her parents' sedan for trips out to the lake to go swimming, boating, tubing, or fishing. When she grew older, she took this road in her own car or in a friend's car, and usually to the lake still, only this time to go sunbathing, skinny-dipping, or just to hang out, drink beers, and smoke weed. It was on the shore of that lake that Hope, just thirteen at the time, kissed her first girl.

Maggie Munson. How do I remember that name still? She must have told me that story fifteen years ago. I can't believe I still remember that girl's name. Wow.

I wonder if she ever went to this state park? I'd imagine she must have, considering how she spent nearly every summer of her first eighteen years of life out in this area. Her parents seemed every bit as outdoorsy as Hope always was, so it stands to reason they may have hiked, camped, or at least visited the park on several occasions over the years.

I'm not sure if Hope ever mentioned it to me before, though. We certainly never went there together. Somehow, we never even made it out to the lake together. Did she ever invite me? She must have. Which means that I must have said no. But why? Why would anyone ever say no to that? How could I have been so dumb?

"What's the name of this park?"

In the reflection of the rear-view mirror, I watch Brett turn his head to face me. He must have been staring out his window.

What is he looking at out there? Is he seeing something I'm not, or is he just lost in his own thoughts? What could those thoughts be? It's been so long since I've been in such intimate quarters with another human being for so long, and it makes me jumpy.

"Spider Falls."

I nod as if that means something to me.

For some reason, I glance at the Glock in the cupholder and then at the rifle on the floor of the passenger seat. I look up at the rear-view mirror, and Brett is still looking at me instead of looking back out his window. Did he see me look at the guns? Does it matter? Why am I acting this way all of a sudden?

Everything is under control. He is literally tied, taped, and chained in place. On top of all that, he has a nasty wound in his side that's still healing, and the last thing he wants to do is rip his stitches open. Not that he even could, because once again, he is physically incapacitated.

Besides, why wouldn't he want to get home to his wife and his unborn child? He has every reason to be telling the truth. I'm just being paranoid again. I asked him a question, and he answered me; that's why he's still looking at me in the mirror.

Make conversation. That's what people do. You're

still a person. You haven't lost that yet. At least, hopefully not.

"Why is it called Spider Falls?"

Brett stares back at me through the dual layers of his facemask and the rear-view mirror glass.

"I don't know."

There's an uncomfortable moment where we're both just silently looking at each other.

"I'd never been there. Before all this. Vicki had, though. She's the one who suggested we go there."

"Why?"

"Why Spider Falls?"

"Yeah."

He pauses briefly.

"She said she used to go there as a kid with her family. Mentioned there was lots of open space and not a whole lot nearby in terms of civilization. I told her that could be a bad thing to be so far removed from the types of places that would have the things we might need, but she told me it could also be a good thing to get off the beaten trail and go somewhere people wouldn't think about."

Absurdly, I find myself wondering if Hope and Vicki ever crossed paths as children or adolescents. I almost ask Brett what his wife's maiden name is, but then I think better of it.

Even if he told me, I don't honestly believe whatever name it is will suddenly jog some long-forgotten memory of a story Hope told me once from her past. This area is sparsely populated, even in the summertime, but Brett also looks to be about a decade younger than me. Unless Vicki is a cougar, I think the odds are slim that she and Hope ever ran in the same circles.

"Like I said, though, we haven't been there very long. Maybe a week, tops."

"Where were you before?"

I'm trying to sound conversational, but it still feels like my tone is coming across as interrogatory. If Brett minds, though, it's impossible for me to detect it by his face, and he's not really showing much resistance to my questions in his answers. It'd be easy and understandable for a person in his position not to say much at all, but he's speaking like an open book so far.

"Are you asking where we used to live… before all this? Or after?"

"After. Before the ranger station, were you on the move constantly, or did you have another spot for a while?"

Now Brett twists his head to stare back out his window into the passing darkness.

"We've holed up at a number of places over the years. Came from the city originally, probably like everybody else. It was especially hard, since neither one of us really knew much about surviving on our own. Don't get me wrong, though, Vicki and I both came from poor families, so it's not like we ever had it easy. But I just mean we never really got into the whole camping, hiking, backpacking lifestyle. So, all of this… it's definitely been an adjustment for us."

Understatement of the century for almost everyone left alive on Earth, I'm sure.

"We were lucky, though, in the very beginning. When shit really started to hit the fan, Vicki got a call from her sister who lived out in a trailer home, kind of up near the foothills. Her sister and her sister's husband convinced us to get out of the city and to come shack up with them until everything blew over. I wasn't particularly keen on the idea at first, but it's a good thing Vicki's so damn persuasive. Her sister, too. Between the two of them, we didn't stay in our old house very long after that."

"What happened?"

"To the house?"

"No, to her sister. And her sister's husband. Are they still with you?"

This is something Brett should have mentioned yesterday when he first told me about his pregnant wife and their place in the state park. Dealing with Brett and his wife—two against one, even if one of the two is chained up and restrained—is already a dicey enough proposition as is.

But if it's actually Vicki, Vicki's sister, and Vicki's brother-in-law who are all there—four against one—I'm better off pulling over, tossing him out the side, turning around, and heading straight home right now. That sounds like a recipe for disaster on my end, heading into that kind of scenario. I'd be a suicidal fool to do it.

"No. They passed."

My eyes drift up to the rear-view mirror to try and catch any clues that I can from Brett. He's still staring out the window, which makes it impossible to try and see his eyes through the mask.

"They're dead? Both of them?"

"That's right."

"How?"

He turns to look at me in the mirror. I realize I'm acting like a cop again, so I try to tone it down.

"If you don't mind my asking."

Brett shakes his head.

"I don't mind. The virus took them. Both of them."

My eyes bounce back and forth rapidly between the road in front of us and Brett's reflection in the mirror above me.

"But not you or Vicki? Obviously, since you're both alive. But you weren't worried, especially since you were living together?"

Brett pauses again but keeps his focus on me.

"We had a system, the four of us. We took turns going out in pairs on any trips to get supplies. Any time a pair went out, they'd quarantine separately from the other pair for ten days."

"At a trailer home?"

My voice is at least a bit less accusatory this time, though the skeptical tone is probably no less offensive. I just can't help myself, though.

"It wasn't easy, don't get me wrong. We basically set up a tent under a shade canopy a little way off from the trailer, and that was the quarantine area. We'd divvy up all the stuff first—the supplies whichever pair that went out brought back—and then that was that for ten days; we'd keep to ourselves to be safe. And unfortunately, one time after they went out, they came back and quarantined, and when the ten days were up, and we went back to check on them… they didn't wake up."

Brett's voice has become husky and hoarse again. Is it rustiness from talking too much and screaming bloody murder last night, or is that true emotion bubbling up?

"That was hard, obviously. On both of us, but especially on Vicki. At first, she didn't even want to stay there any longer. She said she didn't think it would be right, considering it was their place and that they were the ones who told us we could stay there with them. But I told her that they would want us to stay and be safe as long as we could, and that there was no good reason for us to leave."

"So, why did you leave then?"

"We didn't have a choice. It got taken from us… by force. Men—I don't know how many—they came in the night. If it wasn't for our dog—not our dog, the dog that belonged to Vicki's sister—I'm sure they would have caught us completely unawares, and we'd both be dead now. But thank God that dog started barking and going crazy like he did, because it was enough to wake us up and get us on our feet. I grabbed a gun, but I realized it was pointless when I saw at least five or six of them or so moving in fast on the fence along the property line.

"Vicki and I ran out back and got away in our truck just in time, because the last thing I heard was a gun go off, and then the dog stopped barking, and from that point on, we didn't look back. We left everything behind back there; there was no time. I just drove and drove, and we've been staying wherever we could ever since. Sometimes in abandoned houses or buildings, but more often than not just out in the forest."

Brett goes quiet again.

"Until now?"

"Until now. It was the baby that got us serious about finding someplace we could make permanent… or at least as permanent as you can get nowadays. Once we knew we were pregnant, that's when I decided we couldn't just have a baby and raise a kid out in the woods like that. We needed a roof over our head. Something solid, someplace safe. Or again, at least as safe as can be. It's hard enough for two people to be on the run constantly, but then when one of those two people gets pregnant? That's damn near impossible. And it won't get any easier once the baby comes, either."

No, it will not. On that point, Brett Taylor is absolutely correct.

I cannot begin to imagine raising a child in this world, let alone trying to do it with a newborn baby. Especially without modern conveniences and technology. It's a struggle for me to take care of myself each day, and I'm almost forty-four years old.

Besides, knowing what I know as an OB-GYN, I can't even fathom going through childbirth without the proper supplies and equipment. That's not something you can just go out and scavenge for and find everything you need at different houses, farms, or stores. Whether in the city or in the country, there's really not a whole lot of available options. And the hospitals and pharmacies were the first places to get picked dry, no doubt.

I keep all of this to myself, however, because I don't need to pour gasoline on the fire. Brett sounds like he has a fairly good idea that he and Vicki are about to embark on a brutally difficult, nigh-impossible new challenge together.

It's a cliché to say that becoming a new parent is one of the hardest things a person will ever have to go through. But doing it without the necessary support or resources, not to mention doing it in the midst of a global pandemic and the final systemic breakdown of human society as we know it?

Good luck, Brett and Vicki Taylor. You're going to need it, and you're probably going to also need more than a few miracles to happen along the way, too.

While I decide to spare Brett on the parenthood

topic, I can't completely let him off the hook just yet. He said two things earlier that piqued my interest, and one of them especially warrants immediate clarification.

"You mentioned you have a gun and a truck. Are both of them back with Vicki right now?"

The gun has to be with Vicki, unless the two of them somehow lost it along the way, which would be almost as impossible to believe as the idea of them raising a baby together in this world. I know this because Brett didn't have anything on his person when I searched him; he only had the knife he used to kill that one guy in the basement.

The truck could also be with Vicki back at the ranger station, but it's probably more likely parked somewhere nearby that house where Brett and I first crossed paths in the basement. I did confiscate a vehicle key when I searched Brett while he was unconscious.

I'm curious to hear his explanation for both objects, since whatever he says will teach me a lot about Brett Taylor's trustworthiness as a person, but also a lot about what I need to be ready for when I meet Vicki Taylor.

"The truck… the truck is parked a block or two away from that house we met in. It's probably gone by now, if someone knows how to hot-wire, or even if it isn't, I'd imagine it's been stripped clean. I don't even know where the key's at anymore."

"I have it. I can toss it out the window along with the key to your lock when I drive away later."

Brett laughs. The sound startles me because it's so unexpected and unusual, and my heart races a bit as I check in with his reflection.

"Thank you. That's very generous. I don't suppose I could bribe you into giving me or Vicki a lift over there, too, once you're done taking whatever you want from our place?"

A wry smile spreads across my face that Brett will never see.

"Afraid not. I'm sorry, though. I know that must be a trek."

I also know there's no way he'll make that trek. Only a fool would set out that far on foot to try and recover their vehicle. Better to start over and steal a new one. I know this, and I know Brett knows this, too. Maybe he also has a wry smile spreading beneath his mask right now.

"No worries. Thought not. Probably for the best. I'm sure it's a goner by now, anyway."

My smile fades quickly. On to more important matters.

"The gun, though, Brett. Was it in the truck, or does Vicki have it?"

This is crucial now. Whatever he says, it is key to how I continue forward with this situation in multiple respects.

If Brett says the gun was in the truck, it will call into question everything I think I know about him so far. Because why on Earth would anyone go out to gather medical supplies for their pregnant wife with a gun and then leave it behind in the car? Especially while entering a strange house that may or may not now be occupied since the last time you visited? That's the time you'd need a gun the most.

If Brett says the gun is with Vicki back at their place, it still begs the question why he wouldn't take it with him for such a dangerous assignment. But then again, I suppose I also understand the idea of leaving a weapon behind for your pregnant wife to defend herself while she's alone.

Of course, the most important aspect of that second possibility being true would mean that Vicki Taylor is armed. And that would definitively alter my plan of how this whole exchange is going to go down.

Brett looks at me in the mirror.

"Vicki has it."

Good news: Brett's probably not a liar. Bad news: Vicki has a gun.

"What kind of gun is it?"

"I—I'm actually embarrassed to say I don't really know my guns that well. It was my brother-in-law's gun. Maybe a pistol or a revolver? Are those the same thing?"

Spoken like a man who brought a knife to a gun fight back in that basement.

"Not at all. But your wife—Vicki—she has the gun now? You're sure of it?"

Brett hesitates for the smallest nanosecond.

"I am. I left it behind with her… so she could protect herself. But I wouldn't worry too much about it. She's never used it before. I'm not sure she'd even know how."

I find that hard to believe. No one could have possibly survived the last five years in this country without having at least a basic knowledge of how to operate a gun. It's just not realistic. Whether she knows how to use it or not, though, the sheer simple fact that Vicki has easy access to a firearm changes the entire complexity of this operation.

My brain works quickly to analyze and dissect this information, hypothesize as many different scenarios as possible, and work my way backward toward a new plan that accounts for Vicki Taylor being armed and who knows how dangerous.

This mental process isn't helped at all when Brett unexpectedly chirps up from the back seat.

"We're coming up on it now, the entrance to Spider Falls. See the sign up ahead?"

Sure enough, I glimpse a brown sign looming out of the darkness up ahead on the right side of the road. As we get closer, the words 'SPIDER FALLS STATE PARK 3 MILES' with an arrow pointing to the left are visible.

"How far do we go into the park before we hit the building?"

"Hmmm… I gotta be honest, I'm not much better with judging distances than I am with knowing guns. Maybe a few miles? Two or three?"

He has to do better than that.

"How long does it normally take you to drive in your truck? From the ranger station to the entrance here on River Crossing?"

Brett thinks a good few seconds before answering.

"Oh, you know what? I'm sorry, but I've never timed it. I've never needed to. Usually, I've got my eyes on the road, and I'm worried about a million other things. It won't take long, though. There's a short drive in, and then you'll see a hut in the middle of the road where I bet they used to take cash and give maps and parking passes and do all that stuff. The ranger station is right off to the side from there."

"Is it on the right or the left?"

"What?"

I'm growing frustrated. If Brett wants me to turn the heat back on, I will. He's quickly forcing me there.

"The station, Brett. Where you and Vicki have been staying. Is it on the right or the left when you drive in and pass the welcome kiosk?"

Again, he thinks for a few seconds. Why is this so difficult? Even if they've only been there a short time, this shouldn't be a hard question to answer.

"Left side. You'll drive up, the kiosk will be on your left, and the station's right after it, just a little way up on the left. Can't miss it."

Speaking of 'can't miss it,' I see a large wooden sign coming up on my left. That has to be the turn.

"Is this it? Is that the entrance on the left up there?"

"Yes, this is it."

I slow just a bit to make the turn.

Almost immediately, we're ushered into a narrow two-lane road with overgrown trees on both sides. The road itself is paved, so it's not like we're traveling on bumpy terrain; the road we started on after I woke Brett up was far worse than this one.

Still, though, there's something that's claustrophobic right away about having all these branches and bushes creeping in on both sides. It was dark before on River Crossing, but it's even darker now with the dense vegetation that surrounds us.

I'm definitely taking my time now. The speedometer needle hovers just above fifteen.

"All right, listen, Brett. Slight change of plans. When we get close to the kiosk, you're going to let me know it's coming up soon. I'm going to park right next to it, but on the other side of it, away from the ranger station, okay? So that the kiosk is between me and your place. I'm going to roll the windows down, I'm going to cut the ignition, and I'm going to aim my rifle at your place.

If Vicki comes out to see who it is, you're going to call out to her and you're going to explain exactly what's happening. You're going to tell her the truth, and the truth is that I have two guns on me in here, and one of them will be trained on her this whole time. You following me so far?"

"Of course."

"When I tell you to call for Vicki, you will call for Vicki. Here's what's ultimately going to happen no matter what: Vicki is going to have to come out at some point, and she's going to have to bring out the gun you guys have in there. If she doesn't have the gun on her, if I don't see the gun on her person, you're going to tell her to go in, get it, and bring it back out.

"You're going to tell her, in your own words, not to do anything stupid or crazy, because I have a gun pointed at her, and I can also just as easily turn and blow you away in the back seat, too. Feel free to tell her that, because it's important she understands what the situation is and how this is going to happen.

"When she does bring out the gun, I will tell her where she needs to throw it near us, and I will tell her when she needs to throw it. And once she does that, I will get out, still with my gun pointed at her, I will pick the gun up, and when I have both guns, I will move back to my jeep, and I will then have three guns in my possession, and you and Vicki will have no guns. You still following?"

"Yes."

"Vicki will prove to me she is completely unarmed at this point. She will then stay completely still as I come over to her. Again, I will have several weapons on me at this point, and she will have none. You will stay right where you are, of course, strapped in, locked up, not moving a muscle. Together, Vicki and I will go, slowly, inside the station, and I will keep a gun pointed at her back the entire time she retrieves each and every item I ask for, brings it out to the jeep, loads it up, goes back in the station, over and over, repeating this process methodically until I have taken what I want.

"Then, and only then, I will have her help you out of the back seat, again with a gun aimed at the both of you, and the two of you will walk as far away as I tell you to. Same plan after that: I'll drive away until I feel safe, you'll both stay still—and I'll be watching in the mirrors—and when I feel good about this whole thing, I'll throw the keys out the window to your lock and to your truck. If you do all of this, and she does all of this the right way and we have no problems, I might even throw your gun back out the window, too, before I drive off. Sound good to you?"

Brett nods.

"Absolutely. And by the way, the kiosk is coming up soon on your left, I believe. You told me to tell you so you're ready. But I'm ready, too. I'm ready to do everything you just said."

I guess I am ready—as ready as I'll ever be. Obviously, I would have vastly preferred being the only one with a gun during this whole transaction, but I suppose it's better to know what I'm getting into up front than to go into this blindly and get surprised. That would have been much worse; that could have been the end, once and for all.

The kiosk materializes up ahead, and I slow the jeep even further so it's barely moving forward at all now. Ten miles per hour. Five miles per hour. As slowly and as quietly as I can go, I go.

When we finally pull up to the small hut, I turn the steering wheel gently to angle the vehicle so that the passenger side is facing the structure—and thus, the ranger station that is farther up on the left beyond it. I can only just barely glimpse a larger building, but I do see it there, which is good. Another thing Brett has so far been truthful about.

Once I've got the jeep just where I want it, I lower the windows, turn the ignition off, and slide the keyring necklace back down the front of my shirt.

Spontaneously, I decide to change my own plans just a bit now that I'm here and now that this is actually happening. I slide the Glock into the waistline of my pants where I normally keep it, grab the rifle, and quietly open the driver door. Brett doesn't say anything, which is smart on his part. Keeping the door ajar, I move myself back into position near the left rear passenger side.

Yes, I like this better already. Now, I have three things separating me from Vicki: the kiosk, the jeep, and, most importantly I think, her husband. I lower the end of the rifle where the back window would normally be and rest it on the metal frame so that it's pointed at Brett's head. He watches me do this in silence.

"Call for her."

There are a couple seconds of hesitation. Maybe he's unnerved that I'm deviated from the script. If he is, he needs to get over that fast if he wants to live. This is my show, and I reserve the right to make any last-minute changes however I see fit.

"What do you want me to say?"

I give him a look that might be lost because of the

mask, but I give it to him anyway.

"What would you normally say?"

"I wouldn't normally be in this situation."

"Just call for her, Brett. I don't care what you say. Call her by her name."

He does just that.

"Vicki!"

I jump when he yells. Everything has been so quiet up to this point. For that matter, my entire life is lived in quiet now. It has been for years. It's startling every time something loud and abrasive occurs, whether it's a cat shrieking in the night or a man shouting out for his wife.

Nothing happens. It's all just dark, quiet, and still, save for the sound of my rapid breathing in the mask, and Brett breathing just in front of me from inside the car. He turns to face me.

"Should I call her again?"

"Yes. Call her and tell her to come out here."

"Vicki! It's me. It's Brett. Can you come out here, please?"

Silence. Stillness. Darkness.

He looks to me again, and I nod.

"Vicki! Please, baby. Come out here! It's me. I need you to come out here, please. It's Brett!"

Still nothing happens for a few seconds. But then a woman's voice rises timidly out from the distance.

"Brett?"

"Vicki! Yeah, it's me. I'm out here. Can you come out, please?"

A couple seconds pass again before she answers.

"What's going on?"

"Baby, I'll explain everything. But I need you to come out here, please. And baby—bring the gun. If you don't have it on you, go back in and get it."

"What's going on?"

"I told you, honey, I'm gonna explain everything. Don't worry, though. I'm just fine. Everything's gonna be just fine. But I need you to trust me right now, okay?"

Silence.

"Vicki?"

"I'm here."

Brett shifts in his seat. He's clearly uncomfortable with all the tape, rope, chains, and the seatbelt holding him in place. I know it can't be pleasant being bound up like that so tightly for so long now, but I don't regret it. It's a necessary precaution.

"Vicki, I need you to trust me. I'm—I'm with somebody. I came back here with somebody. A woman. Alex."

My eyes flash at him in surprise and anger. It takes me longer than it should to remember that I actually for some reason introduced myself to him last night. I must have told him my name. I'm momentarily shocked that I did that, and I'm even more shocked that he remembered.

"Why are you with a woman?"

In another universe, that could be a funny yet loaded question. This could be an entirely different circumstance with an entirely different set of stakes. More classic sitcom or romcom misunderstanding than tense action thriller meeting.

"This is Alex. She's a doctor. She was nice enough to bring me back here. This is her car, her jeep; she drove me all the way back here. Vicki, baby—she saved my life. I got hurt trying to get those medicines, and she stitched me back up. I owe her my life."

When did I tell him I was a doctor? I remember now when I said my name was Alex, but I have no memory of telling him I used to be a doctor. Did I really reveal that to him, too, last night?

Jesus. I must really be slipping. Either that, or it's just been too long since I had social interactions with a real-life human being. Honestly, both are probably true.

Vicki is still invisible to me. Her voice is coming from the direction of the ranger station building, I know that. I'm also keeping my ears primed and a careful lookout on the peripheries of my vision for any sound or movement that might happen elsewhere.

Everything has been as Brett said it would be so far, but that doesn't mean it won't change unexpectedly at any second. For all I know, Vicki's sister and brother-in-law are still very much alive, both armed, and closing in on me from both sides in a surprise pincer-move attack.

I mean, for all I *really* know, those five or six men in his story could be friends, family, or other allies of theirs. Brett's entire story on the way over here could be made up. I have to stay constantly vigilant, or risk getting surprised and then killed.

"Did you hear what I said, Vicki?"

"I did. What happens now? What's going on, Brett?"

Brett turns quickly to face me. I flick the end of the rifle back in the direction of her voice, hoping the gesture is enough for him to compute. This is on you, buddy. You need to make this happen. Stop looking to me for help. She's your wife. Convince her.

He turns his head back around.

"It's like I said, honey, I need you to come all the way out here. Slowly, though, babe. And you need to bring the gun. Do you have our gun on you?"

"Yes."

"Good. That's real good, honey. Just hold it up in the air. I know this seems strange, and it doesn't seem right, but you have to trust me. Everything's gonna be just fine."

There's another brief silence before she speaks again from somewhere up ahead.

"I'm coming out. I don't want to get hurt. Please don't hurt me. I'm pregnant. I'm gonna have a baby. Please don't shoot."

"No one's gonna shoot anybody, baby. Alex knows you're pregnant. I told her all about you, and all about us. She saved my life, Vicki, so she's not gonna hurt me, and she's not gonna hurt you. If she wanted me dead, she would have let me die. But she saved my life, and she drove me all the way out here so I could come back for you."

"What does she want?"

Brett is the one who hesitates now, though at least he doesn't turn around to check in with me for once.

"I don't know, baby. That's the God's honest truth. She told me she has a list, though, just a few things, I think. But even if it's not, even if it's more, we owe her that much. I owe her that much for what she did for me. Remember in the movies, babe, the movies we used to watch together? Whenever they traded a hostage for money or a ransom or whatever? That's kind of what this is. It's just like in the movies. As long as everyone keeps their cool and does what they're supposed to do, no one gets hurt. Just like in the movies."

Something in me bristles at the analogy he's concocted. I know he's not wrong, not exactly, but it still leaves me feeling like I'm somehow the villain in this situation.

It's important for her to realize that I saved her husband's life. Without me, there is no happy homecoming. There is no Mr. and Mrs. Taylor. This isn't some hostage handoff or ransom. I didn't do this intentionally; I didn't capture Brett or spend all that time, energy, and medicine on saving his life just so I could use him as a bargaining chip.

And yet… and yet, he's not exactly wrong. I can't deny it. At least on some basic level or at face value, I suppose this is a kind of exchange.

Am I a villain then, bartering another human being? Trading a husband back to his pregnant wife so that I can make off with some extra supplies that I don't *really* need?

Fuck. Thinking of it all that way, it's hard not to see this situation in an entirely different light.

"What does she want, though? We barely have enough as is!"

Brett shifts in his seat, but no matter how uncomfortable he must feel physically right now—and mentally, since she just essentially outed him—it's not nearly as uncomfortable as I'm starting to feel.

Yes, there's an immediate flare that goes up inside my brain, reminding me that Brett said last night they had plenty to go around, which means that either he was lying then, or Vicki is lying now.

But there's also another flare—a brighter, hotter one—that forces me to consider the ramifications if Vicki is in fact telling the truth.

What if they *do* barely have enough supplies to get by? What does that mean for them? What does that mean for me and what I plan to do next, assuming this all continues to work out as planned?

Brett turns again to face me, shakes his head quickly from side to side, and lowers his voice. Though his volume dips considerably, he's still just as impassioned when he speaks to me now as he was before while yelling out to his wife.

"Alex, I am so, so sorry. I didn't tell you the whole truth last night. I know I said we had plenty to go around and last us for months, even with the baby coming, but that's not exactly true. Far from it, actually. Vicki's right. We… we're still getting set up here. We have just enough to last us a week, maybe a little longer. That's why I went out for supplies. It wasn't just to get the pills and the medical supplies—it was to get food. Water. Weapons. I didn't mean to lie to you, but please—you have to understand—I had to get back here. I couldn't leave her alone by herself. I couldn't do that to her, especially not pregnant. You have to understand. You have to believe me."

My mind is whirring. Meanwhile, I'm also trying to tell my heart to shut up, over and over again.

"Tell her to come out here. Tell her you're going to count to three out loud, and if she doesn't come all the way out where we can see her, all the way out into the headlights, right in front of the kiosk, with both hands and with the gun pointed straight up in the air, by the time you say 'three' I'm going to shoot you."

I can somehow see Brett's eyes in the glass visor of his mask now clearly. Why now? They're wide and white with fear.

"Really?"

"Yes, really. Tell her that. I mean it, too. I'm not

fucking around. This is taking too long."

And it is. Things are changing. My position is changing.

Or it's not. I'm not sure yet. Everything was going so smoothly. How did it all go wrong?

"Please… please, Alex. Please don't shoot me."

"Brett. Tell her you're going to count to three, tell her what I just told you, and then start counting. Do it. Do it now."

I press the end of the rifle right up to the glass of his facemask visor where I can see his eyes clearly for the first time, maybe ever. Definitely ever. They're green. Bright green. Brett's green eyes narrow on the gun and his voice shoots out into the night with a newfound sense of panic and urgency.

"Vicki, she's got a gun on me. She's got it right here, pressed up against my face, right here in the car. Please, baby. Come on out. Come walk out here, out into the light, right in front of that hut thing where the gate is. Keep your hands high up in the air, both hands, and the gun. She doesn't want to hurt me, and she doesn't want to hurt you, but she says this is taking too long, and she's gonna count to three, and if you're not out here by three, she says she's gonna kill me."

There comes a kind of howl in the distance, closer now than the voice was before. Not far at all I think from the kiosk.

"What?! What?!"

"Please, baby. Just do what she says. We're almost done here. You gotta trust me, Vicki. No one's gonna get hurt."

"But she says she's gonna kill you!"

"She says she's gonna do that only if we don't

cooperate! Now, I plan to cooperate, don't you? We'll figure it out. Whatever she needs, whatever she wants, we can live without. Things are not important. We can replace things. What's important is you and me, Vicki Marie, so come on out now!"

This wasn't supposed to go like this.

But then again, how was it supposed to go? Even without the histrionics, wasn't I still planning on stealing from them? It's either theft or ransom. There's no other explanation. Nothing about this plan can be styled virtuous anymore. It was never virtuous to begin with.

I never really *needed* anything I planned to take from them. This isn't me stripping an abandoned vehicle or taking items off a pair of dead men who probably wanted to rape or kill me or both.

This is me trading a man's life back to his eight-months-pregnant wife. I saved that man's life, but he also saved mine. I don't need their food or water. And unless they have a vaccine, a time machine, or a magic spell book that can raise Hope back from the dead, they couldn't possibly possess anything in the world that I truly *need.*

"Start counting."

"Alex…"

"START COUNTING!"

"One!"

Brett gives it a lengthy pause, and I can't say I blame him in the slightest.

Do I blame myself for this, too?

"Two!"

His voice cracks, and so does my resolve.

Brett Taylor doesn't want to say 'three.' He wants for all the world not to say 'three.'

I'm right there with him. Silently, I hope and I pray he never says it. We can stay out here all night in silence just so long as he doesn't say 'three.'

Vicki Marie Taylor saves us all. She comes stumbling up from out of nowhere and half-runs, half-falls over the low curb that surrounds the kiosk. With both hands in the air—and with one of them clutching a gun that's pointed up to the sky—she arrives at the designated spot and becomes fully visible in the ambient glow cast off from the low beams of the jeep.

"I'm here, I'm here! Please, God, don't shoot! I'm here!"

There is no mistaking the fact that she is sobbing right now in her gas mask, which must be a feeling akin to sticking your head in a blender, filling it with water, and slowly drowning in it.

The first thing I notice about her is that she is indeed very, very pregnant. Vicki looks like her water might very well break right here in front of us, standoff be damned.

Her swollen stomach is only further accentuated by the way it's not entirely covered by the shirt she's wearing, which looks like it might have once belonged to Brett instead of her. The shirt is baggy up around her neck, shoulders, and arms, but grows tight the further down it goes, until the hem ends rather abruptly at her exposed belly button, which is about the size of a golf ball.

She's short—very short, shorter than I expected her to be, for some reason. Maybe some of this is an optical illusion because of how big her belly is, but it seems that the vast majority of Vicki is concentrated between her neck to her waist. Her legs are minute little things wrapped in stained sweatpants that dead-end in small utility boots.

Vicki must wear her hair short, because I can't see any of it spilling out beneath her mask. Granted, she's facing me, so maybe it's tied behind her and draped down her back.

Her shoulders rise and fall at irregular rhythms with her sobs, which seem to rock her whole body from head to toe. I can easily hear her crying through her mask and all the way over here on the other side of the jeep.

"Please… please don't hurt him! Please!"

"Toss the gun over the jeep!"

"What?!"

"I said toss the gun up over the jeep! Quickly, now!"

She rears back and launches the gun with all her strength. It sails through the air and gets lost for a few seconds against the black night sky before I hear it land with a thud not far behind me.

Slowly, carefully, I take a few steps backward, removing the end of the rifle from Brett's facemask but keeping it trained on him the whole time. I keep walking backward slowly until I almost trip.

A quick downward glance reveals what's under my foot, and sure enough, it's the gun.

I'm impressed, Vicki Marie Taylor. Not a bad arm for a short, eight-months-pregnant woman stuck in the throes of a crying fit.

With the rifle still pointed straight ahead at Brett, I gingerly lower myself down on my hamstrings until I can remove my left hand, my non-trigger hand, reach down, and pick it up. I then spring back up—and maybe a bit too quickly—because the damned stars appear in my vision, and I start to feel lightheaded.

Not now. Please, not now. This is the worst possible

time.

I give my head a quick jerk of a shake and hope that neither Brett nor Vicki Taylor notice anything peculiar.

It sort of works. The stars are still there, but I'm not feeling as faint.

Whatever. As long as I don't pass out, I'll be okay. The hallucinations are annoying but manageable. Going unconscious is not manageable.

My left hand slides the Taylors' gun in behind me so that I now have two guns tucked down the back of my pants in my waistline, plus the rifle, of course, in my hands.

An absurd thought trickles into my brain that I'm becoming some kind of cowgirl vigilante sharpshooter. A more practical thought silences that one by reminding my brain that I'm still seeing stars from simply standing up too fast. Let's keep it together, now, shall we?

"Vicki, I want you to listen to me. My name is Alex. I have no intention of hurting you."

Her body is still convulsing with emotion.

"Please… please just go… just leave us alone…"

"That's exactly what I'm going to do. But first, I need you to do me one last favor—"

"We don't have anything! We don't have enough as is. Please, please!"

I'm moving as slowly and unassumingly as I can. I don't want to spook her, and the last thing I need is for her to run. She'd be a fool to run, since I now have all the guns—at least, I think I do. And, more importantly, I still have her husband locked up in my car.

But she's also probably not thinking straight right now. She's clearly overcome with fear and anxiety, both over what has happened so far and over what she probably thinks is still possible here tonight.

There's no other way to do this, though, than by me approaching her now and holding her at gunpoint. That's how we wrap this whole ordeal up. She has to show me what's in their 'house.'

Do I plan on taking anything? That depends.

If there's more than enough there and they've been lying to me, then absolutely, yes. I'll also probably kick myself for backpedaling at all on this plan and for allowing myself to get conned and to let my own emotions and my sense of empathy get the better of me once again.

But if what they're both saying now, this latest rendition of Brett's story, is accurate, and if they really don't have anything or don't have much, then I might just leave them alone after all like she wants me to.

I'll bring her back out here to help him out of the jeep, and then I'll get in and drive away, and I'll toss the keys out the window as planned. I've decided I might even leave them their gun, assuming this is how it all turns out. That would feel right. It would make me feel a lot better about how everything has gone down tonight.

Wouldn't it? It would be enough. Leaving them with what they have and with their gun for protection. Assuming they have enough to get by. For a week. 'Maybe a little longer,' Brett said. It might be longer than a week. Long enough to get them through the birth. They could make it that far.

I know they couldn't, though. Now I'm the one who's lying, only I'm lying to myself, not to them. It wouldn't be enough, and they couldn't make it that far. Not if it's like she says it is. There's no way they could.

But that's not my problem. They're not my responsibility. I don't owe them anything. What more do I have to do? I already saved his life, dragged his ass up out of that basement, nursed him back to health, and drove him all the way out here. Gas is only less precious than food and water. What more could I do for them, anyway?

Purposefully, I will my brain not to answer that question as I come at last within about ten feet of Vicki.

"Listen. Listen! I'm not going to hurt you. I didn't save your husband's life and bring him all the way out here just so I could hurt you or him. I have no intention of pulling this trigger tonight. But I will if I have to. You understand?"

"Please… please just leave us alone…"

"Vicki! You have to listen to me! I'm going to leave you alone…"

But am I?

"I'm going to get back in my car and drive away just as soon as you show me what's in that building over there. You'll never see me again. But I need to see what's in there first."

Do I?

"Just walk me back there now, let me take a quick look around, show me you're not lying, show me you're not sitting on a whole hoard of food and water and supplies back there, and I'll go."

"Why can't you just leave us—"

"VICKI!"

It's actually not me this time, and it takes all my reflexive power and self-restraint not to spin around in surprise. If I'd done that, she could have reached out and pulled this rifle right out of my hands, I'll bet. That's how shocked I was and am to hear Brett's voice boom out from behind me.

"Do as she asks! Take her inside and show her what she needs to see!"

Brett's voice works a kind of magic on Vicki. Her shoulders stop shrugging up and down, her chest stops heaving, and she catches herself in the middle of a sob.

The last thing that happens is she opens her eyes a bit wider, and now I see them for the first time. They're just as green as her husband's.

I bet the baby's eyes will be green, too.

"Okay. Okay."

She nods, collects herself, and turns around slowly, checking in with me the whole time, like she wants to make sure that's okay with me. I wave the rifle forward as if to say let's go, it's fine, just walk.

And that's exactly what she does. She walks, slowly but precisely, past the kiosk, turning her head frequently to continue checking in with me, wanting so badly to be right, wanting not to make a wrong move, keeping her arms up high and her fingers scratching at the stars.

There's a soft, flickering light coming from the open doorway of where she's taking me, what I assume must be the ranger station.

As we draw nearer, I start to realize the light for what it is: fire. Sure enough, as she crosses over the doorway threshold and I follow in close behind her, the first thing I notice is a modest fire burning in a small stone fireplace in the corner.

Vicki and I stand in the center of a room that's not much bigger than my bedroom at home. There's a twin-sized cot in the corner opposite the fireplace that can't possibly be large enough to accommodate both of the

Taylors, given how pregnant a woman Vicki is. In front of the fireplace is a small loveseat with a soiled, torn blanket and a grubby pillow stacked atop one of the cushions. I'd assume one of them probably sleeps there. Probably Brett.

The kitchen area doesn't have much. There's a fridge that of course no longer functions, a stove that no longer functions, and a sink that no longer functions. A couple cupboards; maybe one of them serves as a pantry. A wooden counter.

That's about it as far as furnishings. The walls are all just plain wood; no décor of any kind. Either the last park ranger to occupy this space was a super minimalist nature freak who didn't believe in making an abode in the great outdoors feel 'homey,' or whoever's been here since has picked this place clean.

I notice the two windows in the building are not reinforced or boarded up in any way, shape, or form. That's another lie from Brett that I'm not the least bit mad at, given the reality that's increasingly setting in for me. There's only one door, it's wide open, and neither side of it features any modifications, defenses, or reinforcements. I'm not even seeing any extra locks on there.

"Where do you keep your food and water?"

Silently, Vicki lowers one arm and points her index finger at the two small cupboards in the kitchen area. Together, they can't be more than twenty cubic feet.

"Where else?"

"That's it."

"Nowhere else? You don't have more stashed somewhere else on the property? Don't lie to me, Vicki."

"I'm not lying. That's all we have. I told you we

barely have enough for ourselves as is. And we're about to have a baby…"

Her voice trails off into a hollow whimper.

I keep the gun pointed at Vicki as I walk a wide semicircle around her to the kitchen. With my right hand holding the gun and my finger still on the trigger, I reach my left hand up to throw open the cabinet doors. I then back up so I can get a good vantage point on what's inside, while still keeping my focus on Vicki.

She's not lying. One cupboard contains all their water: a ragtag assortment of canteens, plastic bottles, glass vases, and converted kitchen pots and pans. The see-through items reveal that not all of these containers are even full. Some are barely filled at all, it appears.

If the water situation is bad, the food situation is even worse. At least the water cabinet was mostly full of containers and storage receptacles, even if they weren't all fully utilized. The food cabinet itself is half empty. What's there isn't much, either: most of the berries, fruits, and vegetables are in various states of rot and decay. Small flies buzz around the items that are the worst off.

"This is really where you two have been staying?"

Vicki nods tearfully.

"And you intend to stay here to have your child? What kind of supplies do you have on hand for that?"

Vicki's head goes from bobbing up and down to shaking left and right.

"Nothing. We don't have anything."

"Vicki–"

"I'm not lying to you! That's why Brett went out. To get more food and water, yes, but also to get the things we need to have the baby."

I'd never say this out loud to them, but I find it highly dubious that either Brett or Vicki really knows 'the things they need to have a baby.' My guess is that Brett was just planning on grabbing every kind of medicine or piece of medical equipment he could find on his foraging trip in the blind hope that something might work for them. It's not as if they can use the internet for research, after all.

I give Vicki a long, penetrating assessment, and she holds up under it from the other side of the rifle and my gaze. Her body still gives off some physical cues that she's working hard to stem the tears, but as far as I can tell, she's staring right back at me now through her mask, daring me to call her a liar.

Is it better to do what's right or to do what's smart?

I've spent so many years doing what's smart instead of what's right. Lately, though, it seems I've been on a real kick of doing dumb shit just because it feels like it's the right thing to do.

Will that catch up with me eventually? It sure seems like a virtual certainty.

But then again, what do I really have to lose anymore?

A voice in my head instantly answers 'your life,' but that answer just doesn't move me like it once used to. I'm not actively looking for death; I'm too much of a fighter, a survivor. I can't help that, since I've spent my whole existence trying to foster new life and help those in need stave off the specter of death, loss, grief, and loneliness. It's just how I'm wired.

But loneliness… loneliness is beginning to feel worse than death to me.

The cat is one thing. Is it enough, though? Could

there be a world where I rediscover my true purpose again before the world finally ends?

"All right, Vicki. I want you to take that blanket off the couch over there."

It's impossible to read her expression as she maintains eye contact with me. She doesn't move, though, so I gesture to the loveseat with the rifle.

"Come on. Quickly now."

The gun prompts her into action. Vicki moves over to the couch, picks up the decrepit blanket, and holds it out to me.

"Not yet. We're going to walk back outside now, all the way to my car, okay?"

It's still taking her longer than I'd like to follow my commands, but I try to give her the benefit of the doubt, because I'm assuming she's fantastically confused right about now.

I follow close behind her as we exit the ranger station, and I don't bother to close the door behind me as we make our way toward the jeep. Brett watches us from the back seat. I wonder if he's as confused as Vicki must be.

For that matter, I wonder just how confused I might be in the head for making this whole about-face.

"I want you to walk around to the other side and get in the back seat with your husband."

Vicki immediately turns and puts her hands together in a praying motion, blanket and all.

"Please, no, you said you wouldn't hurt us!"

"I'm not going to hurt you. Just… *please*. Please get in the back seat with Brett. I just want to talk to you both for a second if I can. I… I want to help you."

Vicki is still for a moment or two. But then she

turns, opens the car door, and slowly eases her way up and into the back seat, with one hand on the blanket and one hand on her belly.

When she's fully in and clear, I close the door gently behind her, and then I lower my rifle for the first time since we arrived.

"Listen to me. I want to help you. I want to help you both… with the baby."

They both just stare at me from inside the vehicle.

"Back… before all this… I was a doctor. I was an OB-GYN, as a matter of fact. Chief resident at my hospital. Before all this happened… before the world went to shit… I helped deliver hundreds of babies. Probably more than a thousand, actually. I'm very good at it."

They're still just staring. Waiting, I guess, for me to say more?

"Now, obviously, it won't be the same today as it was back then. That goes without saying. I don't have a hospital, the proper equipment, a staff of doctors and nurses to assist me. But you know all that. What I do have, though, is a decent store of medical supplies, tools, and medications, some of which I got from the same house you were at, Brett, down in that basement. You know all this, too."

He slowly nods but is otherwise silent.

"Here's what I'm willing to do for you. I will bring you back to my home, provided you agree to ride there blindfolded. I'm not comfortable allowing you to roam around free, which I'm sure you'll understand. But if you're open to it, you can stay and sleep in a spare bedroom, provided you accept the fact I will keep the door locked from the outside. Maybe… in time… we can relax some of these rules, or modify them, to make it feel a bit less like you're being held prisoner. That will depend entirely on trust, however, and on how you both behave and choose to act."

Since I'm making this all up on the fly, it sure would be nice to have some kind of verbal reaction, or even just a visible facial reaction or expression, to go off of right now. If it weren't for Brett nodding a second ago, I'd wonder whether they're even listening to me.

"While you're with me at the house, you'll do as I say, and you'll follow all of my orders like your lives depend on it. Because they do. In exchange, you'll receive food, water, shelter—and I mean a *real* shelter with a *real* supply of food and water, not whatever this is. I will also help you deliver the baby when the time comes, which I'm sure won't be long now."

Perhaps self-consciously, Vicki's hands rub her stomach in small circles.

"Once the baby is born, however, that will be the end of this arrangement. As much as I'd like to believe you're both good people, and I'm sure you are, I'm also sure you'll understand that I can't take any chances. I'm already taking what most people would consider too big a chance right here in suggesting all this. But the truth is that I want to help you, so if you're willing, I'm willing to lend a hand.

"And then, once it's done and once the baby's born, I'll drive the three of you out to your truck if it's still there, I'll give you the key, I'll give you back your gun, and that will be that. If I can spare some extra rations, I'll spare those, too. Maybe, assuming this all works out all right for the next couple weeks or however long it takes for the baby to arrive, maybe you both can even earn your keep, so to speak, around the house. You can earn the rations and supplies you consume while you're with me, and you can earn what you take when you leave. We'll see how it all works out."

Vicki is still rubbing her stomach. Brett slowly lowers his chin to his chest.

"What do you think?"

Vicki turns to look at Brett. He keeps his chin to his chest for another second or two, then lifts it up to face me.

"Why are you doing this? Why are you helping us?"

I fidget with the gun at my side.

"Because… because it's the right thing to do, I guess. Is that a good enough reason for you?"

Vicki beats Brett to the punch as she turns back to me.

"Yes. Oh my God, yes, it is. We don't need a reason. We're just so grateful, truly so grateful you'd be willing to do any of this at all for us. Whatever you ask of us, we'll do it. Anything. God bless you. God bless you for this… Alex. God bless you, Alex."

Brett nods again.

"You truly are an angel sent to us from above. We'll never be able to thank you for all that you've done for us. First for me, and now for both of us, and for the baby. Thank you. God bless you."

I guess I shouldn't be surprised that the Taylors seem to be God-fearing Christian folks.

Anyway, it's best to get this show on the road before they start breaking into song or Vicki starts weeping again and tries to kiss my feet or something similarly strange. This interaction was always doomed to be awkward, but it's currently borderline unbearable.

"All right. Good. I'm glad we're all on the same page. I guess… is there anything you two need in there?"

Vicki shakes her head profusely.

"Not a thing. You saw it in there. We don't have anything worth saving."

That's for sure.

"Well, all right, then. Vicki, I need you to tear that blanket in half. Like I warned you, there are parts of this arrangement that aren't necessarily going to be pleasant for the two of you, but unfortunately, they're non-negotiable. I'm going to get some duct tape from the glove compartment, and when I come back around, I'm going to ask you to put your seatbelt on and to try and relax as I tie your hands together. Again, it's only temporary, and I'm sure you understand the precaution, since we only just met. I'm also going to tape half the blanket over each of your heads. I'll make sure you have plenty of room to breathe and I'll tear holes for airflow at the bottom. But again, this is how it has to be, especially since I wasn't planning on bringing anyone back for this return trip."

Vicki and Brett Taylor share a look.

"Are we good on all that?"

Together as one, they turn to face me, each nodding, as Vicki begins to tear the blanket in half. She's the one who speaks.

"Whatever you ask of us, it shall be done."

TEN

Hope was right. She was right about everything.

If I wasn't still in shock and in mourning, maybe I'd find it funny, and maybe I could muster up a bitter laugh. Even from beyond the pale, she's managed to prove once again that she really did know best.

I'm not sure I'll ever drive again after everything I've endured today.

As if it wasn't enough to have to wheel my dead wife out to my car shortly after taking her off life support, as if it wasn't enough to have to lay her out in the back seat without any kind of shroud and then to hear her roll up against the back of my chair every time I had to punch the brakes hard, as if it wasn't enough to hit and probably kill another human being by running him down in order to escape in one piece, as if it wasn't enough to make a mad dash to rescue Ruthie from our home and then to flee the city with our lives… these episodes were more than enough to convince me to never go back, and perhaps never to drive again in general.

But you know what? Hope was right. Because I'll be damned if as soon as we started to get out into the country, everything just became so much easier and lighter by comparison.

No more crazy, evil people rushing out onto the road to try and jack the car while I'm in it. No dodging and weaving around all manner of improvised projectile weapons being hurled at the windshield. No dodging and weaving around all manner of *human beings*—human beings who were lost, confused, terrified, or desperate— wandering out into traffic or running from some terrible threat I never want to see or imagine. No more fire. No more gunfire. No more dead bodies, abandoned vehicles, and burning buildings.

Whether that destruction and devastation has made it to our house as of yet, I don't know, and I don't care anymore. I wasn't about to stick around to find out.

It was already far too close, just seeing it all on the way there, speeding along against time and against the most wicked aspects of human nature. I thank my lucky stars the house wasn't up in smoke when I got there, and that Ruthie was unhurt and utterly unfazed by all the chaos raging in the world around her.

There wasn't time to grab much. Again, maybe there might have been more time than I knew, but it wasn't worth risking. In my mind, it was a miracle just making it there at all. I didn't press my luck. I grabbed our dog, I grabbed Hope's keys to the summer house, and I grabbed a large plastic tub of mementos and important documents from out of our closet. That was it.

Why the tub? I don't know. I guess because my brain always equated that container with being the receptacle of important things to save in an emergency or in a fire. Hope and I had been meaning for a while to invest in a fireproof safe and had just never gotten around to it. In the meantime, we'd been putting important things—things like our college diplomas, our marriage certificate, our social security cards, etc.—in the tub, along with random artifacts and bits and pieces of memorabilia we deemed special and worth preserving and protecting.

So, I grabbed those three things—the tub, the dog, the keys—and I got back in the jeep, started it up, drove away from that house, and didn't look back.

That's not entirely true. It's actually not true at all; I looked back the whole time. I looked back so much I nearly ran into a mailbox while driving.

Because that wasn't just a house: that was our house. It was our first house together as partners. Our first house together as a married couple. And I knew then, as I swerved to miss the mailbox by inches, that it would be our last house together, as well.

I had Ruthie up front on the floormat below the passenger seat because I didn't want her to see Hope. Keeping them separate and away from each other felt like the best course of action at the time until I could come up with a plan. Fuck, until I could let out a breath and just process all of it myself.

But she was right. Hope was right. The further and further we got away from the city and civilization, the less crazy it all got.

Soon, the smoke and the bullets and the angry or horrified faces were all just bad memories in one big, bad dream. And by the time the houses stopped altogether, you never would have been able to tell the world was starting to end in the first place.

Thankfully, no matter how much society feels like it's on the brink of collapse, the last thing to go is the corporations. There's too much money invested in all the big companies that work with all the other big companies, and as a result, the people with stakes in all those companies would rather have their own neighborhoods get razed than their offices, corporate headquarters, stock portfolios, and bank accounts.

Because of that greed, my phone has service, and because my phone has service, I'm able to navigate to the Bergstroms' summer house without issue.

This is my first time ever coming here by myself. No matter how close you get with your in-laws—and I never really got *that* close to Hope's parents before they passed from NDV—it's still just not something most people would ever do, going to your in-laws' house without your spouse accompanying you on the visit.

Technically, Hope is accompanying me on this visit. But I don't want to think about it that way.

The property is exactly the way I remember it. It's been a few years since we last made it out here, on account of Hope's parents getting sick and then becoming some of the first victims claimed by the virus, but it hasn't changed.

That's part of the magic of this structure, way out here by itself in the middle of the woods. There's just something timeless about it. The biggest change that happens is the cycling of the seasons year after year as the leaves change color in the trees, fall off, and regrow all over again.

As for the house itself, it still looks the same today as it did the very first time Hope brought me out when we were still just dating casually.

That was an experience. Hope had made it clear to me that, at least according to them, her parents had no problem with her sexual orientation. What Hope failed to realize in retrospect, I believe, is that although her parents might not have said aloud they had any problem with her sexual orientation, they may have inwardly harbored their misgivings and judgments. Because believe me: there was *plenty* of judgment to go around in the way they looked at me and talked to me that whole weekend when we first met.

It doesn't matter now, though. None of this matters now. The Bergstroms are dead, and so is Hope.

Now it's just me and Ruthie, setting up shop—I guess?—until this whole thing blows over, and we get the official word from on high that it's safe to go back to work; that a vaccine has been secretly developed, mass-produced, and widely distributed from some underground government bunker, that all these 'patriots' have finally been imprisoned, and that sanity has been restored.

Ruthie lets out a low whine as soon as the car comes to a stop. I recognize the sound as being her signal that she needs to use the restroom. It's only now, now that we're here alone far, far away from home, that I realize just how long she's been holding it.

The poor thing no doubt expected I'd be letting her out as soon as I walked in the door. Instead, I yanked her up, threw her in the jeep with me, and took her for a long car ride. I'm actually stunned she didn't wet herself on the floorboard. Hope raised her well.

That thought causes a bubble of despair to sneak up into my throat, so I clear it forcefully, blink my eyes a couple times, loop around to the passenger side, and open the door for our nine-year-old fur-baby to use the facilities of the great outdoors. Ruthie is too good of a dog to need a leash out here, so I'm not worried about her running away when she darts off into the bushes to find the perfect spot for relief.

Besides, where would she run off to, anyway? There's nothing out here for miles in any direction.

As our dog—as my dog—answers nature's call, I lean against the hood of the jeep and wonder what happens next. There's no playbook or manual for Armageddon, assuming that's what this is. I still haven't given up hope that order will eventually be restored along with normalcy, but I'm also not dumb enough to think that today's events are ordinary.

There have certainly been times in my life where I wondered just how close we were as a race of creatures on this planet to exterminating ourselves, but never— *ever*—did I really think it would actually happen. Call it optimism, call it naivete, call it whatever you want, but I was always right, at least. No matter how dire things got nationally, internationally, or even personally, we always found a way to get through it. This too shall pass, and all that. One of my favorite personal mantras.

Today, though… today felt different.

All of this, these events these past five years, it's all felt like a snowball rolling down an icy mountain. At first, there's not much cause for concern; it's just a snowball. But the faster it rolls, the more it picks up speed and additional snow, and before you know it, this thing is the size of a boulder, and then it's the size of a house, and then a hotel, and then it's just a full-fledged avalanche that comes down from God to bury you alive and leave you cold, dead, and breathless.

That's the point we're at now, I fear. Hope predicted this would happen two years ago, and I scoffed at the notion. Fast-forward to today: Hope is dead, I killed her, and here I am now at her childhood summer home with absolutely no idea what I'm supposed to do next.

Survive. That's the word that keeps tickling the back of my brain.

It's an annoying sensation, and one I've been trying to ignore, but it won't go away… and perhaps for good reason. If this is truly the end, as she predicted—and clearly, I'm overdue to start listening to her—then I need to start doing what she wanted us to be doing when she was still alive. Back before she contracted the virus and before she slipped away from me.

We're here now, at the house in the forest. So, that's a start.

This is what she suggested two years ago. She thought this would be the safest place for us to go, and though it's early, she's already proven herself once again to be preternaturally wise. Maybe it's all the butterflies floating around and the birds singing in the trees, but this place feels like a utopian paradise. It feels like I just barely escaped the snapping fiery jaws of hell and have now stumbled upon my own private slice of heaven, or at least the Garden of Eden. Pre-snake Garden of Eden—that's an important distinction to clarify.

What now, though? I'm here. Better late than never. I have the keys to the place. What are the necessities in a survival-type scenario? Food, water, shelter. I've got one of those three. Unless it's secretly even worse out here than it is in the cities and I just haven't realized it yet, I'm assuming I have running water inside, along with electricity. So that's all good.

Food is probably the best place to start. I don't have any cash on me, but based off my prior assumptions and beliefs concerning the corporations and how money is the true fabric and lifeblood of America, my credit card should work just fine. All I need to do is search for the nearest general store and/or supermarket on my phone and then load up like it's Y2K.

Out here in the country, I bet that sort of thing happens all the time, actually. Not to stereotype, but these rural folks are usually the ones buying into all that nonsense and building the bomb shelters.

Of course, now I have a new perspective on that. I guess they were right all along. And here I am, out in the country, about to join them.

Ruthie trots back out from the edge of the woods looking like a brand new dog. She's absolutely clueless about what is happening, both on the grander stage of the world as well as right here at home with our little family. Poor thing has no clue that it's just her and me now. I wonder if the smell of Hope in the car was a comfort to her on some specifically canine level.

That thought leads to a new one that is far less pleasant. The smell of Hope in the car... I can't leave her in the car. It's too hot outside.

As hard as I am working to not constantly think about Hope—and I acknowledge I am doing a horrifically bad job—I also can't just forget everything I know about human beings from almost twenty years of medical practice and study. Thanks to all those popular police and doctor shows on TV, even most people without an M.D. probably can guess what happens with a dead body unless it's kept properly cooled and maintained.

My brain goes to the plastic tub. I know that somewhere in there, probably towards the bottom, is a manila envelope that contains both of our wills. I also know from prior conversations with Hope—usually morbid but funny ones where we'd both been drinking too much beer or whiskey—that neither one of our wills took into possible consideration a death occurring in the midst of global upheaval and societal breakdown. Does anyone's will take that into consideration?

Enough. I'll dig out those documents later and see what can realistically be accommodated still and what will require modification. First things first, I need to get her inside, and I need to turn the thermostat way down low. After I do that, I need to quickly make a list of everything I think that I'll need to survive.

For how long? I don't know. Maybe I should just max out my credit card and get as much of everything that I can until there's no room left in the jeep. That's probably the best call. Better to be overprepared than underprepared. That's what these country folks have believed this whole time, and now they're getting the last laugh. Although it's hard to believe that anyone is actually laughing right now with what's happening out there.

RBG sits on her hindquarters and pants in the hot sun, watching me patiently and waiting for whatever happens next.

It's time to get both of you girls inside where it's cooler. Sad as it may make you though, Ruthie, I think it's best to keep you separated from one another while I'm gone.

Ruthie comes in with me first as we do a quick walkthrough of the house to assess its state in various capacities. She's not much help. This is her first time here—Hope's mother was allergic, so we always had to board her when we visited in the summer—and she's already making the most of it, running from room to room enthusiastically, sniffing away at all the fascinating new smells and generally acting like a dog half her age.

Not for the first time today, I wish that we could trade places, Ruthie and I. Ignorance might not always be bliss, but it absolutely is on today, of all days.

Much to my relief, the water runs unencumbered from every faucet I turn on in the kitchen and bathrooms. The toilets flush, the lights all turn on, the A/C comes whirring to life with only a second or two of notice. When I turn the knobs on the stove, blue flames pop up, and the oven coils grow red when I fiddle with the buttons above. The digital clocks on the oven and microwave are flashing the wrong time, but that's easily corrected. Probably the work of the most recent thunderstorm that came through here and caused a temporary loss of power.

Ruthie is not pleased when I corner her in the second bedroom—the one Hope used as a kid, and the one we always slept in when we visited as adults. She seems confused and disappointed when I close the doors to the bathroom and the upstairs hallway, bend down, scratch her beneath her chin, and promise that I'll be right back. I truly hope, for her sake, that I will.

After I've ducked out the door and closed it behind me, I mentally steel myself for the next task in what seems like an endless slate of mentally and emotionally exhausting tasks.

Task. I can't believe I just called what I have to do now a task. This isn't a task. It's a nightmare. This whole damn thing is a nightmare.

When am I going to wake up?

Nearly four hours later, I return to the house with the jeep stuffed full of supplies.

Canned goods, non-perishables, gallons upon gallons of clean drinking water. Batteries of all shapes and sizes. Gasoline, oil, propane. A small generator. Rope, tape, twine. Tarps, a sleeping bag, a tent, a blow-up air mattress. Starter logs, firewood, matches, lighters, a fire extinguisher. Vegetable and fruit seeds. A hammer, a saw, a wrench, a drill, a machete, an axe. Nails, screws, drill bits. Flashlights. Pepper spray, bug spray, bear-repellent spray. A water purifier and a solar-powered USB charging station. Extra clothes, hats, gloves, boots, socks, gas masks. Three first aid kits, thirteen NDV testing kits, a whole menagerie of medicines, drugs, ointments, salves, bandages, and other common medical tools and goods you can find outside a hospital. Two bottles of Templeton Rye.

Basically, everything you'd find by doing a Google search on how to survive a zombie apocalypse, because ashamedly, that's one of the searches I actually did. Though it certainly wasn't the only one. I also consulted far more reputable articles and sources for my impromptu shopping list.

The only items I consciously omitted were the weapons. I debated back and forth on whether or not it was worth arming myself with guns, knives, or even some of the more extraordinary weapons I came across, such as a barbed-wire baseball bat, a crossbow, and a battle-spear (all from the zombie apocalypse survival website).

Ultimately, I passed on all of these weapons. I've never been a fan of guns, and I have no idea how to use them. If ever there was a time to learn, that time looks

like now, I'll admit. But still, I'm holding out hope—
perhaps a vain, ludicrous hope—that all of this will end
before I'm ever forced to fire a gun or learn how to use
one.

Worst-case scenario, I can always defend myself
with the machete or the axe.

Actually, true worst-case scenario, I can use the fire
extinguisher. I've sadly already had practice with that
one; at least mentally.

Even out here in the most rural parts of our nation,
you could tell something was wrong in the stores.
Outside, driving past the occasional farm, ranch, or
cabin, you'd never know a thing. Ditto for all the nature
out here as well.

But once *inside* the stores, it became impossible to
forget just how rapidly and how severely things had
taken a turn for the worse. I was shocked to see how
picked over every place was that I visited, considering
the remoteness of this location and how sparsely
populated it is. The overall feeling I got inside each store
was that I was already somehow too late, even out here
in the boonies. People had beaten me to it and picked
clean most of the items I had on my list at any given
location, which forced me to visit far more locations
than I really felt comfortable or safe doing so. But I did
it anyway, because I had to.

Those people I did encounter moved quickly and
wordlessly about their business, every bit as intent on
getting in and getting out as I was. No one spoke to one
another. The only sound being produced came over the
intercoms at the local grocery store, where classic 80s
soft rock hits somehow took on a ghastly, haunting
quality with most of the market aisles abandoned.

One store I went to didn't have anyone in there at all. No customers, and no employees, either. I walked in the door of this establishment—a kind of cross between a convenience store and a post office, I believe—and realized right away that I was utterly alone, even though the door was unlocked, and all the lights were on.

Did I feel bad stealing from that place? I'll admit that I did. I probably even lingered longer than I should have at the checkout counter, yelling some variation of "is anybody here?" more times than I needed to. There was never any doubt in my mind from the moment I entered that place that I was by myself, but I still had doubts that I'd actually just grab whatever I needed and walk right out without paying, survival of the fittest be damned.

But that's exactly what I did. I did what I had to do at the few places I could check out. This area doesn't have a whole lot of offerings to begin with, and unsurprisingly, most of the spots I came across were locked up, had their lights turned off, and bore no signs on the windows or doors to explain why.

All the explanation necessary could be found easily by listening to the car radio or going absolutely anywhere online. Everything was dire; everything was bleak. Nothing was promising or optimistic. Whole cities were on the brink of collapse. It wasn't just happening here in America, either. The world was suffering. The planet was dying.

No, that wasn't quite accurate. The *people* on the planet were all dying.

Halfway back to the house, I turned the radio off entirely. All that anybody knew wasn't good, and most of what they wanted to discuss, it seemed nobody really knew for sure anyway. Wild theories, doomsday conjectures, melodramatic monologues or rants about random trivialities. After a while, it just became intolerable. I finished the long drive in silent reflection, preparing myself as much as I could for what comes next.

What comes next. I'm here in the driveway, and I can't even begin to imagine what comes next.

Immediately, I know that what comes next is I'll unlock the door, I'll unload the car, and I'll let Ruthie out of Hope's old room and take her outside again. But after that… that's where all this gets impossibly surreal and impossibly difficult.

I can do a more thorough inventory of the house. That's probably my smartest move. Honestly, I should have probably done that before I took off to gather supplies. Maybe I bought some things that are already here.

And then I remind myself that it doesn't matter. If I open that kitchen pantry and I find ten thousand cans of Spam and twenty thousand gallons of drinking water, it doesn't matter. There's no such thing as having too much of anything right now.

Hopefully, that won't always be the case. But for the time being, it most definitely is.

***

The last time I was this drunk, I was this drunk with Hope. That fact is not lost on me. Neither is the fact that Hope is no longer alive.

And neither is the fact that her body is wrapped in

blankets and lying in the dark all alone on the mattress in her parents' bedroom, probably directly above my head right now.

I look up at the ceiling and imagine for a minute that I hear something. My ears and my brain try to collaborate and cook up a fantasy where I hear footsteps up there that move out and to the staircase. They get my eyes in on it, too, and I pretend that she materializes now at the top of the stairs, smiling that devilish, playful, fuck-me-or-fight-me trademark smile of hers down at me. I can hear her voice calling out to me, asking me what I'm doing all the way out here at her parents' place, at the vacation house, by myself. She's wondering why I'm drinking alone and sitting here without the TV on or any music, and she's giving me a hard time about it. I miss the way she teases me.

Yeah, that's right. Go on. Drink up, me hearties, yo-ho. Yo-ho, yo-ho, a pirate's life for me.

I miss Disneyland. Why did we never do that together? She would have been so cute with Minnie Mouse ears on her head.

Fuck.

There's so much we never did together. So much we had planned to do together and never got the chance.

Or, we got the chance, we had chances, and we didn't take them.

Because of me. Because of my job. Because of my ego and my pride.

Fuck.

I pour myself some more.

This was not on the itinerary tonight, this drinking myself drunk and wallowing in self-pity and guilt. But on some subconscious level, I guess I expected it would happen. Why else would I buy two bottles of whiskey? I didn't buy them for the damn dog.

The damn dog sleeps on the sofa next to me in the living room, her head in my lap. Still blissfully ignorant, that one.

If dogs are supposed to have a sixth sense about knowing when something's wrong, this one apparently lost it somewhere along the way. Ruth Bader Ginsburg is conked out without a care in the world. She has no idea what she's lost. I'm only just beginning to grasp it all myself.

Though I bought the whiskey with the intention to drink it, I didn't intend to drink this much until I found the envelope in the tub of documents and mementos. Rifling past polaroid photographs, handwritten cards, her birth certificate, her passport, our marriage certificate… it's a wonder I didn't reach for the bottle right then and there.

But when I found what I was looking for, opened it, and started reading, that's when I knew it was time to start drinking. Particularly when I got to the sections where Hope indicated it was her wish to pass down all her worth and assets to a child, or to split it up evenly amongst multiple children, that her and her partner Alex planned to adopt one day.

This did not come as a surprise. Hope and I had long discussed the possibility of children in our future. With my job being what it was, I found myself constantly around newborn children and their parents, so it never really felt as high or as immediate of a priority for me as it was for her.

But for Hope, motherhood was a must. It was a mandatory destination on the roadmap of her life, maybe even her manifest destiny, and she spent our entire time together gently but consistently pushing and prodding me toward it, with the pressure only intensifying after we moved in together, and especially after we got married.

Seeing it in writing, though, there in black and white on official legal documents, was a stark, brutal reminder of just how much I failed her.

Hence, whiskey. Lots and lots and lots of whiskey.

Bitterly, I think to myself of the one bit of good news I found in the will. Not that 'good news' and 'will' can ever coexist in any way.

I knew she wanted to be buried one day, but I never knew exactly where. If I had to guess, I would have guessed out here, but then again, I wasn't sure. She was never super close with her parents, but at least she had a better childhood with them than I did with my mom. And though she still saw them on the odd holiday and brought me around for a few of those, as well as some trips out here during the summertime, I never knew for sure just how much this place actually might mean to her.

Until I saw it there in writing. She wanted to be buried right here. Out in the forest somewhere.

Legally, I'm not sure you can do that. You can't just put a body in the ground wherever you see fit.

But it's not the official legal will where she specifies this. She actually, at some point or time, typed out and printed a piece of paper, addressed to me, declaring her desire to be buried here if at all possible.

As a backup plan, she said she would be willing to get cremated so her ashes could be scattered in the forest if burial proved to be unfeasible legally or logistically.

But she made it perfectly clear in her letter that her preference was to go 'au natural.' She didn't even want a coffin. Just put her in the earth where she could immediately get absorbed and become one with the soil, the plants, the animals.

This is the sort of thing I never, ever would have accepted had she brought it up with me; which, no doubt, explains why she never did, instead choosing to write out this document on her own in secret and slip it in the envelope inside the tub without my knowledge.

Oh, Hope. You sly devil. You dirty, sexy, hippie devil.

I pour myself some more as I re-read the letter.

Did she know? Could she have somehow known on some level when she wrote this what would happen?

Maybe she wrote it sometime these past two years. It's not improbable to think that at all. She wouldn't have had to be psychic. Maybe she saw the writing on the wall the night I turned her down on fleeing out here permanently.

No. There's no way. Even if she thought the world was coming to an end soon, she couldn't have predicted that she'd be the first to go. She had no idea she'd contract the virus and neither did I.

Morbid as it is to think about, she probably believed deep down that it would be the bigots that got her, not NDV. Knowing Hope, she might have had premonitions of getting gunned down while peacefully protesting or standing her ground at a women's rights rally. She would have wanted to go out like Joan of Arc. Getting sick was never part of her plan.

It's never part of anyone's plan. Unless you're religious and you think it's all part of God's plan. Like mama with her lung cancer. Or like Drake.

Drake. How am I thinking about Drake at a time like this?

Still, it doesn't stop me from opening Spotify on my phone and clicking on "Hold On, We're Going Home."

The beat starts. I sip from my whiskey and nod my head with the music.

How many refills have I had now? Who gives a fuck?

When the vocals come in, I clamber awkwardly to my feet. Ruthie doesn't appreciate me removing my leg from under her muzzle, but she'll just have to chill for a minute. My eyes are closed, and my head is bobbing on my neck. Before I know it, I'm dancing.

I'm dancing. How is that happening? The world is ending, and I'm dancing. The love of my life is dead, and I killed her with my negligence and my stubbornness, and she's wrapped in blankets upstairs, but I'm down here drunk dancing to Drake like we're back in the clubs we used to go to when we were in our twenties and had no idea what was coming and didn't care about anything except each other.

I'm smiling and dancing and trying not to crumple and fall.

In my mind, she's here with me, swaying and moving her head from side to side. I can see her curly brown hair bouncing around her shoulders and face as she taps her feet and slides her hands behind my neck and strokes the back of my head, mouths the words to the song, pulls me in close, bites my earlobe, whispers the lyrics to me. She's here with me in my mind, but also right now in the room, I can smell her and taste her and touch her, and I can't ever let her go.

Tomorrow, I will bury my wife.
But tonight, we will dance together one last time.

ELEVEN

Last night, I did something reckless. I filled Brett and Vicki Taylor in on my little secret.

And you know what? They repaid my trust in spades.

It's been roughly twenty nights since this experiment in cohabitation began. I say roughly, because to be honest, I haven't been keeping as good of a count lately as I was in the very beginning.

Time is already such a nebulous, irrelevant concept in today's age. Trying to keep an exact tally of the days, weeks, months, or years just seems like an inherently pointless exercise and a waste of, well, time.

I'd say maybe halfway into that period, though, approximately a week or a week-and-a-half ago I'd bet, I started leaving their room unlocked at night. I didn't tell them what I was doing. But I prepared myself, especially in the beginning, for what might happen.

It was what I considered to be a necessary exercise in trust. I unlocked their room from the outside, went back to my room—the master bedroom that used to be Hope's parents' room—and waited. With the rifle close at hand, plus my ever-trusty companion and nocturnal watchcat Coretta Scott King, I went without sleep those first couple nights, ready for anything, but also hoping with every fiber in my being that nothing at all would occur.

The Taylors came through. Again and again, night after night, nothing happened. Each and every morning, when I opened the door to their room, I'd find them still sleeping.

I certainly took the proper precautions in the beginning. The Taylors were, more or less, glorified prisoners in the house those first few days and nights. Though I did remove Brett's chains, and I upgraded his living quarters from the basement to the second bedroom—Hope's old room—I still kept him and Vicki locked away most of the day and night in there. When I took them outside to relieve themselves of their bodily wastes, I did it one at a time and at gunpoint. I brought them their food and water. Their door was locked while I performed all my daily chores.

Gradually, I began to allow and accept their help in certain areas. Even though I'd known Brett just a little bit longer and a little bit better than his wife, I let Vicki have more freedoms first. Realistically, it just made more sense.

Vicki is short, stocky, and very, very pregnant. Allowing her the opportunity to get some exercise and some sunshine also was part of my plan for her pregnancy, since I knew it would be good for her and for the baby. Not only was she a more logical choice to have with me gathering eggs, tending to the garden, refilling rainwater jugs, and completing other tasks than her husband from a safety standpoint (still with me being armed and not far behind her at all times), but these tasks were also good for her from a health standpoint.

Eventually, I started bringing Brett out from their room as well, maybe once to every two times Vicki got to come out and stretch her legs for a while.

Later, I started having my meals with them, though from a short distance and always with either the Glock or with the Taylors' pistol in one hand.

Last night, though, I did something truly reckless. I told the Taylors during one of these dinners in their room that for the past ten or so nights, I'd been leaving their door unlocked. With a bizarre, almost desperate interest, my eyes roved their facial expressions to see what kind of reaction my confession might get.

The Taylors did what they always do. They were pleasant, they were polite, and they were grateful.

Brett bowed his head to me.

"Well, we certainly appreciate your trust in us, and we'll continue doing everything we can to maintain that trust and earn more of it."

Vicki smiled the kind of smile that only gets sent and received without a mask on.

"It's a lovely gesture, Alex, but it's also unnecessary. This is your home and your rules. We just thank God every day you opened it up to us when we were in need."

After dinner, I left them alone, retired to my room with Coretta, and waited. Most of last night and into the early morning hours, I waited to hear the telltale sounds of footsteps on wooden floorboards as the Taylors explored their newfound freedom and perhaps tested its limits as well.

But the sounds never came. More than once, I got out of bed, pressed my ear to the door, and listened just to make sure. I even opened the door and made up reasons in my head to go down the stairs and then climb back up them again, willing something unusual to occur when I did this. But nothing did. Their door remained shut. There was never a peep from within it, either.

So, this morning, we're celebrating.

Maybe 'celebrating' is too strong a word, but I'm also not opposed to commemorating in some tangible way the progress we've made just in these past two or three weeks as a trio of individuals.

It wasn't long ago at all that I was absolutely alone here, robbed of the final link that connected me to my prior life when Ruthie passed away.

Now, I have a new pet, Coretta the cat, who adores me and who sleeps in my bed with me at night, and who never fails to bring me unexpected doses of pleasure when I least expect them.

And, perhaps just as importantly, if not more so, I have come into close personal contact with not just one, but two human beings, both of whom respect my authority and understand the nature of this situation, yet both of whom provide me with certain comforts and benefits in my life that I didn't even know I was missing until I found them again.

When I open the door to the Taylors' bedroom, they're exactly where they always are each morning: sound asleep in bed.

Vicki used to sleep on her back, but I've convinced her to shake up her natural preferences while she's still carrying the baby and sleep on her left side in the fetal position instead. I won't deny it gives me a certain sense of pride and satisfaction every time I open this door and see that she's indeed sleeping the exact way I recommended.

Brett is more of a wild card when it comes to sleeping habits. I've come in here before to find him sleeping on his stomach with his arms tucked under his pillow, on his back with his arms stuffed under the sheets like he's a mummy, and on his side facing either direction. On more than one occasion, I've discovered him spooning his wife in his sleep, with his face nestled in her hair and usually with one heavily tatted arm draped across her protectively.

There was even one morning not long ago where I walked in on them, and his hand was on her stomach and her hand was on his hand. That was something to see, I won't deny it.

This morning, Vicki is on her left side and almost invisible, buried underneath a sheet, blanket, and comforter. Brett is doing the 'mummy sleep' this morning, flat on his back, arms at his sides and feet straight out, mouth open as he snores at the ceiling.

There are some mornings where they both wake up when I enter, there are some mornings where it's only one of them, and there are some mornings where neither one of them wake up at all until I start to speak to them. This already has the look and feel of that third scenario to me.

I clear my throat, and Brett's eyes flash open. He sits bolt upright in bed as if he's just realized he forgot to do something extremely important.

His movement causes a chain reaction, because I now see that Vicki stirs—or at least, what looks like Vicki stirs beneath all the layers of cotton and fiber. Like a tortoise head slowly popping out from its shell, I see her round, pink face ease its way up from below the hem of the comforter until she slides it far enough up the pillow that she can see me. There's a soft smile on her lips as she comes to consciousness.

"Morning, Alex. What have you got there?"

I'm holding in my hands three plates, each with a fork set on the edge. It wasn't long ago at all that I didn't allow them forks. But now look at us.

"Don't laugh, but I tried something new today."

I set two of the plates down on the bed by their feet. Brett gazes down at his curiously as Vicki slowly and methodically works her way up to being seated in bed with her back against the headboard. Once she's finally upright, she gasps.

"Alex! Oh, my. Is that—are those—are those omelets?!"

I'm trying hard not to grin from ear to ear.

"I figured: why not, right? We all like eggs. You've both been helping me out so much with the garden, and with the weather cooperating, too, it just seemed like the time was right to try something new. Do something a little special for once, you know?"

They don't need to know that I've never made an omelet for myself since I moved in out here, or that it took me an extra hour or so, at least, I'd bet, to make sure I had all the right ingredients and that I'd split them all evenly.

Brett reaches for his plate, brings its up close to his face, and takes a deep inhalation with his eyes closed. When they open again, he's smiling ear-to-ear as well.

"Wow. That is just... wow."

The Taylors have never had eggs here. I've never even made them the scrambled eggs that I treat myself to. They've subsisted on nuts, berries, vegetables, and my famous breakfast raccoon-shit paste I'm known worldwide for. This is the first time I've allowed them eggs, and it's not even eggs—it's an omelet. One omelet each, to be exact.

Vicki looks like she might cry.

"I'm so, so sorry."

Now, she is starting to cry. Brett looks as surprised and concerned as I imagine I might look.

"It's... it's so beautiful. It really is. I just... I'm sorry, the eggs, they... I don't know why..."

Brett still appears flabbergasted, but I know exactly what's going on. I lean over the bed, take her plate, and scoop the omelet off onto Brett's plate. He accepts it without understanding what's happening; it's clear as day on his face.

"I totally understand, Vicki. Believe me, I do. I'll make you something else."

That just makes the tears intensify.

"*No*, please no, Alex! I already feel bad enough as is. You... you go to all this trouble to... to make this beautiful breakfast omelet... and I can't even... I'm so sorry..."

I hold up my hand to stop her.

"Really, Vicki. I understand. It's completely natural. Certain foods, certain tastes, certain smells. There's nothing to apologize for. You're pregnant. It's your body being your body. Don't worry about it."

Brett has sat this whole time with first one omelet and then with two omelets on his plate, alternating his focus between Vicki and me, listening intently the way men always do when they're bound and determined to be a rock for their woman, even though they don't know what that means or fully entails. I can tell his self-restraint is nearly at a breaking point, so I do him a solid by picking up my fork and taking a bite out of the omelet on my own plate.

He sees me do it, takes this as his cue that it's okay—just as I intended—and then dives right on in, devouring the dual omelets on his plate. Brett only stops long enough between greedy, hedonistic mouthfuls to check in with his wife.

"Is this bothering you if I still eat it? Because I can stop."

He says it in such a way that makes it abundantly clear he does not *want* to stop, whatever her answer may be.

And luckily for Brett, Vicki's in a magnanimous mood this morning. She closes her eyes, leans back against the pillow, and wipes at the last remaining tears there above her cheeks until they're gone. Vicki lets out a deep sigh and then speaks to her husband.

"No, you're fine. Thank you for asking, though."

In a normal world, I'd go find a suitable breakfast alternative for a pregnant woman who's a guest in my house. But unfortunately, this isn't a normal world and that's just not possible. I can make the paste for her, or she can probably even make it for herself.

For now, though, I'm going to eat my omelet, because this is as much a delicacy and a treat for me this morning as it is for Brett Taylor.

***

As the day progresses, the Taylors help me around the house.

Today is Vicki's day to join me outside for chores.

We delay the start of those chores so she can have the breakfast paste and eat it at her leisure. Her stomach's not right today, and she's not afraid to tell me. I'm also not afraid to get a late start on the day's tasks because of it. There's no great rush.

Only when she's good and ready do we set out for the basement and then the outside world. I have the Glock in the waistband of my pants behind me, but I'm using both of my hands to help guide her down the stairs to the basement. She waits at the foot of the steps for me to grab our masks from the workwoman's bench in the corner, and after we're masked up and ready to go, I walk up the steps to the cellar door with my janitor's keyring necklace, unlock the chains, and open one of the heavy doors with my back.

It's only after I've gotten the door and all the camouflage materials on the other side clear that I return down the steps into the basement for Vicki, who's still standing patiently waiting for me at the bottom of the stairs that lead to the rest of the house.

Yes, I have a loaded weapon on me at all times while I work with the Taylors, but nowadays, that's less about the Taylors and more just about common sense and habit. Even when the Taylors weren't here, I had a loaded weapon with me every time I went outside. Carrying the Glock around is nothing new. Whether it's the Glock, the rifle, or the pistol I'm holding for the Taylors until after the baby comes, nothing has really changed.

I'm being cautious, as always, but it has less to do with them and more to do with practice and general precaution. The world is still every bit as fucked up today as it was before the Taylors arrived. They have nothing to do with that.

After the day's work is done, I help Vicki back down into the basement and then lock the cellar doors behind us. There was a time where I'd use the flashlight during this whole process just to make sure nothing unexpected might happen between us in the dark. Today, and for a number of days now, I find that unnecessary.

Once the house is secured, we make our way back up the stairs to the first floor. I keep expecting to see Brett there somewhere, whether in the kitchen or the living room or really anywhere in the house other than their bedroom. It's the same thing when their roles are reversed and it's Brett I take outside with me for the day's chores and Vicki stays inside.

Either way, though, the result is always the same: whichever Taylor stays inside, that Taylor stays in their bedroom. Even knowing the bedroom door is unlocked and knowing they are free to go where they will in the house, it seems both Taylors are content with our previous arrangement and with respecting those old boundaries.

When I walk Vicki back into their room, he's doing pushups on the floor. She lowers herself onto the bed and stretches her legs out in front of her. It's abundantly obvious to me that the baby could come at any point now, and I've made this known to the Taylors, who say they are ready for it to happen.

Whether or not I'm ready for the baby to come, I'm not sure. Am I ready to try and make good on my promise and fulfill the main objective behind this whole relationship in facilitating Vicki's childbirth?

Of course I am. I'm not worried about helping a mother deliver her child, although I'll admit I'm a bit nervous about doing so for the first time outside of a hospital and doing it all by myself without the usual tools, supplies, and professional help. I think that's to be expected, though.

What I'm more surprised by is the lack of readiness I feel about what comes *after* the baby. The anticipated birth of the Taylor child has given the three of us common ground. If I'm being honest with myself, it's also given my life a purpose again that was sorely lacking before.

But what happens after the baby is delivered? Assuming there are no complications and that everything goes well, do I stick to the original plan?

The *original* original plan was to drop Brett off back at the ranger station in Spider Falls State Park with his wife and never see either of them again. Although, I suppose the *original original* original plan was to let Brett bleed out in the basement of that house with those other two men.

Clearly, the original plan has been altered several times now. It was never my intention to bring Brett back to my safe haven. On top of that, it certainly was never my intention to bring Brett back to my safe haven a second time, this time with his pregnant wife in tow, and with the understanding that I would provide for them both and then help deliver their child for them, too.

When that child is delivered, do I then continue on with the final part of that revised plan and send the Taylors and their newborn babe packing?

Do I drive them out to that neighborhood—a place I now know to be extremely dangerous after Brett and I were both nearly killed the last time we visited?

Can I really just drop them off at their truck, toss

the key out the window, and drive back home without a second thought? Especially knowing that they have nowhere else to go? I saw the state of their previous residence at that ranger station.

If that's the life they're returning to—only this time with another mouth to feed in a baby—I'm not sure I'll be able to sleep at night, honestly.

So, what, then? They can't just stay here forever with me.

Can they?

Brett finishes his pushup routine, stands, and uses an old t-shirt that I've lent him to wipe the sweat from his torso. It used to belong to Hope's father once upon a time.

For some juvenile reason, it gives me a sense of satisfaction to know that Mr. Bergstrom would probably be appalled seeing his shirt used in such a fashion. He'd no doubt be mortified in general knowing that his beloved family summer home had fallen into the hands of his daughter's Black lesbian wife and the two random strangers she decided to take in. It makes me smile.

Brett pulls the shirt on over his head.

"Gotta stay ready for when the new world order forms. No matter what happens, America will always need soldiers, right?"

I don't think that's right at all, actually. Besides, America doesn't exist anymore. And a new world order? That baby has a better chance of coming out looking like me than we have of forming a 'new world order' as a species.

It's not my place to share those truths with Brett, however. If he wants to keep preparing himself physically, mentally, and emotionally for a future that he still somehow believes in, then far be it from me to tell him no.

"Were you a soldier? Before all this?"

He laughs.

"No, not at all. I wasn't much more than a waste of space before all this. But then I met Vicki, and she turned my life around. Now my life has purpose."

Vicki beams from the bed at her husband but is otherwise silent. I watch the two of them watching each other for a moment, and a piece of my heart lurches in my chest as I think of Hope and of how much I miss her.

Clearing my throat much the same way I did this morning when I came in to rouse them, I back into the open doorframe and place a hand on the knob. Oddly, I suddenly get the feeling like I'm somehow intruding, as bizarre as that is, given the context. It is what it is, though, and it's how I feel right now.

"I'm going to do some reading… in the other room. In my room, I mean. If you need anything."

They both just look at me but say nothing, so I continue, trying to be a bit less awkward.

"I was thinking maybe… I know it's not much, but I was thinking maybe we could have a drink tonight. With dinner. It's not really fair, since you're pregnant and all, Vicki, and I don't want to leave you out. But lately, I've been craving whiskey, and I haven't had any in… God, I don't know how long. But it's been forever. I don't even know if you drink, though, Brett?"

Brett turns to his wife.

"I *love* whiskey. Always have, always will. Haven't had whiskey in five or six years now, I'll bet. I would absolutely love that and to take you up on such a generous offer, Alex. However, it all depends on my wife. Whatever Vicki Marie says, goes."

Vicki Marie massages her stomach absentmindedly as she sleepily alternates her gaze between us.

"I think it's a great idea. I'm only sad that I won't be able to join you. Maybe, assuming all goes well, maybe after the baby's born, we can do one final toast together, how about that? One final toast before we say our goodbyes and part ways. I know that I'll have to nurse, so I won't have much… just a sip maybe. Assuming you think that's all right, Alex? What do you think?"

I think that in a normal world, we'd be having a different conversation, and I'd be providing a different answer. But here and now in this world?

"I think that'd be fine. One final toast won't hurt."

Vicki looks relieved, and so does Brett. He leans over, kisses her loudly on the mouth, and then turns to me.

"Wow! Omelets in the morning and whiskey in the evening. Could this day get any better?"

He laughs, she laughs, I laugh.

Brett's right. It's been a very good day. Maybe the best day I can remember in a long time.

We've each had two glasses of whiskey, Brett and me. It's been years since I drank with someone else. Though Brett Taylor is probably the furthest thing from my ideal drinking companion, it's nice just to have a drinking companion once again. It's nice just to have a companion once again.

Two companions, actually. Vicki Taylor is every bit as lively as her husband, laughing and smiling until she has tears in her eyes as she sits next to me on the living room couch and regales me with stories from her past. You'd never know that she was stone-cold sober based off how boisterous, involved, and talkative she's grown tonight over dinner and now over drinks.

Three companions. I stand corrected. Coretta has deigned to bestow her company on us this evening.

The orange tabby cat has never been far from me after I brought her into my home and healed her up from the injuries she accidentally suffered in my traps. Ever since the Taylors moved in, however, she's been a bit more standoffish and skittish around them, coming and going only when she pleases.

Tonight, though, she is bound and determined to join in on the festivities and to not get left out. In true cat fashion, she makes the rounds between the three of us in the living room, going from one person to the next, absorbing all the pets, scratches, and cutesy words, before suddenly and without warning moving on.

It gives me immense pleasure when I realize that I'm the only one of the three of us she decides to plop down on, however. All it takes is a couple pets behind the ears and a few scratches below the chin, and Coretta collapses languidly between my thighs on the sofa, saying without saying that she'd really love it if I use both hands to rub her jawline and run my fingernails down her spine all the way to the base of her tail. Who am I to argue with her?

Vicki can't stop laughing as she tries to finish her story of how her and Brett first met.

"…I keep thinking to myself, 'Does this meathead

have no self-awareness? No sense of personal space?' Every time our row lowers the pews to get down on our knees, it seems like he's gotten closer to me somehow. After Communion, we're practically bumping elbows. I actually remember turning to you at one point—do you remember this?"

It's a bit harder to see Brett than it is to see Vicki, given the fact we're all sitting in mostly darkness. The only light comes from a solar-powered camping lantern in the center of the coffee table; a light the Taylors brought down from their room just for this very occasion.

Brett smiles and nods from the armchair he sits in.

"I do."

"Of course, you do. I turn to him, and as quietly as I can whisper, because you know, the reverend is still up there talking to everyone on the loudspeaker, but I turn to this guy, this stranger, to Brett, and I whisper, 'Excuse me.' And I'll be darned if he doesn't even *look* at me. He goes on listening to the reverend talk, doesn't even blink. It's like he didn't even hear me, even though he's made sure we're not one foot apart at this point."

Brett glances over at me to interject.

"Oh, I heard her. I just pretended that I didn't."

"You stinker! I knew you did. You just wanted to make me work for it, I guess."

"I wanted to make you notice me. And I wanted you to keep talking to me, that's all."

"Well, it worked! Because I'll be darned if I didn't whisper over again, 'Excuse me, sir, do you mind?' And my older brother, who was sitting next to me on the other side, he turns and *shushes* me, like we're back at Sunday school or something. My parents even looked down the row at me with these disapproving looks on their face. And I'm *nineteen*, mind you. It was humiliating. I turned beet-red for the rest of the service, and I remember thinking to myself, if I ever catch this deaf biker gang hillbilly trying to sit next to me in church again, I'm gonna pop him straight in the chin."

I chuckle into my whiskey glass.

"Did you?"

"Did I pop him in the chin? Or did he try and sit next to me again?"

"Either. Both."

"Well, neither, actually. After church lets out, we're all walking out to the car as a family, when who should I see running up after us?"

Brett raises his hand guiltily.

"He comes running up, and I'm still flushed and *hot* from everything that's happened, so I can hardly believe the nerve of this guy. I wheel around on my high heels in my fancy red-and-black Christmas dress, plant my hands on my hips, and say something to the effect of, 'Now what the heck do you want?'"

She leans closer.

"I normally would have said 'hell,' but I was with my folks at the time."

I smile at her.

"Plus, you had just come from church."

Vicki's eyes light up as she laughs girlishly.

"Yes, that too! And plus, it was Christmas Day. Lots of pluses, and lots of reasons not to swear. Well, anyway, this rotten, no-good creep, he gets all sheepish suddenly and holds out his hand to me. And you know what he says?"

Brett does.

"I say, 'Excuse me, miss, but I think you left your cell phone in there.'"

Vicki glares at him playfully.

"And you know what, to this day, he still denies it, but I would bet money on the fact that he *stole* that cell phone right out from my purse while he was cozying up next to me at the pew. He did it all intentionally just so he could rile me up and then have an excuse to come talk to me afterwards."

Brett finishes his whiskey and mumbles his thanks as I reach over with the bottle to pour him some more. We've nearly finished the bottle, though to be fair, it was probably only three-quarters full to begin with.

"I didn't steal it. I've never stolen a thing in my life. Other than your heart."

Vicki laughs despite herself.

"Liar! There's no way that cell phone just magically fell out of my purse and into your possession. I know what you did!"

Brett holds up his hand.

"Finish the story already. Poor Alex is probably bored out of her mind."

I pour what's left of the whiskey into my glass.

"Not at all! I'm enjoying myself."

And I am. Frankly, I am *stunned* at just how much I'm enjoying myself. I had no idea I missed the art of conversation this much. I had no idea I missed just being around people this much.

Vicki gives me an apologetic look.

"Well, to make a long story short, I have to thank this man for bringing me my cell phone that I *supposedly* left behind, only because I've got good manners and only because my whole entire family is standing right there watching me.

"And then Brett, without a care in the world, as if it's just the two of us at a bar or restaurant and not five people standing outside a car in the church parking lot, he actually has the gall to ask me for my phone number and see if I want to go out with him sometime. Right there in front of my parents! And my brother! And I'm nineteen! Can you imagine?"

"Where's your sister in all this?"

Vicki shakes her head.

"I don't have a sister. Just one brother. Thomas. He might still be out there somewhere. Who knows? We weren't really keeping in that great of touch before all this happened, anyway."

"I thought Brett said you had a sister? Weren't you staying with her and her husband for a while?"

Vicki looks as confused as I am. She turns to Brett, and so do I.

Brett's eyes flicker between the two of us. His whiskey glass is suspended in mid-air, about halfway between his mouth and his lap.

"I said I had a sister and brother-in-law. The ones who got sick and who we were staying with, together at their trailer, until they got sick. Bill and Sadie. Is that what you're thinking of?"

My brows furrow for a second before I purposefully relax them and then reroute my focus to the cat on my lap. I pick up where I left off with Coretta, dragging the nails of my right hand along her vertebrae. The whiskey glass in my left hand feels heavier than it did before, and my brain takes this opportunity to remind me without being prompted that the Taylors' pistol is behind me, wedged between my tailbone and the back cushion of the couch.

"That must be it."

There's an uncomfortable silence as I try not to overreact or overthink what just happened.

I've been drinking, after all. Maybe I did remember incorrectly whose sister and brother-in-law it was. That's not that farfetched at all.

There's no reason to sound the alarm. Everything has been going so nicely. Don't let this minor detail screw it up.

But the silence… it's this sudden, uncomfortable, loaded silence that really bothers me.

Brett breaks it.

"Anyway, I'm sure it will not shock you to learn that Vicki turned me down that day in the parking lot and did not give me her phone number. But I was a persistent bugger, and I made sure that we kept running into each other around town until I finally wore her down. Best decision you ever made, right, baby?"

Vicki laughs, though it's not quite as natural as before. I notice.

"Well, I don't know about *best* decision. Certainly, it's up there with getting knocked up during the apocalypse. That's gotta be in the running for one of the best decisions anyone's ever made."

She laughs again.

I look up from the cat, meet her eyes, and smile.

A new thought pops into my head. I'm probably wrong. But if I'm right…

"I think we've all made some decisions in life that we wish we could take back. Believe me, though, you getting pregnant should not be one of them. That's a beautiful thing, and something you should never regret."

Vicki seems genuinely touched.

"Thank you, Alex. I really appreciate you saying that."

I down the last of my whiskey.

"Now, the truck, on the other hand. Really? A bright yellow Hummer? Tell me you two snatched that gaudy-colored gas-guzzler from someone else."

Vicki laughs and opens her mouth to say something, but no words come out. Instead, she glances over at Brett, then laughs again breathlessly.

"You didn't actually pick it out at a dealer, did you, Vicki? Tell me that was Brett's ride before you two ever got married."

Vicki and Brett both start talking at the same time.

"We don't have a yellow–"

"We found that car–"

They both stop talking at the same time, too.

Another uncomfortable silence follows.

Vicki laughs. Her face is as bright red right now as she described it to be in her story earlier.

"You go for it, hun."

Conversely, Brett's face is blanched. He clears his throat.

"If you're talking about a yellow Hummer, that sounds like my brother-in-law's truck. The one we took when we got away from those men."

"You took your brother-in-law's truck rather than your own vehicle?"

"There was more gas in the Hummer. And it was a safer choice to be in. Our vehicle at the time was a beat-up Chevy Impala, I think. Could barely run at the time."

"So, the Hummer is yours, though, then? That yellow one I saw on the street while driving us away from the house with the men and the medical supplies in the basement? The one I'll be taking you to after the baby gets delivered? The one I have the key to still?"

"That's right."

"The one with all the stickers on the back?"

Brett frowns.

"My… my brother-in-law had some… opinions… opinions that I didn't share. That I don't share. You know how family is. Especially where politics are concerned. Brother against brother, and all."

I nod.

"Families can be tough. My mama and I never saw eye-to-eye on anything, but I still loved her, and I know she still loved me."

Vicki tilts her head at me.

"Do you know where she is? Your mama?"

"She's dead. Lung cancer. She died twenty years ago."

Vicki lays her hand on my arm, her face a picture of sympathy.

"Oh, I'm so, so sorry to hear that."

"I appreciate that. It was probably for the best, though, based on how things turned out."

"And your father? I take it he wasn't in the picture?"

"Why would you take it that way?"

She pulls her hand back at once like she's just touched something hot.

"Oh, I'm sorry. I didn't mean it that way. Is he still around somewhere?"

"I don't know. He wasn't in the picture for me."

Vicki looks confused.

It's time to get moving. I wish right now I hadn't had so much to drink. That being said, my tipsiness may well be the least of my worries right now, and I'm still sober enough to know it.

I get to my feet, much to Coretta's dismay.

"All right, well… this has been fun. I think I'm going to turn in for the night."

Brett has his eyes on me, but Vicki's looking at the spot I just vacated on the couch.

I realize far too late that what she's really looking at is the gun, her gun, which has somehow fallen out behind me on the cushion.

As casually as I can, I reach down and pick it up. I have the empty bottle and glass in one hand and the gun in the other.

Both Taylors have their eyes on me now, but neither one says anything. Cat got their tongues? Coretta is already at the foot of the steps waiting for me.

I walk over and stand in front of Brett.

"Can I take your glass?"

In a sort of daze, he offers it to me first, nods second, and speaks third.

"Sure, thank you."

"Don't mention it."

I can feel their eyes on my back, watching me carefully as I carry the two glasses and the empty bottle into the kitchen and set it all on the counter.

When I return to the living room, they're both standing at the foot of the stairs. Coretta is gone; probably up in my room already. Brett has one arm draped over Vicki's shoulders. Vicki has one hand resting on her belly and is holding their light in her other hand. I'm trying to hold the gun at my side like I'm not conscientiously holding the gun at my side rather than holstering it behind me in my waistband like I normally would.

Vicki smiles and tilts her head again to the side.

"Alex, tonight was just lovely. This whole day was, really, between the omelets, the whiskey, the stories and laughs. Maybe tomorrow night, you can share your story about how you and Hope first met. I'd love to hear more about her."

Something about Vicki saying Hope's name doesn't sit right with me. I grit my teeth through that feeling and fake her a friendly smile anyway.

"That sounds like a great idea. Let's plan on it."

Brett gives Vicki a squeeze, and then the two of them start their ascent up the stairs. I give them plenty of space before following up with the gun in one hand and a flashlight in the other.

At the top, Brett turns his head to me.

"Goodnight, Alex. Thanks again for the whiskey."

"You're welcome. Thanks for giving me a good excuse to drink it."

They move off slowly down the hall. I take my time coming to the top of the stairs and rounding toward my own doorway, waiting to see if anything will happen. The door closes to the Taylors' room uneventfully.

That's good. Uneventful is good.

Coretta is already asleep on top of the blankets of my bed. Her coloration is completely different from Ruthie's—not to mention her species—but there's a moment where I just stand there taking in the furry animal curled up on my bed and lose track of time, place, and context.

I shake that off in a hurry. This is no time for nostalgia or for letting the ghosts of my past in. Not now, not when everything's changed.

I check to make sure the rifle is still tucked underneath the mattress and just above the bedframe. Thankfully, it is.

Unless the Taylors have somehow managed to crack the code on the safe, I know that the Glock is secure, along with an extra flashlight, a full canteen of drinking water, the chains and U-lock I used on Brett, and all of the pills I took from that basement.

As much as I let my guard down with the Taylors these past couple weeks or however long it's been, I'm also not a moron. I put the important things—the things they could either use against me or the things I could use against them as leverage—in a place that I knew would be safe. Literally, a safe.

But then again, maybe I am a moron, given the discoveries I've made this evening. I'm not sure how I could have known better, but I should have known better.

Brett lied to me on the way to the ranger station. He lied to me on multiple fronts. I even found out about some of those lies there and then, but I wrote them off at the time and excused them for what they were, thinking Brett lied out of justifiable motivation to return home to Vicki and their unborn child at any cost.

But now? Now everything's different.

It doesn't matter how much whiskey I've had. I know what Brett said in the jeep on the ride out to Spider Falls. He said the couple they stayed with for a while at that trailer home were Vicki's relations, not his. It was Vicki's sister and brother-in-law. I know that's what he said.

Actually, does it even matter? Given the switcheroo tonight, I'm not convinced any of it is true.

Did they even stay with a couple at all, whether that couple was related to them or not? Does Vicki even have a brother named Thomas? Was that whole story about how they met in the church and the cell phone getting left behind, was all that just improvisation meant to lull me in and make me sympathize with these characters more?

It *felt* real, though. At least on Vicki's end.

Maybe Brett's been keeping her in the dark, too? Maybe all of what she said tonight and all of what she's said to me these past few weeks has been true and genuine, and she had no idea that Brett was making things up in order to get home to her.

The truck, too… this business with the yellow Hummer. I know what I saw while driving away from that neighborhood. It's impossible to miss a vehicle that big in that bright of a color.

And I'll never forget seeing that giant white noose with the upturned white fist inside it as well. That's not the kind of thing someone like me sees and then forgets easily.

How bad is all this, though? Is this just Brett Taylor embellishing stories and lying unnecessarily because he thinks it's a good idea, even though he's wrong?

Or is this plot deeper? Are both Taylors in on it? They didn't seem to be in on it together tonight. They said different things when I asked them about the Hummer. What does that mean?

I wish I didn't drink so much. My mind is spinning, and I can feel that it's trying to click into gear. All the parts and the machinery are ready and oiled up for action, but something keeps slipping, and it's because of the alcohol. I had too much alcohol, and now I can't formulate the right plans and strategies. My mind can't do what it's best at.

I need to lie down, so I do that.

No matter. Everything's fine. I still have the upper hand.

They don't know that you know. Whatever it is that you know. Or think you may know. Whatever it is, you still have time to figure it out, and figure out what you plan to do about it.

You smoothed everything out at the end, talking about your parents. They thanked you for the whiskey and the omelets. Everything is fine for now. Nothing needs to change until you decide it's time for a change.

Just lie still and wait. Give it some time.

Enjoy Coretta curled up nice and warm at your feet. Keep the Taylors' gun close at hand. Don't fall asleep. Do what you did last night, but do it better. Listen for sounds. Keep your ears and eyes open. If you hear anything... if you see any light spilling on the floor beneath the crack under the door, then react... and react quickly. Keep the gun... in hand. Stay ready... stay sharp.

Don't... fall asleep.

Don't fall... asleep.

Don't... fall...

There's a bloodcurdling scream, and for once, I feel like I wake up the right way. As soon as I hear it—what I hope is the first scream, as well as the only scream— I'm up out of bed and on my feet.

What happened? How long have I been asleep for?

It was a woman's scream. Vicki, no doubt. It sounded like a scream for help, and it sounded like it was right outside in the hallway.

I reach for the flashlight on the nightstand and switch it on. Coretta is nowhere to be found, but the Taylors' pistol is nearby on top of the comforter.

How could I fall asleep?

It's the whiskey. I couldn't have been asleep long, though, because I feel it still. The spins, the dizziness, the dry mouth.

As carefully as I can, I move across the room to the door. With my finger on the trigger of the pistol, I use my flashlight hand to turn the knob and throw the door open.

Someone is crying. It's Vicki's voice. I recognize what she sounds like when she cries.

My flashlight moves down the hallway until it finds her there, sobbing in the open doorway of their bedroom. Veins throb at her temples, her hair is plastered to her forehead, and her skin shines with sweat.

Vicki's wearing only that oversized t-shirt of Brett's that I know she wears to bed, and nothing else. There's a large, clear puddle of liquid on the floor between her legs. She holds her hands out to me, which are dripping, and then bends forward, presses her hands into her stomach, and half-screams, half-cries again.

"It's happening... oh my God, Alex, it's happening! Please... please help me!"

Her body convulses as she tries to contain and withhold the mounting pressure inside her.

I've seen it before. It's happening. Instinctively, I

start to move down the hallway to her.

"It's okay, Vicki. Everything's going to be–"

The back of my skull splits open with a searing pain, and then everything goes dark.

TWELVE

After two years of surviving off fruits, vegetables, nuts, and foods I either bought back in the early days or stole in the later days, I have done something wondrous: I have constructed a chicken coop and a chicken run.

Perhaps even more wondrous: I have filled that coop with chickens.

Six hens, to be exact. All 'rescued' from a farm maybe fifty miles from here on my latest foraging trip. Whatever happened to the farmer, he was not there when I was there. Maybe he was out foraging himself, but more likely, he is dead somewhere, never to return to his hens.

That's the story I'm spinning to myself as I look upon the majesty of my work. I didn't steal these chickens from a dead man. No, I rescued them all from certain death after they were unintentionally abandoned by their previous caretaker.

If I'd never come upon them, someone else might have. Maybe that person would have kept them for eggs like I intend to do, but more likely, that person or people would have slaughtered them and cooked them. Good thing I'm not a meat-eater. Or maybe some*thing*, some predator or fearsome animal, might have come for them.

Whatever may have happened, these chickens can rest easily now knowing they will be well-protected and cared for by me. At least they now know where their next meal will be coming from, and at least they now know they won't be someone or something's next meal themselves.

I've made sure of that by attaching a lock to the coop. The key has been added to the ever-growing inventory of keys I now keep around a ring like a janitor. Except instead of having that keyring on a utility belt, I wear it on a silver chain as a necklace.

Why? I'm not exactly sure. I guess it just feels inherently safer to me to do it this way, and to keep them close, right against my heart, as corny as that may sound.

We'll see. I'm still trying it on for size. I can't go full custodian just yet.

There would have been a time not so very long ago where I would have laughed at this Alex Washington, a woman who gazes upon a makeshift poultry housing structure the way ancient Egyptians probably once gazed upon the Great Sphinx of Giza.

But like it or not, this is the crowning achievement of my current life. Collecting chickens and building them a shoddy wooden apartment. That's what my life has come to.

And you know what? Absurd as it is to contemplate, I'm not ashamed, either. Because what else am I supposed to do?

All of my old barometers for success and a life well-lived are long, long gone. I can no longer hang my hat on how many mothers I've helped bring new life into this world or on how much I'm getting paid per year. Hope and I don't have trips to look forward to taking together. Whether I ever would have consented to adopting and becoming parents ourselves, now I'll never know.

Romantic relationship, family, friends, career, wealth, retirement, vacation. Weekdays and weekends. Seasons. Holidays. It's all gone. None of that exists in a world where civilization has ruptured, and society is no more.

Even before I lost phone service, wi-fi, heat, air conditioning, electricity, gas, running water… some of those modern conveniences began to lose their luster for me.

Obviously, not all of them. Having heat when it's cold outside and A/C when it's hot outside is a luxury, sure, but it feels like a borderline necessity depending on *how* hot or cold it gets. And a life without running water and electricity at first felt like it wasn't a life worth living at all.

But the wi-fi, phone service, internet, radio stations in my car, television in the house… these are some of the conveniences that I began to do without long before I didn't have a choice in the matter.

In the beginning, I wanted to absorb as much information as was humanly possible. I regularly depleted my phone's battery and probably racked up crazy overages in terms of wi-fi costs on my credit card just from constantly scouring the world wide web for anything I could learn about what was happening, both domestically and internationally.

And then, something funny happened. As the situation grew more dire, so too did my hopes. Before long, I found myself subconsciously weaning off the internet addiction.

I guess I finally figured: what was the point? None of the news was good. One by one, cities fell, states crumbled, countries folded. People killed other people for reasons good and bad. The virus killed all people for reasons unbeknownst to anyone, except maybe God.

I found a comfort in books. Maybe 'comfort' is the wrong word, since there's no such thing as comfort in this ugly new frontier of existence. But books allowed me an escape, albeit a temporary one, where I could forget about how fucked up everything was and how I had little to nothing left to live for anymore.

When I finished all the books that once belonged to the Bergstroms, I started 'permanently borrowing'— again, I don't want to say 'stealing,' even though I know that's what it was—books from the houses I went to during my scavenging expeditions. Obviously, I never wasted gas or risked my life just to get a new book to read, but when I found my supply of something more crucial starting to wane—something like batteries or gasoline—I would make sure to mentally add books to my wish list for resource gathering.

In the early days, it wasn't uncommon to see other cars on the road or even other people coming and going from rural homes and farms while I was driving. No one interacted, though, or waved hello. If someone saw me, they went running. Usually that meant running away. And on the odd occasion it meant running toward me, I made damn sure to hit the gas and swerve as necessary.

The first time someone shot at me in the jeep, I didn't understand what was happening. Worse, I didn't know where it was coming from. Thankfully, whoever it was must have been a lousy shot, because I didn't get hit and neither did my car. But after that occasion, I stopped foraging during daylight hours.

Unfortunately, the nighttime soon proved it wasn't a much safer time to be on the road, either. I had a pickup truck chase me for several miles with the brights on right behind me the whole time at one point. There was nowhere to go but forward on that stretch of two-lane highway. If they had a gun, they didn't shoot. They just drove up on me and rode my tail until finally they either lost interest or ran out of gas, slowed down, and finally became a distant light in the mirror. I went a different way back home that night.

It wasn't long after this incident that I finally invested in a gun. I'd passed on buying one when I had the chance years ago, which proved to be an unwise decision. It forced me to have to go out and find one, and guns—unlike many other supplies—aren't something you can find in any given house, even out in the country.

The Glock came into my possession in a most unsavory but also most fortunate fashion. I was in the basement of a farmhouse rooting around for tools when I rounded a corner and nearly had a heart attack.

Some poor elderly man had holed himself up and perhaps taken sick with the virus, because there were no wounds or injuries on his body that would have indicated a struggle. He had been down there for some time, though, because the rot had set in.

If it weren't for Jim Carrey, I don't know if I would have been able to endure the smell of his maggot-ridden body decomposing and falling apart as I searched it for useful items. Just the sight of this happening right in front of me had nearly been enough to make me quit.

But I'm glad I didn't, because if I had, I never would

have discovered the gun tucked into his jeans behind his back—or the box of bullets he had hidden behind the musty, stained mattress I found him on.

Scavenging at night and keeping the Glock loaded and on my person every time I went outside weren't the only habits I developed over the past couple years. Whether by choice or necessity, my routines and daily activities slowly altered and then solidified into the best, safest incarnations I could make them.

For example, I stopped parking in the driveway and started leaving the jeep further away from the house in the woods. If anyone saw me on the road or even came across the vehicle while on foot, I didn't want them to automatically come upon the house as well.

I added the jeep key to my keyring necklace and made sure that whenever I left the vehicle a safe distance away from the house in the woods, I also covered it up with branches and leaf cover. I even tried hard to start covering the tire tracks up as best I could before heading home on foot.

What started out as the Bergstrom family's summer vacation house slowly became a fortress. Not overnight, of course, but gradually, over time, those first two years.

I realized that just because I'd been fortunate enough to remain undisturbed since I fled out to the forest, that didn't mean I'd always be undisturbed. All it would take would be someone like me, fleeing the city for the safety and sanctuary of the country, who happened upon the house, and then I'd be dead. They wouldn't need one of the two keys on my necklace for the front or the back door; they'd just need to pick the locks or break the windows and climb on in.

Painstakingly, I took the necessary precautions to

avoid those types of nightmarish imagined scenarios. I boarded up the many windows in the house and added tubular steel security bars over the windows on the ground level. One foraging trip was devoted entirely to finding materials to use as reinforcements and home defenses. Large sheets of metal that I happened upon in some junkyard maybe sixty or so miles away from here proved to be perfect for the doors. This project was not easy, but at least I still had electricity for it.

The same could not be said for my chicken coop. It's probably been about a year since the power went off, and the coop represents my first real structural project since then.

Maybe that's why I'm so proud of it… because I know that I did it all the old-fashioned way, with a hammer and a saw and nails.

Ruthie watches the chickens with interest as they cluck and strut around, exploring their new digs. I was worried she might try and lunge at the chicken wire if one of the hens got too close. Do dogs eat chickens? I can honestly say I have no idea. It's something I'd look up if I still had a smartphone that functioned. I know her dogfood used to be chicken and rice flavored. Is that the same thing, even? Were real chickens used to make it?

Thankfully, she's been good about the chickens so far. Now eleven years old, she's less curious and impulsive than she used to be as a pup. I would've bet she might have gone for these chickens in her younger days.

Today, she seems like she's just more curious about them than anything, and the chickens don't seem particularly concerned by the dog's presence nearby, either. Maybe they had a dog friend or two at the farmer's ranch I found them on once upon a time? Who knows…?

What I do know is that I can hardly wait to have fresh eggs again in my life. I have no clue how long it might take for the hens to start laying them. If I came out tomorrow to find six eggs waiting for me, I'd be just as surprised as if I found zero eggs or sixty eggs. This is another instance where it would be nice to have Google or Wikipedia or something, but oh well.

Like everything new, I'll just have to learn as I go.

It's not unusual for me to dream of Hope. I'd say I dream of Hope at some point every night, actually. Whether the dreams are good or bad, happy or sad, she is still here with me, even in death. Though not really, and that's why even the good dreams and the happy ones never end well, because I always wake up.

No, it's not unusual to dream of Hope. But what is unusual—what may actually be unprecedented—is to dream of Hope *here*.

Usually, my dreams are of the past. I'm replaying old memories or reliving them in a whole new way. We're typically much younger in my dreams—most often in our twenties, back when we first met and started dating.

But not tonight. Tonight, she appears as she was… or as she would be today, if she were still alive. Not old, but not as young as we once were. Just starting middle age. What we were supposed to do together. We were supposed to celebrate being 'over the hill' together, or at least mourn it together. But then, that never happened, because she died.

And yet, here she is now, standing right in front of me. We're *here*, too; here in this house, the summer home of her family. And it looks like I know it does today: dark, quiet, empty. This isn't the vacation house we came to a few times as a couple while visiting her parents. It's the place I now inhabit alone.

Well, not entirely alone. I still have RBG.

Ruth Bader Ginsburg is here, too. The dog, not the Supreme Court justice, of course. She runs right over to Hope, tail wagging vigorously, with her chin upturned and ready to receive scratches.

Hope laughs and squats down in the bedroom doorframe, eager to oblige her dog.

Her dog. I love Ruthie like the child we never had together, Hope and I, but Ruth will always be Hope's dog. Hope was always number one, the alpha in our pack.

I've been so mesmerized seeing my wife as she should be—healthy, present, alive—that I'm just now realizing where I am and where we are exactly as a family. They're in the doorway to Hope's parents' bedroom, which of course is now my bedroom. I'm in my bedroom, in my bed, sitting up in bed, seeing Hope, who is not dead but who is right here with me as she should be. Or as she should have been. As she is?

"How's my girl?"

True to form, she's neither talking to me or about me—she's talking to the dog about the dog. Nothing changes, even in death.

"What are you doing here?"

Hope keeps scratching Ruthie below her chin and

behind her ears. It's been years since I've seen the dog smile like that. No matter how much attention I give her, no matter how inseparable we've become around the house and outside during chores, no matter how much I've tried to essentially be like Hope always was to her, I'm still no Hope. It doesn't make me mad… it just makes me wistful.

"This is my house, is it not?"

Hope keeps loving on Ruthie but does angle her face up so she can meet my eyes for the first time. God, she's beautiful. The last time I saw her, she was nestled in blankets at the bottom of a hole I dug for her in the earth.

I don't want to think about that now, or about what her face and her body looked like that day. This Hope, as she is right now and as she should be, this is my Hope. This is the real Hope.

"I love what you've done with the place. Very industrial chic. Some serious Mad Max vibes. I'm surprised I didn't find you in a blonde wig and a slinky chain-mail dress holding a crossbow pistol."

I laugh despite myself. She always knew how to make me laugh.

"What are you doing here, though, really? I'm dreaming, aren't I?"

Hope finally stops lavishing all her attention on RBG. She stands up and moves across the room to sit on the edge of the bed. When she does, I feel the weight of her change the mattress beneath me.

She's real. This has to be real. She's so close to me now and so perfect.

And the detail… dreams don't have this kind of detail. Do they?

"Am I dreaming?"

Hope smiles her smile at me and makes my insides burn.

"How about I pinch you so we find out?"

Slowly, she leans forward across the bed until she's close enough to lay her hand on my breast. With her eyes on me the whole time, she pinches my nipple between her fingers, not too hard, but not too soft, either. Just the way I like it. I close my eyes and moan in my throat. She knows me; she knows me like no one else ever did, and like no one else ever will again.

And then, she lets go. I open my eyes and I want to ask her why she stopped.

But I don't have to. Hope reads my mind.

"Sorry, babe. It's not that kind of dream."

I groan and lie back against the headboard.

"So, it is a dream, then. This isn't real."

"You're the doctor."

"I'm not that kind of doctor."

"I know."

"I know you know. *Ugh*... I don't know if I can do this tonight. It feels different tonight. Too real."

"You say that like it's a bad thing."

"It is a bad thing if it's not actually real. Unless you're actually you—you're actually alive, I mean—I don't know if I can do this willingly. Usually, it's different. There's not this kind of intense self-awareness. Reality-awareness. I don't think I'm strong enough to handle it."

Hope reaches out and runs her thumb across my lips.

Fuck. It feels so good. It feels so real. She's killing me.

"You're stronger than you think you are, old lady."

"Excuse me. You're older than I am."

Hope smiles sadly.

"Not anymore."

She pulls her hand back and slides to the edge of the bed.

"You're not leaving me already, are you? You just got here!"

Hope stands.

"You're waking up soon."

"What? Really? Well, then, I change my mind. I don't care if it's different or if it feels too real. I want to feel it. I want to feel *you*. Please… please don't leave me."

"I never have. I never will."

She moves toward the doorway. Ruthie is gone.

"Hope. Please."

She is starting to fade in the darkness. I'm losing her again. I can't lose her again.

"Hope… forgive me."

She turns to look back.

"Alex… forgive yourself. It's time. I love you."

THIRTEEN

When I wake up, Brett Taylor is staring down at me from above. That alone lets me know that something's not right.

My head is killing me. Specifically, the back of my head. Something feels wet back there, like my hair is matted with sweat or goo… or blood.

I go to reach for it with my fingers, but I can't, because my wrists are pinned behind me. It feels like they're tied and taped together. My arms throb from the awkwardness of the position. I feel pain everywhere in my body.

But pain's not important. I can deal with pain. What's important is that Brett Taylor is standing above me and that I'm on the ground.

I'm in my basement. Even in the dark, I can recognize it, because Brett is holding a flashlight. He's holding my flashlight, actually.

And my gun. His gun, technically, but the gun that I took from Vicki. The gun he should not have in his possession.

And he has my keys—my keyring necklace. He's wearing it around his neck over his shirt like he's mocking me and flaunting his hostile takeover and his treachery right in my face.

None of this should be happening right now. My back is against a hard surface that I realize is the same support pole I chained Brett to. It would be ironic if it wasn't inconceivable.

How did this happen? What's going on?

"Theeeeere she is. Rise and shine, doctor."

Brett pushes the flashlight closer to my face. It's far too bright for my eyes, so I close them and turn my head away.

"Must be nice, having your neck free so you can do that. Wish I had that luxury back then."

I don't understand. Why would Hope release me back into this? Maybe this is the dream… maybe this is the nightmare.

"Is that flashlight a little too bright for you? Maybe I should grab a stinky old pillowcase and pull it over your head. Would that make you feel better?"

Something flies through the air and collides with my stomach. The pain is excruciating, but I can't double over like I want to, not with my hands pinning my shoulders back against the pole. I grit my teeth against the pain and try with all my might not to cry or scream. It's so very hard to breathe right now.

"Not so fun, is it? Kind of sucks to be in horrible pain and not be able to do anything about it, huh?"

"That… that wasn't my fault…"

Without warning, it comes again for my stomach. It's his boot, and it's every bit as unbearable the second time as it was the first. I can't contain a wrenching gasp.

"It wasn't your fault? Whose fault was it then that I got strapped to a pole with a bag over my head? Who was it that had me locked up down here like I was a fucking prisoner? Who was it that made me piss and shit myself and stuck me with needles and drugs? Who was it who did all that, huh?"

"I… I saved your life…"

"Oh, here we go again!"

He paces around with the light in front of me.

"I am so fucking sick and tired of hearing you say that. *'I saved your life.'* I saved your life, too! You know what I didn't do afterward? I didn't lord it over your head day and night. And more importantly, I didn't fucking put you in *chains!*"

"It was for my own protection…"

"Oh, yeah? How'd that work out for ya?"

Brett squats down on his hamstrings so he's level with me.

"Newsflash, by the way: I didn't mean to save your life. You were next. Did you know that? You do now."

He spits in my face. There's nothing I can do to avoid it except to keep my head turned and my eyes closed. He uses the gun to force my face toward him, but I keep my eyes closed.

"Look at me."

Brett whips the gun across my cheek, and I bite my lip to stifle a scream.

"Open your eyes, or I'll hit you again."

I crack them open by force.

Brett pushes the tip of the pistol to my forehead and sneers.

"I would never, ever, *ever* risk my life for a nigger."

He spits in my face again and then stands back up.

"Especially not a queer one."

Brett and the light move across the basement floor until he's over at the foot of the staircase.

And that's when I see her. Vicki is perched on the very last step above the concrete with her back to the wall. She's holding my rifle in her hands—which means they found it.

At least the Glock is still in the safe. So are the chains and the U-lock, otherwise I'm sure I'd be wearing those now around my neck and my torso. All of the pills and medical supplies are in the safe as well. Do the Taylors know that?

"Surprise."

Vicki sneers just like her husband. What a lovely couple they make.

"My water didn't break, but I bet you sure thought it did!"

She acts as if I'm only just now figuring that out.

"Don't you worry, though, doctor. When the real thing comes, you'll be close at hand."

Brett bends low enough to kiss his wife's baby belly.

"We're gonna make it nice and simple for you, since it turns out you're not too smart, for a doctor. Two options. You can help deliver our baby like you said you would, and we'll let you go after it's done. Or you can refuse, and we'll shoot you. Pretty simple, huh?"

I say nothing.

Brett waves the light at me.

"Why don't you think about it for a while? No rush. When the baby's ready—really ready this time—you'll know. And then I know you'll do the right thing. Won't you?"

I stare back into the light defiantly.

"Come on, babe. Let's give Alex the privacy she deserves down here."

The Taylors start up the steps.

About halfway up, Brett stops and shines the light back on me.

"You know what there is a rush on, though? The combination to that fancy hidden safe of yours. I want what's in it, and I think you know why. I'll be back down here in a bit. When I come back, I expect you to tell me the combo. I don't wanna have to work for it. If I have to work for it, I'm gonna have to hurt you. I'll hurt you real bad. You get me?"

I spit toward the light.

Brett only laughs.

"Yeah, you get me. I'd save your spirit, girlie. With that kinda attitude, you're gonna need it for when I get back here."

Brett and the light disappear up the stairs. I hear the door close, and then it's pitch black down here in the basement. Except for the occasional sounds of feet shuffling across the floor up above, it's mostly dead silent, as well.

Now that they're gone, I allow myself a whimper as reality sets in.

First, it's the pain. My stomach still throbs from where he kicked his boot into the softness there. It's hard to keep my brain from immediately rushing to conclusions and lighting on words like 'internal bleeding' and 'organ damage.' Even as an OB-GYN, I certainly spent enough time in med school and residency to know better than to overlook the possibility of injuries you can't see above the skin.

If there's a silver lining, it's that my stomach muscles tensed up reflexively after the first kick. Hopefully, I've avoided anything serious, though there's no real way for me to check, especially not now and not like this.

After I register and really absorb the physical pain for what it is and what it could represent, my mind shifts right into analysis. The only alternative is to get emotional and go down the wormhole of woe-is-me, and that leads to nowhere productive.

If there's one thing I know without a shred of doubt, it's that Brett and Vicki Taylor have absolutely no plans to keep me alive after the baby comes. Releasing me isn't an option. They know it, I know it, we all know it.

So, what are my options?

Escape is the most obvious one, though I'm still very much in shock and physiological agony. I know I need to let those go and surrender to my analytical mind if I want to have any chance of staying alive.

Escape to where, though? I've spent five years building and retrofitting this refuge to keep people out and to keep me in, safe, and alive. Am I really prepared to abandon it now?

If it means my life, then sure, I suppose.

But where could I go? And am I really prepared to start over from scratch again?

A vision of the abandoned ranger station in Spider Falls State Park manifests before me in the gloom. I saw firsthand what life was like on the run. Even in that home I found Brett in, and in every other house, store, farm, junkyard, car, tent, ranch, or whatever, the chances of survival—even short-term survival—are slim to none.

I'd have to start foraging constantly. All of my supplies and my comforts—my food, my water, my medicine, my chickens, my cat, my jeep—all of it would be gone. I'd have to make a run for it and hope I could somehow evade the bullets fired from not one, but two guns aimed directly at me.

And who's to say I'd even have all my limbs free? I have no idea how the Taylors expect me to be of use to them in delivering their baby if I'm tied to a pole in a basement.

Do they expect me to just coach them through what needs to happen? To talk them through the process and provide expert insights and analysis real-time while I'm strapped to a pole with only the knowledge that my death is imminent on the other side of delivery as a kind of sick, twisted comfort?

There's no way I survive like this. Not tied up and with my hands taped behind my back and my ass on the floor. The only way I get out of here is if I free myself somehow before Vicki goes into labor. Once the baby starts coming, it's all over for me. The sands in the hourglass of my life will nearly be run out at that point. If I'm not out of here by then, I'm out of time and out of life.

And that could happen any day now. That could happen any second now, really.

Out of here. What does that even mean?

I can't wrap my head or my heart around it. It's not just the sentimental side of me that is tied to this home I've created for myself, although that's also not inconsequential in my decision-making. My wife is *buried* here. This house belongs to her family. My dog is buried here. I had—no, I *have*—every intention to die here. Am I ready to do that *now*, though?

It's a rare occurrence, but my head and heart align again on this. I cannot leave here. It's not just the ties I feel; it's also just good common sense.

All of my supplies are here, all of my home defenses, all of the hard-earned fruits of my labor. Countless hours spent building something from the ground up and from the inside out, as well as numerous trips over the years spent risking my life to gather the materials and stockpile the resources I needed to make this my last refuge and a final resting place, not just for those I love and care about, but for me as well. Somewhere in the back of my mind, I always knew that this would be the site of my final stand.

Also… he has the keys. Brett has my keys around his neck. Even if I wanted to make a run for it—and I don't—I wouldn't be able to. The cellar door is locked twice over, the front door is locked and barricaded, the back door is locked and barricaded. The only way in or out of this house, by my own design, is the cellar door that I'm staring blindly at right now in the darkness. And the only way to get through that door is with the keys around Brett's neck. Which means the only way to get out is through Brett.

And if that's the case, it means I don't really need to get out. I just need to get Brett.

Can I kill Brett Taylor? Absolutely. Whatever empathy I once held for him is now long, long gone. It goes without saying that I regret ever taking pity on him as he bled out in that basement. I should have left that racist motherfucker down there to rot and die alongside his racist motherfucker friends. They would have made good company for one another in hell.

What about Vicki Taylor? She seems every bit as evil as her husband, but he's not the one carrying an innocent child inside his body. I'm not sure I could pull the trigger if I had to in good conscience on her. Maybe if it was a life-or-death situation, I suppose. But even still… the very idea of it just doesn't equate for me, given who I am, what I've done, and what I believe in.

Enough, though. I'm getting ahead of myself. There's no sense in wondering how I'd react in hypothetical scenarios while I'm still stuck down here in a very real, very tangible, very *lethal* scenario. How in the world am I supposed to kill anybody when I can't even move?

My hands are tied and taped together as best I can tell without being able to see anything or have someone describe the situation behind me on the other side of the pole he has me pressed up against. But if there's to be any hope of resistance and of fighting back to reclaim what is mine, I need to free myself.

But how?

Patience. Patience, planning, and careful deliberation. That's the mental aspect of this.

And the physical aspect is moving whatever I can however much I can for as long as I can without detection. He's got me restrained, but at least I'm not chained up in metal and iron. If he had access to the chains and the lock, I'd be done for. As is, it feels like he's just used duct tape and some of that same rope I took with me from the basement we first met in.

The *bad* rope. I remember it now for what it was and what it is. This is the rope those two buffoons used on me, the same rope I was able to break free of with relative ease while stalling for time. Brett doesn't know how bad the quality of this rope is, but I do.

And even though I can tell he's done a better job tying me up back there than they did, I'm still able to rub my wrists against one another behind my back in a way

I wouldn't be able to if he had done a better job.

These stupid men. They get careless because they assume their physical advantage over most women negates the need to take extra precautions. Hubris and dumb jock mentality. Classic.

All I need is to stay patient and to buy myself time. More time than what I needed the last time I found myself in this kind of predicament, judging by the tightness of the bonds and the extra added layer of the sticky, strong duct tape, but with enough steady pressure and enough time, I think I can maneuver my way out of this one as well.

Pressure and time. That's all it takes really, pressure and time. I feel like that's also a quote from a movie I once loved.

What I wouldn't give to watch an action or a drama on the television screen again rather than living one out every single fucking day.

When Brett finally tires of torturing me, he wipes sweat from his forehead with the back of his hand, flicks it off in my direction, spits into my face one more time for good measure, and then slowly ambles off toward the staircase, panting all the while. Even though he has the flashlight beam aimed away from me at the stairs, I force myself to swallow down and mask the immense, sudden relief that surges up inside me.

Finally, *finally*, he's almost gone. Don't give him any excuse to come back.

The light returns to my face.

"I'll give you this: you're stronger than you look."

One eye flutters helplessly against its brightness. My other eye is already swollen shut.

"But it doesn't matter. Sooner or later, I'll break you. Everybody breaks. Some just require a bit more… convincing, that's all."

He stands there another few seconds in silence, observing me, I suppose. Perhaps taking in the wreckage he's wrought. No doubt proud of his accomplishments the same way a boy is proud when he plucks the wings from a butterfly or burns an ant under a magnifying glass.

I hope he's at least a little bit ashamed he didn't succeed in getting what he wanted, though. He's certainly mad; I could hear it in his voice as he screamed in my ears, and I absolutely felt the brunt of it through the pain he inflicted as his patience waned and the assault became more vicious and uncalculated.

Whatever he's feeling, even without his mask on, I can't see him. Not with one eye closed and with the other blinded by the light.

At last, the flashlight sweeps away, and then the sounds of his heavy boots trudging up the wooden stairs commence, and my chin dips to my chest as blood and spit drools out from my busted mouth to the concrete floor. I hear the door slam shut and listen as he moves across the floor upstairs and then finds his way to the other staircase, and now his footfalls are getting fainter as he moves up to the second story, perhaps to go harass and paw at his pregnant wife, since he's still riding the high of his violence and brute masculine strength.

What's the damage, doctor?

A voice in my head tells me to keep my chin up,

while another voice tells that one to shut the hell up. I'm so, so tired, but I'm terrified I won't be able to fall asleep.

Somewhere in the midst of that endless barrage, my nerve endings seemed to short out and shut down. The beginning was the most excruciating part because I had no idea what to expect. No matter what you see on TV or the movies or what you read in books or news articles, torture is something you have to experience for yourself to truly understand. Even if the mind doesn't break, the body does, whether you want it to or not.

What's the damage, doctor?

It's a miracle I can see at all out of my right eye. My left eye is swollen shut. There is no doubt in my mind that my nose is broken. My tongue roves the cavity of my mouth and tastes blood everywhere. Whether I'm missing a tooth or missing several teeth is unknown. There seem to be holes where before there weren't any, but maybe if I'm lucky, they're just chipped or cracked. Three of my five fingers on my left hand are broken. Both of my thumbnails are missing. There are cuts up and down my arms and my legs, though he stopped doing that when he realized I was losing too much blood and he risked killing me before the baby came.

What you do see in the movies that's true is the desire to die while being tortured. At least for me, that was accurate. Again, not right off the bat. As blisteringly horrific and wicked as it is to experience, humans are fighters by nature.

I saw it for years at the hospital. Even while facing extraordinary pain and having the sensation you're being ripped apart at the seams from the inside out, mothers of all ages, races, shapes, sizes, and personalities manage to draw on some primal biological well of strength and perseverance that otherwise remains dormant throughout most of our day-to-day lives.

Such was the case for me at the beginning, despite encountering pain I could have never previously conceived of, let alone describe now in words.

But as time wore on and then stopped altogether, and as the pain continued, worsened, intensified… something changed. That resistance, that indefatigable human spirit, the 'never give up, never surrender,' all that and more… it changed for me.

It didn't abandon me altogether, I guess, because at the end of the day, Brett still doesn't have the safe combination.

But what did abandon me was the hope. The desire to come out somehow on the other side, against all odds, and be a better, stronger person because of the ordeal suffered. Somewhere, sometime, I lost that entirely.

And all I wanted, more than anything, was to die. To feel that relief. Not so much even just to escape the pain, which would be justifiable in its own right. But truthfully, just to give in. To surrender to the unknown and accept that things didn't go as planned, at least not in this life and this particular go-around on this particular planet, and to shuffle off this mortal coil and try my luck maybe somewhere else. Or not.

Either way, I just wanted it to end. And I'm not ashamed of that.

Through the haze of strobe lights, lasers, and fog, I see her, writhing and shaking her hips from side to side with the beat.

Every now and then, there's a spotlight that catches her perfectly, bouncing off the mirror ball on the ceiling and bathing her in electric moonlight for all the world to see. She is without question the most beautiful thing I have ever seen in my life, and she is looking right at me.

I am not a dancer, but tonight, I will make an exception. I've had just enough whiskey to throw out all decorum and follow through on my baser instincts.

Normally, I'd be home and in bed by now with Netflix playing on the screen and a bowl of popcorn under one arm. But tonight, I am here in this club, I am drunk, and I am utterly enchanted by this woman in the tight blue jeans, white t-shirt, and black leather jacket.

In a daze, I half-walk, half-dance my way through the crowd until I'm standing right in front of her. She smiles at me now, and it's unlike any smile I've ever seen before in my whole entire life. This smile makes me want to rip her clothes off or rip my clothes off or just be nearer to her than before.

If I can just keep getting close to her and keep getting to know her, maybe forever, then I think maybe I'll be okay. Maybe I won't explode.

"You okay?"

She speaks. She just spoke to me. It's impossible to hear over the music, but there's no question she just opened her mouth and said words to me.

"What?"

I hate the sound of my own voice even if I can barely hear it. I need to make sure everything I do is perfect and that nothing is out of tune or out of place. That's what she deserves. Oh God, I cannot blow this moment right now.

"You okay?"

She laughs. I want to tell the DJ to shut it all off just so I can hear what her laugh sounds like. It's enough, though, seeing the way her face ripples out and her eyes light up as she laughs.

"What's your name?"

"Hope. What's yours?"

"Alex."

"Hi, Alex."

The way she says my name makes my head swim. The way she says 'hi' makes my heart sing.

Hope leans her mouth close to my ear to be heard over the music.

"I'm glad you came over here."

I turn to look at her, and our faces are unbelievably close now. The air is pressurized between us.

"Why is that?"

She smiles again, and my legs almost give out.

"Because you're cute, Alex."

The most beautiful woman in the world thinks that I, Alex Washington, am *cute*. Am I dreaming right now? Is this real life?

"I think you're cute, too."

"Oh, yeah?"

I stop dancing and stare her dead in the eyes.

"Actually, I think you're gorgeous. You might just be the most beautiful person I've ever seen."

Hope throws her head back and laughs.

"That's very sweet of you to say."

"It's true."

She sees the look on my face and stops dancing.

"Do you want to kiss me?"

My heart explodes into fifty-thousand fireworks.

"More than anything."

Hope's expression changes.

"So, do it, then."

I hesitate, but only for a moment.

And then I do it. I kiss her.

And it's amazing, like no kiss I've ever had before, because she's unlike anyone I've ever met before, and I don't know anything about her other than that she tastes like whiskey and cherry Chapstick and her hair is curly and she dances to Taylor Swift in a leather jacket and her smile could melt the polar icecaps and her name is Hope and I don't know what I did to deserve this brief incandescent moment of perfect bliss in my life but I'm going to savor it and stay in it for as long as I can, and no matter what happens afterward, I'm going to remember this moment for as long as I live and until the day I die because this is what it means to feel happy and to experience true joy and connection with another human being and to just be in the moment and be present and trust your instincts and listen to your heart and oh God I think I love this woman and I don't even know her.

I awaken to the bizarre sensation of something *licking* and *chewing* at my wrists.

With a start, I remember where I am and what has happened to me. Hundreds, if not thousands, of body parts scream out everywhere on me for my attention.

Brett. That's right. Brett is responsible for what I feel all over and why I can't see or move or breathe properly.

He is not, however, responsible for whatever is happening behind me right now.

I start to scream, but no sound comes out. It has to be a rat. Or multiple rats. Just like the one I found mutilated in my garden that day—what feels like a whole eon ago now. Maybe it's the same one, and there's a rat ghost that haunts my basement, and it's gnawing on my open wounds and sucking my blood like a vampire bat.

Though it's pointless to try and get away when I'm tied to a pole, I can't help human instinct. Horrified and disgusted by what's happening behind me, I pull forward at the shoulders and try to writhe my hands away from the creature's mouth.

And I *do*. My hands *move* in a way they haven't been able to until now—a way they shouldn't be able to.

Everything changes. I test them again, and yes, it's not my imagination. Unless I'm still dreaming, my mobility has changed back there behind me. There's a newfound looseness where before there was only the loss of feeling that comes from having your blood circulation cut off for too long. I can *feel* my missing thumbnails and the dull ache of my broken fingers.

More importantly, my wrists are somehow suddenly free to shift back and forth *significantly* against one another, despite the tape and the rope that's still there. Whether it's a result of the slow, laborious, steady grinding, twisting, and pulling I've been doing on my own down here in the dark to try and loosen the bonds, or it's a result of this vampire ghost rat wetting my wrists and nibbling on my constraints, or both, I'm finally making progress.

I curl my good hand, my right hand, inward, and my

fingertips reach for my palm. There's a wetness there that's undeniably blood, but maybe something else. Saliva, maybe? From the rat or rats? And also, a texture… a sticky, stringy texture. I think it's a bit of duct tape that's come apart.

My fingers wiggle some more until they feel that licking sensation right against them. I stifle another scream. It doesn't feel hungry, this licking. There's a warm curiosity almost to it. I can feel the creature's tongue and its mouth… and its fur. It could be the rat, or it could be…

"Coretta?"

Is that my voice? It's unrecognizable.

The licking stops.

"Coretta, is that you?"

A soft meow comes from behind me, and it might just be the most comforting sound I've ever heard before.

"What are doing down here?"

The cat meows again and then picks back up where she left off, gnawing at the tape and the rope around my bloodied wrists.

"How did you get down here?"

Did the Taylors take pity on me and put my pet down here to keep me company?

There's no way. She must have slipped past them somehow… maybe bolted down the steps when Brett opened the door to come down or come up.

But even that seems unlikely. He would have seen her, and he never would have allowed her to stay down here. I would have heard it happen, too. I've heard him come and go each time he's arrived down here to torture me.

How did she get here, then? Am I hallucinating? Maybe this is another dream?

It feels real enough, though. I can't see anything down here, but I can feel the cat nibbling away.

Absurdly, a laugh starts to tickle at the walls of my throat and chest. The idea that Coretta the cat is somehow unimaginably down here with me in this hellhole basement and trying to free me from my bonds is absolutely insane. Maybe if this cat was a Hollywood animal star that had been trained to do extraordinary things before finding its way out here, I guess I could *maybe* fathom a universe where this makes sense.

More likely, she's just a cat being a cat: curious. Cats love to chase and chew on string, right? I guess rope isn't that far removed from string. And maybe they like to chew on tape, too? I don't know. I've never been a cat person.

But that all changes now if this particular cat somehow manages to do enough back there to get me out of this jam. I'll be a cat-person forever if this works.

How did she get here, though? That's what I can't stop wondering about...

From the back of a catamaran gliding atop turquoise waters stained orange and violet by a Caribbean sunset, I watch the wake behind us spread out and froth over until it's all one again. It's mesmerizing, and I let my mind wander, but I keep my hands busy with their present task, which is massaging the freshly manicured feet of my new bride.

Hope is stretched out across the taut grid of belt straps that forms a kind of above-water hammock between the two ends of the boat. She's wearing a white one-piece swimsuit, because she wants everyone to know that we are married and that this is our honeymoon. And just so there's no doubt at all, she has a wide-brimmed straw hat pulled down over her face with 'JUST MARRIED...' written on one side and '...BITCHES!' written on the other. It's perfect for Hope, obviously, so I wasn't surprised in the slightest when she ordered it off Amazon before we left for this trip.

We've been quiet for a long time; so long, in fact, that I'm wondering if she's fallen asleep as I hold her feet in my lap and massage her soles. Other passengers around us laugh and talk and drink their tropical cocktails out of plastic cups. The crew have been very hospitable and loveable, in a corny sort of way. I've had fun, but this right here, this moment of silence where I can just keep touching her and stare out over the waves at the sunset, I already know that this is going to be the memory that lasts for me. This is my favorite part.

"Tell me a secret."

I look down at her. The hat is still covering her face, but there's no doubt she's awake, since she just spoke to me, and I heard her clearly.

"A secret?"

"Yes. Tell me something I don't already know about you."

My eyes drift from her back out to sea.

"A secret. Something you don't already know about me. Hmm..."

It's hard being put on the spot like this. I don't

mind, of course, but it's still surprisingly difficult trying to come up with a good answer. Hope knows everything there is to know about me. I'm not sure if I have any secrets left.

Thankfully, we have time for me to think. We're still miles from shore, and Hope doesn't seem antsy at all as she lies perfectly still and serene with a half-finished drink sweating in one hand and the hat shielding her face from the setting sun.

"This probably isn't what you had in mind, and it might not be the best thing to share on your honeymoon, but I never saw myself as the marrying type. You know how girls love to talk about their weddings and how it will be one day when they grow up and they meet that perfect person and all that? That was never me. Maybe just because it was only my mama and me, but I never had much respect for the institution of marriage. Marriage didn't keep my dad around, and my mama still wore that ring every damn day on her finger until she died. I wasn't sure why she did that, and I think for many years, it actually annoyed me and turned me off on the whole idea of pledging yourself to one person for all eternity. But now… well, now I suppose I get it."

Hope uses her free hand to lift the brim of her hat so she can peek out at me from under it.

"You 'suppose' you get it, now?"

She winks at me. I smile and squeeze her feet in my hands.

"No 'suppose.' I definitely get it now. This—you and me—this is all I need. This is all I've ever wanted, even before I knew what it was I wanted."

Hope lowers the hat brim back over her face.

"I'm glad."

"Your turn."

She's quiet long enough to make me wonder if she's actually fallen asleep this time. Only when she's good and ready, Hope responds, because that is Hope.

My Hope. My wife.

"Mine is sort of the opposite of yours. It will come as no surprise to you that I've always wanted to get married. A wedding, some kids, some dogs, a house out in the country. That's always been the dream for me. Even as a little girl, I'd cut out pictures from magazines that I found inspiring or influential and tape them to the walls. I was doing the whole vision board manifestation thing *before* it was trendy, just so you know."

"Oh, I know. I've seen your childhood bedroom."

"What you *haven't* seen, though, is my secret lair."

"Come again? Your 'secret lair?' What is that?"

"I don't know how old I was—maybe eleven or twelve?—but there was one summer where I discovered a secret room in the basement of our vacation house. Not really a room, actually... more like a crawl space that everyone must have just forgotten about. I obviously did not tell my parents about my discovery but decided instead to make it my own secret lair. There weren't really walls down there, more just insulation and plaster and wooden beams, but I still taped up all sorts of stuff... and I mean, all sorts of spicy stuff."

"Really? Like what?"

"Cutouts from my mom's Victoria's Secret catalogs. Pages from my diary that I tore out. Cartoon drawings and sketches I did of body parts and of what I thought grown-ups used them for. Love letters I wrote but never sent to Mary Kay Kappelhoff."

"Wow, you're really gonna bring Mary Kay

Kappelhoff into this, huh? On our honeymoon?"

Hope sits up, pulls the hat back onto her head, and wraps her arms around my neck.

"What can I say? She's the one that got away."

"Is that so?"

"Is someone jealous of Mary Kay Kappelhoff?"

"Maybe I am. What are you going to do about it?"

"How about this?"

She leans forward and pulls me into a long, slow kiss. When we finally break apart, I can see the last remnants of the setting sun reflecting in her eyes.

"You'll have to show me this secret lair the next time we're out there. I'd be curious to see it."

"As long as you promise not to get jealous."

"I don't know if I can do that, now that I know what happens for me when I get jealous."

She laughs.

"I have another secret for you, Alex."

"Oh, yeah? What's that?"

Hope puffs out her lips and brings our faces within inches as she whispers under her breath.

"This is what happens for you all the time now, whether you get jealous or not."

"Lucky me."

And I mean it with every fiber of my being, even if I don't exactly get the words out before we're kissing once again.

As is my lot in life these days, I awaken to the sounds of screaming.

Right away, though, I know this is different.

This isn't the cat shrieking in the night from outside the house, tangled up in traps with broken limbs and losing blood.

Where is the cat, by the way? I don't feel Coretta's rough tongue lapping against my wrists or her whiskers brushing along my skin as she chews at my bonds.

It's also not Brett Taylor calling out from the basement with his head in a pillowcase, because now our roles are reversed, and it's Brett Taylor that's probably asleep in my bed upstairs while I'm the captive in my own house, tied up to a support pole in a pool of my own blood and wastes in the basement.

The screaming I hear is a woman's screaming, and I recognize it immediately for what it is and for what it means.

Time's up.

I can only pray it's just begun. If she's been screaming for a while, and I've been sleeping through it like a fool, then I'm as good as dead. Brett will be here any second now to whisk me upstairs. Or perhaps he'll be whisking Vicki downstairs. I still don't know what they have planned for me or how they imagine I'll help them deliver a baby while I'm tied up like this.

What I do know is that any scenario where Brett unties me is also going to involve him having a gun— maybe two guns—pressed right up against me to prevent any kind of 'funny business.'

And the minute—the second—that baby pops out and everything looks good for Vicki, Brett, and the newest member of the Taylor family, he's going to pull that trigger. Because why wouldn't he? I would, too, if I were him.

This is it. This is my last chance. If I have any hope of staying alive, it comes down to right now. I have got to get free of this rope and tape.

It's looser back there than it was. My efforts have not gone unrequited, and neither have Coretta's.

It's still not enough, though. I'm wrestling with the bonds, but they're just not breaking. I would have hoped that we'd done enough between us to get them compromised by now so that I could tear free of it all, rip the tape and snap the rope, and bound forward and up onto my feet like some wild beast erupting from its restraints.

But it's not happening. The screaming is intensifying up above, a full two stories above my head, it sounds like.

He'll be here any minute. She will, too. Or just him. It doesn't matter. None of that matters right now. All that matters is getting free.

I bite my lip as I twist my hands in on themselves. In some sick, twisted way, I'm grateful to Brett for breaking three of my fingers and for bloodying my hands and my arms. I truly believe that if I was whole right now, unbeaten, unbroken, and unbloodied, I might not be able to stomach this new kind of pain that sears up behind me and thrashes at my brain. As wretched as it felt when he was ripping my nerve endings to tatters, I just don't have that much left to lose anymore because of it.

Something cracks hideously behind me, and I gasp into the darkness. I've either broken or dislocated a bone in my wrist, but there's also an accompanying fluidity that makes my heart rush faster and my muscles quicken their pace at this task.

Vicki screams bloody murder as the contractions intensify, and it's the soundtrack to how my body feels as I contort and writhe and wriggle my way, sweat and blood and stink clogging up my pores and burning my one good eye, until finally with one last magnificent heave, my mangled left hand comes free.

There's no time to celebrate. Blindly, dumbly, shakily, my two good fingers—the index and the thumb—work against the knot behind me to free my right hand as well.

It's slippery and tattered, probably more from the cat than from me, but it comes away at last, and then I press my shoulders out and the tape snaps and the ropes fall away as I fall forward with a lurch.

Everything is tingling and throbbing, but there's just no time. My legs are dead asleep, but I pound on them, beating my thighs and my calves and my feet with my pulpy fists until everything starts to kind of come back alive just a bit.

The screaming is getting worse upstairs. I'm hoping that Brett is scared shitless by what's happening and that he's momentarily afraid to leave her side right away, but I know that won't last.

The worse it gets up there, the more motivation he's going to have to come get me, and when he does, it will be too late. Especially if he sees I've broken free, he'll probably just kill me and take his chances with the childbirth on his own.

Half-crawling, half-stumbling, I slide and shamble forward across the concrete floor in the pitch-blackness until I run headfirst into the bench.

Unless he's found it, and I feel like I would have seen or heard him if he had, it's still there… and it is.

Mercifully, far in the back of a drawer cluttered with tools that no longer work without power, is another flashlight. It's a small one, one I only put back there for emergencies, and I have no idea if the batteries will work when I click the button on the side, but it does, and I close my good eye and shudder appreciatively from head to toe.

There's still no time, though.

I switch hands and wrap the small flashlight between my thumb and index finger on my left hand so I can grab the screwdriver out of the drawer with my right hand, my good hand. It's not going to do me any good from a distance if he sees me and he's armed, but maybe in close proximity. Better than a fire extinguisher, perhaps. Or worse. I guess I might have to find out the hard way.

When I turn, something moves on the floor at the edge of the flashlight beam. I track it all the way over to the far corner of the basement until I see the orange fur and the glowing yellow eyes reflecting back at me.

Coretta opens her mouth to meow at me, but I can't hear anything over the screams. I move toward her, and she flees further back into the recesses, darting beneath a pipe and around an old water heater.

"Coretta!"

I'm compelled to move after her, somehow dumbfounded that this cat who has grown to love me is now repulsed and terrified of my presence. With everything that's happening and everything that is about to happen, some part of me knows this is unimportant, but there's also some deeper, unknown part of me that whispers into the bowels of my soul that this is extremely important what I'm doing right now, and to trust it, and to move with instinct, even if it goes against my rational brain and the decades of skills and experience I've built on practicality, logic, and reason.

Listen to your heart. Even if it betrayed you before with the Taylors. Don't give up on it now. Don't lose hope just yet.

I crawl after this cat as pandemonium sounds from on high, and now there are footsteps hastily crossing the wooden floorboards up above, and I just know in that same earthy subterranean place of my subconscious that this is it and that he is coming for me now for real.

I must keep moving, even as I start to crawl on hands and knees, dragging myself along the floor through cobwebs across pipes and wood and insulated walls.

Just up ahead, there is a large tear in the pink insulation. Bits and pieces of splintered wood and sawdust are on the ground, and behind what I think was once the Bergstrom family furnace, there is an empty space where a square of plywood has fallen flat on the floor.

Guided by the light and by the flick of a white and orange tail, I squeeze my body through this hole in the wooden paneling and up over the plywood square that must have until recently rested vertically against this wall, blending in and covering it up.

I've never had a reason to go back this far. Why would I? I thought it was only household appliances and electrical systems that no longer functioned.

I enter on my belly into a small space that isn't much larger than the linen closet upstairs. But Coretta is here, with chunks of wood, insulation, and plaster nestled in all over her coat. She meows at me and blinks, and I take in the walls around me for the first time.

There are yellowed pieces of paper taped up to the wood. Faded magazine clippings of underwear models and thin women in lingerie line the beams that crisscross the ceiling. Crudely drawn pictures and notes written in a handwriting that I recognize on some level, even if it's all the work of a much younger, still developing human being that I wouldn't meet for many years to come.

Tears well up at the corners of my good eye, and I have to blink back the memories and remind myself that it's not over yet. This is no time to sit and examine the treasure trove I've found here. If and when I can survive and liberate my home—Hope's home—from these fucking intruders, then I will be able to take in all that her secret lair has to offer, as wonderful and as painful as that exercise might be.

As if I needed another reminder, the footsteps are closer now, just above me on the first floor, and I hear the unmistakable sound of the door opening.

There has to be a way out of here. If Coretta was able to crawl around inside the walls of the house, then I should be able to do the same, right?

Coretta is a cat, though. I am a full-grown woman.

Footsteps thunder down the basement stairs.

It's too late. Even if there was a way out of here, out of this secret lair to the first floor, or even just to another part of the basement, it's too late now. He's going to see that I'm not there. And he's going to be able to follow the blood trail.

I try to stand up, but there's not enough overhead space. The best I can do is crouch with my head and shoulders bent forward and wait.

Maybe I didn't leave a trail. Maybe he'll go back

upstairs when he sees I'm not there.

But why would he? He knows I can't get anywhere.

Does he? I suppose he doesn't. He doesn't know this house like I do. Hell, I don't know this house like I thought I did, either. But still.

The footsteps have stopped, and it's only just the terrible high-pitched screaming that's still filling the whole house up as Vicki battles to give birth. It's otherwise quiet on this floor.

I would have heard him going back up the stairs, unless he purposefully did so without trying to make any sound. He isn't calling for me. All I know is that I heard the door open, and I heard him come down the stairs into the basement. That, and I know that Vicki is still upstairs, probably on the second story, though who even knows, given how loud her screams are now.

And then I hear him. It's almost impossible, but I swear I hear him. I can hear his heavy breathing as he's making his way back here. He's following the trail. Brett must have the flashlight, and he surely has a gun, and he's following the path back here to come find me. Whether it's to subdue me or to kill me, it doesn't matter, because death is the same end result in either scenario.

I poise myself as best I can with the screwdriver and the flashlight. It's this moment right here and right now where I wish one eye wasn't swollen shut and I didn't have numerous broken bones and atrophied muscles. That was all fine and good in helping me grit my cracked teeth against the pain as I wiggled my way to freedom out of the tape and rope. But now, lying in wait for a man with all his strength and stamina, I feel like I'm ill-prepared, given my physical and mental state.

Not to mention, given I have a screwdriver as my weapon, and he probably has a loaded handgun.

Coretta is nowhere to be found. Maybe she went into the walls somewhere that only cats can fit, and she's hiding. I wish I could do the same. At any rate, it's better she doesn't see this. She's suffered enough for all nine of her lives. That cat doesn't need to see me get put out of my misery.

The breathing gets closer, and I decide to switch off my flashlight. If he has one himself, I'll use his light instead of mine. No need for him to trace my own beam back to me right away. And if we're both in the dark, maybe that will provide me with some kind of advantage. Or maybe I can try and switch on my flashlight when he arrives and blind him or stun him. I could even throw it at his face.

My light goes off at the same time as a new ray of light comes in, and then a flashlight where it originates from, and then a gun, and then two arms follow, and then at last his head appears as Brett tries to fit his frame into the narrow space.

His face spins toward me, and I see the flashlight and the gun move quickly in the same direction, so I strike without hesitation, stabbing downward with the screwdriver toward the white of his eye.

There's a new scream, much closer now, and a deafening blast as the gun goes off into a cloud of dust and woodchip spray, and then the flashlight beam shoots wildly across the tight space until it connects with my forehead and sends me flying down against the wall and to the ground, seeing stars in my vision even in the dark.

We are wrestling on top of each other, and he is

stronger than me and he has a gun, but he also doesn't have enough room to use it properly. Plus, he has a screwdriver buried in his eye socket, and I have the element of surprise on him, even if I'm dazed from where he clubbed me with the flashlight.

The gun goes off again and again as Brett fires desperately, screaming and gnashing his teeth in agony and unleashing every profanity and slur that he knows.

I am trying to pull the screwdriver free from his eye so I can stab him again in his black heart or his jugular or somewhere that might actually put an end to him, but it won't come free, and he's pummeling me with the flashlight and with his knees and legs and squirming beneath me, and I know that sooner or later he might overpower me, or one of these blasts from the gun might actually catch me in my body rather than just firing off into the wood and plaster.

I release the screwdriver and grab hold of a chain around his neck, twist it in my good hand, and pull with all my might. It's my keyring necklace. I pull it tighter and tighter until the metal cuts into the skin on my fingers, but I know that the tighter I pull it, the tighter it cuts into the skin around his neck, and I can feel him gurgling and sputtering and gasping for air as he chokes, and I strangle the life out of him.

And then, it breaks.

The stupid fucking chain necklace breaks off in my hand, and just like that, the pressure is off, and he's no longer getting suffocated and strangulated, and now he's fumbling for the flashlight so he can see me, and I know he hasn't used all his bullets yet, and he's going to shoot me or club me so hard that I pass out.

Whatever he's going to do, he's going to do it, even

with a screwdriver in his eye, because there's no turning back now, and because he hasn't lost enough blood yet, and because the necklace didn't hold up long enough to cut off his air supply or crush his windpipe.

I see him whirl the gun around, and I take hold of the keys at the end of the broken chain in my hand, and I press them tight between my knuckles and pray to God—whether or not I believe in God—that the sharp ends of the keys are facing out. And then I punch down at his face next to the screwdriver at his good eye.

There's another scream and a squishing hot wetness, and he throws me off him and fires the gun at random in every direction, and I hold myself still at the ground and pray that none of those bullets have found me.

Brett screams and thrashes about until he does what I hoped he would do finally. He drops the gun and the light and reaches for his eyes, clawing at what's left of them, pulling the screwdriver out with another sickening scream and trying in vain to stop the blood flow and just to realize what all has happened and what this now means for him without having eyes.

This is enough. I see the gun on the ground in the flashlight beam, and I reach for it with my right hand, pick it up, point it at his head, and pull the trigger.

Click.

Click.

Click.

The gun is empty. The motherfucking gun is empty.

Brett shrieks, reaches up toward the sound of the gun, and knocks it out of my hand. With blood streaming from his eyes, he tries to get up to his feet, and he can't see now, so he hits his head on a low beam in the crawl space and falls back to the concrete floor hard.

It is enough. I see the sticky screwdriver gleaming on the ground, pick it up, and with one last, concerted, defiant, this-must-be-the-end-of-it-all action, bring it streaking down through the air and bury it deep into his Adam's apple.

His hands fly up to claw at the tool, but I keep my hands and the full weight of my body pressed down on it and on him. They reach up and scratch at me, his legs twist beneath him, he coughs and drowns in his own blood, and still I hold. Still I hold. Still I hold.

Until it's over. Until it's done.

Long after Brett Taylor has stopped wheezing and moving, I hold my position. I know he's dead, but I will take no chances. I'm so very tired I could die right here on top of him, but I won't. Because I am a survivor. Because I will not be broken. I cannot be broken. I will not die today. Not at his hand. Not for the Taylors. Only for me. Only when I'm ready.

When I'm ready, I shift my weight off from him and let go of the screwdriver. In the dim glow of the fallen flashlight, I take in the wide pool of blood that surrounds us.

Brett is still. My fingers move from the screwdriver spiked through the center of his throat to the side of his neck to check for a pulse.

It isn't there. Without me to bring him back this time, Brett Taylor is truly dead.

I take his flashlight, I take my flashlight, I take the gun. Even though it's empty and even though he's dead, I take no chances. I pick up the scattered keys and the broken chain necklace. When I have everything I want, I crawl out of Hope's secret lair and worm my way back out to the main basement floor.

By flashlight, I make my way up the stairs toward the open basement doorway. Slowly, carefully. The vertigo isn't there, nor is the threat of it. I make not a sound as I pull my way up, empty gun at the ready, all bark and no bite, but hoping it's enough to scare Vicki away if she's up there waiting for me.

But she isn't. Everything is dark here on the first floor.

More importantly—and more ominously—everything is *quiet*.

Why isn't she screaming?

I don't know when it happened or when it stopped, but the screaming has stopped.

And it makes me nervous. Does she know somehow that something has gone wrong down below? Did she hear her husband's screams? She couldn't have… not with her own labor happening at the same time. And not while we were way down in the bowels of the house, wedged together in such a small, insulated, covered place, surrounded by wood and stuffing.

Take no chances, though. Use your head and your heart. Trust your instincts and your experience.

I move as quietly but as swiftly as I can to the linen closet. 1-2-2-5-9-1. My forever Christmas baby. One last present. Thank you, Hope.

I swap out the Taylors' gun with the Glock, which I know is loaded. That means I've evened the playing field somewhat. Vicki Taylor has the rifle, but now I'm armed, too. And though I've taken one hell of a beating, she certainly has, too, if she's been going through contractions and all the ensuing complications of childbirth.

Room by room, space by space, I scan the darkened first floor of the house, gun and flashlight at the ready, one eye wide open, muscles trembling, body fatigued, brain splintered, but committed to finishing the job once and for all.

This is my home. This is our home. We will take back what is rightfully ours.

It's still just too quiet, but there's nothing I can do about that until I find her.

Will I be able to pull the trigger on a pregnant woman? Can a former OB-GYN murder an innocent unborn child by slaying her mother?

If I have to. If that's what it comes to. If there's no other way.

I creep up the staircase toward the second story. This is where I bet she is, or at least where I thought she was when the screams were happening.

The Glock is in my good hand, the flashlight is in my bad hand. I slide along the wall until I'm next to my bedroom doorway.

One Mississippi.

Two Mississippi.

Three Mississippi.

Four Mississippi.

On the fourth, I take a deep breath and whirl around the corner, gun at the ready.

The room is dark. It appears very much undisturbed from how I remember it the night the Taylors fooled me and lured me out into this hallway for their trap.

I check every part of the room just to be sure, because I will not take chances and because I know that she's here… somewhere. She has to be. Vicki Taylor wasn't in the basement, and she wasn't on the first floor.

She couldn't have gotten out, not when her husband had the keys. And now I have the keys.

Which means she has to be in Hope's old room. The room I put the Taylors up in when I foolishly brought them back here, thinking they were good people. Thinking there were still some good people out there in the world…

This is it. I try not to shake as I tiptoe down the hallway, past the spot Brett Taylor got the jump on me from behind and knocked me out cold, past the spot Vicki Taylor stood in when she faked her water breaking as bait to lure me out from a drunken sleep.

Midway down the hallway, I hear a sound from behind me. I spin so fast on my heel that I almost topple completely over, but I catch myself and raise the gun in time, utterly determined not to be snuck up on or tricked again.

To my immense relief, the sound didn't come from Vicki; it came from Coretta. My relief swells as the cat strolls calmly into the light. She looks no worse for wear, despite all the chaos, violence, and bloodshed that happened down below in the pit of this house.

I'll do a more thorough examination—both of Coretta and of myself—later on, assuming I'm still around and alive to do anything, that is. There's still one Taylor and one gun unaccounted for.

I turn back around and move forward silently and soundlessly until I'm at the edge of the second bedroom doorway. The door is closed to their room.

Not 'their room,' though. Her room. Hope's room. Hope's house. Our house.

This is it. She has to be inside.

Vicki will be ready for me. It's either her or me. This

is it now.

One Mississippi.

Two Mississippi.

Three Mississippi.

Four Mississippi.

I use my flashlight hand to whip the door open, and then I immediately duck back outside the frame into the hallway, fully prepared for the rifle to go off.

But it doesn't. There's no sound of gunfire.

And there are still no sounds of screams. Not even breathing.

Cautiously, and ever so slowly, I tilt my head forward so I can use my good eye to glimpse inside around the wooden doorframe, angling the flashlight with me as I go.

Vicki Taylor lies still on the bed. The rifle leans against the far wall in view.

In one fluid movement, I cross the room to the rifle and put it behind me, keeping the flashlight and the Glock pointed at Vicki the whole time.

She doesn't move.

Now, with all guns accounted for and with this last adversary squared within my sights, I see her for what she is. Naked, motionless, pale. And... red. Very red.

I move a bit closer.

Vicki is covered in blood from the waist down, and it's smeared on her hands, arms, and all over the sheets and blankets on the bed. The mattress itself seems soaked through. Her eyes are closed. She isn't moving. I don't think she's breathing.

I move close enough to prod her shoulder with the gun.

Nothing happens.

Almost as if I'm afraid that I might wake her, I gently set the flashlight down next to her form and use the good fingers on my crippled hand to check for a pulse.

It isn't there. Vicki Taylor is as dead as her husband. She has died in childbirth.

Vicki might not be moving, but something else is.

Down in the midst of all the bloodied sheets between her legs, a small baby girl stirs. I stare down at it wondrously and feel the gun grow heavy in my right arm.

How could this happen?

Why now?

Whatever am I to do?

For one terrible fraction of a second, I consider that it might actually be a mercy to pull the trigger. Even if it goes against everything I've ever worked for and against everything I dedicated my whole life to doing, this is not that same world. This baby is the byproduct of hate. In the debate of nature versus nurture, anyone siding with nature would scream at me to pull the trigger now and be done with it.

The practical part of me knows that this is no world for a child, and that any newborn infant—especially an orphan—will never survive.

It would be a mercy. It would be the smart thing to do. For both of us.

My finger is on the trigger… but I can't do it.

Of course, I can't do it. And of course, I won't do it.

It doesn't matter if it flies in the face of reason and common sense. It doesn't matter if she's a burden or a drain on my resources, my energy, my time. More than anything, it doesn't matter where she came from or what she's made of… or *who* she's made of.

Because in the nature versus nurture debate, I'm on Team Nurture anyway. Look at my upbringing. Look at what I was able to make of my life before all this happened. How many people told me I couldn't do the things that I did? How many people would be surprised to see me here today, and to learn that I'm still here, still alive, still surviving despite everything that's happened?

I did all that and more. Not because I was hard-wired to do it, or because I was born with privilege and with a destiny preordained for me by my family, my race, my culture, my religion, my sexuality, my gender, or my creed.

Everything that I am and everything that I've done is because of me. I have willed it so. Through the strength of my own resolve and through the support of those who loved me, who truly loved me, and who accepted me for who I was and who I am and who I wanted to be, I have made endless miracles happen.

This child deserves those same rights, those same opportunities. Just because it came from hate does not mean it should not know love. And just because it was born into a hopeless world does not mean I should deny it at least a chance.

That's all any of us deserve, anyway. At least give us a chance. Give us an equal stake in this world and let us show you what we'll do it with it. You might just be surprised.

I am surprised. I am putting down the gun and lowering my shaking body onto the bed beside this new lifeform that is not mine. I am wondering what I will do with it. With *her*, not with *it*. I am wondering what I will do with her and what will become of *us:* me, a cat, and a baby. I am wondering. But I am also sure.

"Hello there, little one. My name is Alex. Alex Washington. Don't worry. I've got you now. Everything is going to be all right. Everything is going to be all right."

COMING SOON

IT WILL END IN DISASTER

by

PATRICK MORGAN

Spring 2022

ACKNOWLEDGEMENTS

This was a difficult book to write on a number of levels, but if you made it this far, I'm going to hopefully assume you finished it and didn't just skip to the back.

If that is indeed the case, I want to thank you for lending your time and attention to this story. I know just how busy everyone is and how many distractions there are out there, along with numerous other options for entertainment, so it really means a lot to me that you chose Hope's Last Refuge.

This narrative made me nervous at times while working on it, if only because it's my first overtly 'political' book. I'm ashamed to admit that, though, since I don't think there should be anything political about remembering to practice empathy and kindness toward other people. Now, more than ever, we all need to be reminded of that.

On that note, I want to specifically thank my family members for encouraging me not to shy away from this subject matter. I know I raised plenty of doubts to you all about 'going there' and about me, specifically, going there, and you all reminded me time and again what it means to be a fiction writer, to have a voice, and to use my platform for positive change. So thank you, Mom, Dad, Megan, and Paul.

This is my fourth book with Phase Publishing, and

once again, I couldn't be happier with how the whole process turned out. I owe so very much of what I'm building to the belief and tutelage of Christopher Bailey. Thank you, Chris, and thanks to everyone on your team for literally making my dreams come true.

My sincere gratitude also to Jenny Rudd and your team at Right Word Express. It meant a lot to me that you said this one is your favorite (so far), Jenny. I'm also truly grateful for the comments your team made about the vehicle on the cover and about Coretta the cat.

Speaking of the cover, my deepest thanks to Deborah and Kylie from Tugboat Design. Somehow, you keep outdoing yourselves, and I'm so thrilled to have finally found a team I enjoy collaborating with. Beautiful work again!

Last but not least, I want to thank all my friends, relatives, readers, and fans. We are the sum composite of the interactions we have and the people we come into contact with in this life, and I feel so truly blessed and fortunate to be comprised of such wonderful, loving souls.

©2020 Patrick Morgan
Photo credit: Robert Atchinson

ABOUT THE AUTHOR

Patrick Morgan is a writer, dog dad, and hammock enthusiast who currently resides in Austin, TX. He is also the author of *Viaticum*, *Realms*, and *Apparent Horizon*.

Patrick's two great loves are the ocean and the New England Patriots, though he's also partial to Nacho Cheese Doritos dipped in cold Tostitos Salsa Con Queso (don't knock it till you've tried it).

You can contact him via his website at:

www.patrickmorganonline.com

www.ingramcontent.com/pod-product-compliance
Lightning Source LLC
Chambersburg PA
CBHW070757190726
48292CB00002B/561